Books by Rebecca Westcott

DANDELION CLOCKS
VIOLET INK

VIOLET INK

REBECCA WESTCOTT

PUFFIN

PUFFIN BOOKS

Published by the Penguin Group
Penguin Books Ltd, 80 Strand, London WC2R ORL, England
Penguin Group (USA) Inc., 375 Hudson Street, New York, New York 10014, USA
Penguin Group (Canada), 90 Eglinton Avenue East, Suite 700, Toronto, Ontario, Canada M4P 2Y3
(a division of Pearson Penguin Canada Inc.)
Penguin Ireland, 25 St Stephen's Green, Dublin 2, Ireland (a division of Penguin Books Ltd)
Penguin Group (Australia), 707 Collins Street, Melbourne, Victoria 3008, Australia
(a division of Pearson Australia Group Pty Ltd)
Penguin Books India Pvt Ltd, 11 Community Centre, Panchsheel Park, New Delhi – 110 017, India
Penguin Group (NZ), 67 Apollo Drive, Rosedale, Auckland 0632, New Zealand
(a division of Pearson New Zealand Ltd)
Penguin Books (South Africa) (Pty) Ltd, Block D, Rosebank Office Park,
181 Jan Smuts Avenue, Parktown North, Gauteng 2193, South Africa

Penguin Books Ltd, Registered Offices: 80 Strand, London WC2R ORL, England

puffinbooks.com

First published 2014
001

Set in 12.5/16.5pt Sabon LT Std
Typeset by Jouve (UK), Milton Keynes
Printed in Great Britain by Clays Ltd, St Ives plc

British Library Cataloguing in Publication Data
A CIP catalogue record for this book is available from the British Library

ISBN: 978-0-141-34901-5

www.greenpenguin.co.uk

MIX
Paper from
responsible sources
FSC™ C018179

Penguin Books is committed to a sustainable
future for our business, our readers and our planet.
This book is made from Forest Stewardship
Council™ certified paper.

For Mum, who always keeps her glow on and without whom this story would not exist

Contents

Izzy

My big sister, Alex, is a letter writer.
She says nobody writes letters
any more,
but they should
because letters are special.

She says you can hold a letter and
keep it
close to you and read it
any
time
you
want.
Emails can be wiped and texts are
gone
if you lose your phone – but letters stay
forever.

This is just one of the ways that
Alex is different
from other people I know
and it's one of the reasons that
I want to be
just
like
her.

Mellow Yellow

I am a hundred per cent determined to win. Never, in living memory, has Alex lost a game of Snap, but tonight history is about to be rewritten. In fact, it's my New Year's resolution. I have decided that this year is going to be the Year of Yellow and that means the Year of Happiness because yellow is a very happy colour. Winning this game against Alex is definitely going to make me happy. I crack my knuckles and wiggle my fingers – best to be flexible and ready for ninja-like moves.

'OK,' says Mum, shuffling the cards. Our deck is ancient, all dog-eared and crumpled. 'Are we all agreed on the rules?'

'Bring it on,' says Alex, sounding confident. I just nod, not taking my eyes off the cards that Mum is dealing out on to the kitchen table. When all the cards have been shared out between the three of us, we each pick up our pile, keeping the cards face down so that they can't be seen.

'Your turn to go first,' Mum says to me.

I put down the first card, turning it over as it reaches the table. Alex slams a card on top and the game has begun.

Jack, Two, Queen, Ace. I am totally focused, looking at nothing but the cards mounting up in front of me. My mouth is half open, the 's' ready on my lips. I WILL beat her this time – there's no way she can win again.

Three, Ten, Jack, King, King.

'Sn–' I start, but unbelievably my noisy, annoying big sister gets there before me.

'Cheese sandwiches!' she yells, nearly deafening me, and whacking her hand down on top of the stack of cards, just in case we're in any doubt about who has won. 'I win! Again!'

I cannot actually believe that this is happening. She's going to be utterly unbearable now. I really thought I'd win this time. I'd just like to win ONCE – is that too much to ask? I think I'd be a pretty good winner too and not do what Alex is doing now, making 'loser' signs at us and dancing round the kitchen bragging. I'd just smile generously and say, 'Good game.' Well, I think I would. It's hard to know what I'd do when I never actually get to win. Ever.

Mum is laughing and Alex sinks back into her chair, looking across at me with a huge grin on her face.

'How, how –?' I splutter, but I can't even get the words out properly. 'It's not right, Alex. You've GOT to be cheating. We made you say "cheese sandwiches" – there was no way you could win.'

'What can I say?' says Alex, flicking her hair behind her shoulder and shrugging. I'm sure she'll think of something though; she's never usually short of a word or two. 'Natural talent, I guess. If there was an A level in playing Snap then I'd get an A star, that's for sure!'

'Well, it's totally unfair,' I tell her, feeling cross. 'We have to play again and this time you've got to say "cheese and mayonnaise sandwiches". And NO cheating.'

I grab the cards and start to reshuffle the deck, but Mum stops me.

'Not tonight, Izzy. Alex has got studying to do and, sadly for her, Snap is not one of her A level subjects, so she needs to put a bit of effort into doing some work.'

Alex groans dramatically. Alex does everything

dramatically actually, like her entire life is really a show and she's the star. It means that she's noisy and bossy and very opinionated, but it also makes her a pretty exciting person to live with. You never quite know what she's going to do next – the only thing you do know is that it won't be boring. In the whole seventeen years that Alex has been alive I don't think she's ever done anything average. Not like me. My name could be the definition of average.

'Do you *have* to remind me? We haven't even gone back to school yet. I was just starting to relax.' She scowls at Mum. 'It's very important that I have rest sessions in between all the hard work, you know – all my teachers say so. Stress can be very damaging at this stage of my life.'

Mum stands up and starts to clear away our leftover dinner plates. 'Stress can be very damaging at my time of life too, I'll have you know. And I think you'll find the most important part of what you just said was the bit about resting in between working. WORKING! And, as I've seen precious little evidence of you doing any actual work over the Christmas holidays, I think you'll survive with a shorter "relaxation" session tonight!'

She is smiling at Alex, but in that way that

means 'do what I say or I'll stop pretending that you have a choice'. Alex pushes back her chair and gets up, pulling a face when Mum has turned towards the sink.

'Sorry, Izzy. I'll have to thrash you at Snap another night.'

'No rush,' I mutter. 'I'm probably going to be really busy with violin practice for the next few weeks.'

'Oh joy. More screeching and wailing to set my teeth on edge.' Alex grimaces at me as she leaves the room, her pile of school books still on the table and her jumper and scarf hanging over the back of her chair. She'll be back down in ten minutes, once she's spent a while making her room right for studying. That doesn't mean that she'll tidy it up. No. Alex says that the ambience has to be right so she'll drape a silk scarf over her lamp and light some incense sticks, and then flit around lighting candles all over the place.

It drives Mum crazy – she's terrified that Alex is going to burn the house down – but Alex says it's her room and she's virtually an adult so Mum should trust her for a change. Mum lets her, but what Alex doesn't know is that, when she's asleep, Mum always creeps into her bedroom and checks everything is safe. I know this because I check on her too, and one night I opened my bedroom door just as Mum was going into Alex's room. I saw her tiptoe round the room, turning off the lamp and making sure that the candles were out. When she came out, I pretended that I was going to the bathroom. Mum gave me a hug and put her finger to her lips and I knew that she didn't want Alex to know that Mum still looks after her.

I'm glad that Alex has got me AND Mum to keep her safe because sometimes her head is so busy with exciting things she forgets to do the things that she really should be doing. We're like her protectors so that she can get on with being Alex.

Red Card

I have certain expectations when it comes to PE lessons at school. I *expect* them to be excruciatingly awful and, in all fairness, I'm not often proved wrong. That's why today's lesson is coming as such a shock. I've been dreading it for ages. We spent absolutely weeks and weeks working on our ball 'skills' last term and today, as a grand finale, Miss Lane has planned a huge basketball tournament. It was supposed to happen at the end of term, but it got cancelled because of the Christmas music assembly. I thought we'd escaped it, but sadly not.

Virtually all of Year 7 have been crammed into the hall and put into teams. Our sports hall is quite small so there can only be one game going on at a time, which means that everybody else is either squashed on to benches along the sides of the hall, rammed up against sweaty armpits (the uncool kids, i.e. me) or hanging over the upstairs balcony and yelling words of support and encouragement (a.k.a. abuse). Only the popular, sporty kids ever get to watch from the balcony. I tried to go up there once, but I couldn't get any further than halfway up the stairs – I'm just not cool enough.

We've been here for what feels like hours and unfortunately it's now my turn to play. My desperate pleadings in my head, to whichever god it is that looks out for kids who can't do sport, have failed miserably. The sports hall has not been engulfed by a massive tidal wave, nor has my leg miraculously fallen off. There's nothing for it except to reluctantly put on the bright yellow bib that is being handed to me and take my place on the court.

The game starts out as I expected. I loiter somewhere near the end of the court, trying to make it look like I've got a tactic. The ball heads in my direction a few times and I trot towards it slowly, doing a little shrug of impatience when someone else races in to get it before me. Really, I should be graded for drama in this lesson: I truly think I manage to look convincingly disappointed when Simon Turner cuts in front of me and snatches the ball as someone foolishly throws it towards me. I even make a little 'tut' sound – which actually represents my terror at the near proximity of an airborne missile that could easily break my nose if mishandled, but which to everyone else might sound like a sigh of regret.

Halfway through we swap ends. I slope down the court, smiling sympathetically at Hannah as we pass in the middle. Hard to believe, but she's even more hopeless at sport than I am. I wouldn't say that's why we're best friends, but it helps that we understand the trauma of PE lessons.

The whistle blows and we're off again. I start perfecting a little dance routine, taking three steps forward, then one to the side and then reversing the entire movement, taking little bouncing steps on my toes. A glance at the clock on the wall and I can see that our ten minutes of torture are nearly up. I'm congratulating myself on a job well done when disaster strikes. I look up just in time to see the ball winging its way through the air, at extremely high velocity, right towards my face. Without even thinking, I put my hands up to protect myself and feel the ball smack into my palms. My fingers tighten instinctively and I, Izzy Stone, am actually holding the basketball.

I freeze. It feels like the whole world has stopped turning. I know that I need to act fast, that I need to get rid of this thing before it explodes or something, but my brain is struggling to tell my body what it should do. I'm not sure how long I stand there, but gradually I start to hear sounds. I guess that makes sense. I remember someone telling us in science that your hearing is the last sense to stop working when you die. I feel like I might have actually died of fright, but I can hear yelling and when I focus on the voices I can hear that they're all shouting the same thing. My name.

'Izzy!'

'Come on, Izzy!'

I shake my head and drag my attention back to the sports hall, the adrenalin pumping through my body making me feel like I can do anything. I've got the ball. And everyone is cheering my name. I can DO THIS!

Tentatively I try bouncing the ball on the ground. It springs back up to my waiting hand and I bounce it back down again, this time taking a step. Yes! I am moving and bouncing and thinking and breathing all at the same time. Go me, Miss Multitasker! Going slowly at first and then gaining speed, I start to head down the court.

'Izzy!'

The shouts have suddenly got louder and I can hear Hannah screaming my name as if she's half hysterical. The yells from the spectators seem to have died down – they're probably all in shock that I'm actually doing OK. I'm running now and I can see from the corners of my eyes that nobody is trying to tackle me; in fact, everybody seems to be standing still, which is weird, but there's no time to think about that. I dare to take my eyes off the ball for a second and adjust my direction slightly so that I'm sprinting straight towards the basketball hoop. It's too much to hope that I can actually get the ball in, but I can try. Everyone loves a trier after all.

Time seems to be in slow motion now and I've got plenty of time to think about what's happening. Maybe I'm not completely rubbish at physical activities. Maybe I just needed to find MY sport. Maybe I'll be invited to join the basketball team and will get to hang out with the cool kids.

I can still hear Hannah screeching my name. Her throat is going to really hurt if she keeps that up much longer. I've reached the end of the court and, without a second's hesitation, I throw the ball up, up, up. The hall goes completely silent as every single person follows the ball's journey towards the hoop. I hold my breath – and it goes in. IT GOES IN!

Turning to face Year 7, I punch my fist in the air. I've never actually done that move before, but it feels right. I'm jubilant! I know now why footballers celebrate their goals and it's all I can do not to pull my PE shirt over my head and run round the hall, whooping.

'Yes!' I cry, jogging towards the centre of the court, where Hannah is walking quickly towards me. The hall is still silent and I wonder briefly when the cheering will start. And then Hannah is next to me, holding on to my arm.

'Did you see?' I ask her, starting to laugh. 'Did you see what I did?'

'I saw, Izzy,' she says.

'Wasn't it amazing?' I say, still unable to stop laughing. I actually don't think I'll ever forget this moment.

'It really was,' Hannah tells me. 'It was also the wrong hoop.'

I can't actually make sense of what she's saying for a moment, but, as the sound of the rest of my team making horrid muttering noises reaches my ears, I stop laughing and feel my stomach start to turn over. Howls of surprised laughter start to flood across the court from every side, threatening to drown me. They're loudest of all from the balcony and I keep my eyes low so that I can't see what's going on up there. I don't think I'd like it.

'What?' I ask her, hoping I've misunderstood.

Hannah starts leading me off the court as Miss Lane yells at everyone to calm down and get changed.

'We swapped sides at half-time, didn't we?' Hannah whispers, pulling me over to the bench where we've left our bags. She's totally mortified on my behalf, which is small consolation when all I can hear is the hysterical laughter of the rest of Year 7.

I close my eyes and replay the last minute in my head. The silence. The fact that nobody ran after me. They were all in shock that anybody could be so utterly, ridiculously stupid as to run the WRONG WAY.

'Nice one, Izzy,' someone hisses as they walk past me and I wonder for a second if I keep my eyes closed for the rest of the day then maybe nobody will actually notice me. It used to work when I was little and Alex and I would play hide-and-seek. I used to hide by standing in the middle of the room with my eyes closed – Mum told me that I was convinced that if I couldn't see Alex then she couldn't see me. Sadly, I'm no longer two years old and, as I feel someone shoulder-barge me, I quickly decide that being able to see could be crucial to my survival.

I open my eyes and look at Hannah. She grimaces at me, a look filled with pity and embarrassment, and picks up her bag.

'Everyone will have forgotten all about it by lunchtime,' she says unconvincingly. I nod and together we head through the sports hall doors, my face bright red and my head hanging down in total shame.

I'm eating my sandwiches in the hall and trying to ignore the looks that are being directed my way by the rest of the school. I suppose it's good that most people think it's funny – well, everyone except the other people who were on my team. They spent most of maths letting me know just how unfunny they found the entire incident. Apparently, we were only one goal away from winning. Actually, I don't think it's called a goal in basketball. Maybe you score a try if the ball goes in. Or is it a hoop? I have no idea and, as I have no intention of ever setting foot on a basket-ball court again, I have no reason to find out. Whatever it is, we could have won if only I hadn't taken it upon myself to randomly run the wrong way and give the point to the other team. I've heard every theory going about why I must have done it.

1. I must fancy a boy on the other team.
2. I must hate the people on my own team.
3. I am rubbish at PE and therefore enjoy sabotaging PE lessons.
4. I am stupid and probably wet the bed at night.
5. I was momentarily possessed by aliens who made me run the wrong way.

OK, so I made the last one up. It just seems strange that nobody has suggested the real reason, which is:

6. I made a mistake. For which I am now paying. And the price is total humiliation.

Anyway, most people seem to have heard about it by now and, contrary to Hannah's theory, it's not old news. So far this lunchtime I've sat through a *hilarious* re-enactment of me sprinting down the court, complete with sports commentary; several requests from the sportier students to NEVER try out for the basketball team; and an invitation to share my shame with the entire student population by agreeing to be interviewed for the school paper. I ignore the first, reassure them on the second that nothing could be further from my mind and politely decline the third, stating homework as my mitigating circumstance. It'll be all over Facebook by tonight anyway, so there's no need for a formal interview. I'm just keeping my fingers crossed that nobody snuck a mobile phone into the lesson – if video evidence of my shame ends up on YouTube then I might as well stop coming to school altogether.

I finish my sandwich and take a deep breath. I'm not a naturally brave person and all this attention is very unwelcome. I stand up and walk out of the hall as quickly as I can, focusing on not doing anything else that will cause everyone to look at me, for example falling over. As I get to the door, I'm gripped by the terror that my school skirt is tucked in my knickers and I end up scurrying out, one hand reaching behind me, smoothing down my skirt and hoping that I don't look too weird.

Once out in the corridor, I breathe a sigh of relief. Most people are in the canteen or tucked away in common rooms and the corridors are pretty empty. Hannah is on duty in the school library so I head to my locker to stash my bag. My locker is on the second floor in C Block so it takes me a few minutes to get there. I only pass a couple of people on the way and they ignore me, so I'm feeling a bit more positive by the time I've climbed the stairs. Reaching inside my bag, I grab my key and unlock my locker and a piece of folded-up paper falls out.

Our lockers have all got slits in the front, like air vents. I have absolutely no idea why they're there – it's not like anyone's going to put an animal inside there (although I did hear that this really small boy in Year 8 got rammed into someone's locker at the end of term last year, so I suppose he was quite grateful for the opportunity to have a fresh supply of air to keep him going). Anyway, the slits mean that people can post notes inside the lockers and, as I bend down, I brace myself for something nasty. A hate letter maybe.

But I don't need to worry. As soon as I unfold

the paper, I see a familiar colour. It's from Alex, written with her signature violet ink fountain pen. That's what she calls it: her 'signature' ink. She says that it helps make her words stand out from the crowd, that everyone else uses blue or black ink, but that she refuses to conform to other people's rules. She says that it makes her distinctive, unique – it shows that she's a true individual. I think that's quite a lot to ask from an ink cartridge, but Alex refuses to use any other colour.

And actually the colour violet really suits Alex. I know quite a lot about colours and what they mean – and people don't seem to realize that you can tell loads about a person by the colours they choose. Violet represents being brave and one of a kind; it means being someone who is good at creating things and has a brilliant imagination. Violet people are independent: they don't need anybody else. All of those things describe Alex completely, so it's good that she writes in violet ink. It's just that Alex thinks it's the colour that makes her BE those things and that's wrong. It's Alex who IS all of those things – the colour just matches her personality.

I look down at the note. Alex's handwriting is

always changing; she's constantly attempting new styles and trying to figure out what each style says about her. This message is short, but written with very flouncy, flowery letters. She won't keep this one up for long – there's no way she could write a 2,000-word essay like this.

Izzy,

My advice? Laugh it off. And pull a sickie next time you have a PE lesson ...

Love you forever.
Alex xxxxxxx

I fold the note up and slip it into my pocket. Alex is right – I just have to grit my teeth and smile this one out. I have a quick practice, but it turns out that smiling through gritted teeth makes you feel like a lunatic so I stop and just hope that I can manage to look calm and serene for the rest of the day. I will use my best 'there's nothing to see here so please move on' face. I wish that Alex hadn't heard about my mess-up, but it feels good to know that she's thinking about me.

I head towards the sanctuary of Hannah and

the library, feeling a little bit more confident about my ability to make it to the end of the school day without dying of mortification. Maybe I'll write about it later in my notebook – that usually makes me feel a bit better. I might not be able to control the things that happen to me in my real, actual life, but I CAN choose the words that I use to write about everything.

Alex and I have got words in common – we both like writing things down. Where we are different is *why* we write. Alex writes letters: she writes letters to Mum and me and leaves them around the house; she writes to her friends all the time; she writes to Granny and Grandpa even though they only live just down the road. And she writes because she wants people to know what she's doing and what she's thinking. Alex chooses to write letters because letters are sent – someone always reads them.

I don't write letters because I don't want anyone to read what I've written. It's private – just for me. I write words down without worrying what anyone else will think. I just let them pour out of my head and on to the page. I don't write stories – I suppose you could call it free verse – it's kind of like poetry although it doesn't rhyme. Nobody knows that I write. I sometimes wonder what it would feel like to show Mum or Alex my words, to read them aloud the way they should be spoken. I think it might feel quite amazing, but I'm not like Alex so it'll never happen. I'm not brave enough to share my thoughts like that.

Rose-coloured Glasses

It's been a long, tiring day so after supper I have a bath and then write in my notebook for a bit. The notebook I'm writing in at the moment is gorgeous – it's got a deep blue cover with swirls of yellow on the front and 'notebook' written in flowing writing.

When I was younger and learning to read, I used to sound out the word 'notebook' and I read it as 'not-e-book', which I *thought* meant it was called a 'NOT a book'. I always think of a notebook as a 'not a book' now because it doesn't come with any words in it, so it isn't actually a proper book. And because proper books are written for people to read and I would never want my writing to be seen by anyone else.

After I've written a few verses, I turn my light out and lie down. I must be totally exhausted because the sound of the phone ringing pulls me rudely out of a deep sleep and I sit up with my heart pounding. I look at the clock – 10 p.m. Nobody ever phones us this late.

I lie back down and try to snuggle under the covers, but I know I won't get back to sleep for ages now. It's dark in my room, but I can still make out the cuddly toys neatly lined up on the end of my bed. Behind them is a weird shape and for a second I panic, but then I realize that it's just my violin case leaning against my wall, the shadows making it seem bigger than it really is.

I yawn. I've got a geography quiz at school tomorrow and I really do need to get some sleep. My understanding of cliff erosion is definitely NOT going to be improved by being tired. I close my eyes and then open them abruptly as I hear footsteps pounding up the stairs and then my bedroom door being flung open.

'Izzy – quick! You've got to get dressed!' Mum dashes back out and runs across the landing to Alex's room.

'What's going on?' I hear Alex moan.

'It's Grandpa. He's gone walkabout again. That was Granny on the phone – she needs us.' Mum runs back into my room and turns on the light.

I wince as the brightness hits my tired eyes, but I've already swung my legs out of bed and am racing over to my chest of drawers to grab a pair of jeans.

I hear Alex swear under her breath and then she slams her bedroom door closed and hurries into my room where Mum is rummaging through my wardrobe, trying to find me a warm jumper.

'Where does Granny think he's gone this time?' she asks Mum.

'She's not sure,' says Mum, thrusting a hideous yellow and pink woollen monstrosity at me. I never wear this jumper because the neck is really tight – putting it on gives me a headache and taking it off virtually removes both of my ears, plus, the colours really clash with each other – but I don't think now is the time to be arguing about fashion. 'Apparently, he was talking a lot today about the car factory that he used to work at, but that's miles away from here. She's wondering if he might have gone to visit Great-grandma – he's done that before.'

I shudder. The cemetery at night is not my favourite destination – it's bad enough when we have to take Granny and Grandpa there in the daytime, to leave flowers on Great-grandma's grave once a year.

'Right, girls, quick as you can. Get a coat each – it's colder than it looks out there.' Mum heads off down the stairs and we follow her.

We drive the short distance to Granny and Grandpa's house. We've always lived near them and I'm kind of used to having them nearby and seeing them all the time. Apparently, they once had dreams of moving nearer to the sea, but that was years ago before Grandpa got poorly. They've lived in their house ever since they got married, and Mum was born there.

I don't remember Grandpa before he was like this, but Alex says she does. She says she remembers him playing tennis with her and taking her out to the park, and she says it was Grandpa who started teaching her the piano. I'm not sure that I believe her. I think she just wants to sound like she knows him better than I do. And anyway she doesn't even play the piano any more; she gave up when she was twelve because she said it was a stupid instrument and nobody cool ever played the piano. I play my violin for Grandpa all the time and he loves it. He sits and listens and sometimes he claps. He doesn't always wait until I've finished before he starts clapping, but I think that's just because he likes my music so much.

We pull up outside their house and Granny is standing on the doorstep, looking worried. Mum turns off the engine and calls to Granny as she opens the car door.

'Any sign of him?'

Granny shakes her head and Mum rushes up the garden path and gives her a big hug.

'I wanted to go and look for him, but I was scared that he might come back while I was out and then he wouldn't know what to do,' says Granny, sounding like she's about to burst into tears.

'I know, Mum, it's OK,' Mum tells her. 'We're here now. You sit tight and put the kettle on. You know how much he likes a hot cup of tea when he's been off on an adventure!'

I'm quite surprised by how Mum is talking to Granny – it sounds like Granny is the child and Mum is the parent. But, instead of getting cross, Granny wipes her eyes and smiles gratefully at Mum.

'Right, I'm going to get back in the car and drive out towards the car factory,' Mum says to Alex and me. 'I want you two to walk from here to the little shopping precinct. Phone me if you find him. And STICK TOGETHER!' She aims the last bit at Alex who raises her eyebrows but nods.

'Don't worry, Mum,' she says. 'We'll find him.' Then she takes my hand and we walk back down the path. I turn at the gate and wave to Granny, who suddenly looks very small standing in the open doorway and looking out into the dark.

We turn right and start heading down the street. There's no sign of Grandpa on this road, but when we turn the corner the houses get grander and the gardens in front of them are bigger and darker. Alex starts peering into each driveway that we pass and I copy her, calling 'Grandpa' every now again, as quietly as possible, but loud enough that he might hear me.

As we get further away from their house, Alex gets more and more on edge, letting go of my hand to check her phone every few seconds just in case Mum has phoned to say that she's found him.

'Come on, Grandpa – where *are* you?' she mutters.

'What are we going to do if we can't find him?' I ask her.

'Don't say that!' Alex says, sounding cross with me.

I walk in silence for a minute and then she picks

up my hand again and gives it a squeeze. 'I'm sorry, Izzy, I didn't mean to snap at you. I'm just really worried about Grandpa.'

'Why does he do this?' I ask her. 'I mean, I know he forgets stuff all the time, but I don't get why he just wanders off.'

Alex thinks for a minute. 'It's part of the forgetting, I think. He suddenly decides he wants to do something and forgets that he's seventy-four years old. He thinks he's still a young man or a boy even.'

'Do you mean he doesn't know who he is?' I ask her. 'That's horrible – imagine not knowing who you actually are.'

'No, I think he knows who he is – he just sometimes gets a bit unsure about *where* he is in his life. So something that happened fifty years ago might seem like it only happened yesterday. Mum told me that it can make him confused and it can be a bit frightening.'

We walk further down the road and I think about what Alex has said.

'Poor Grandpa,' I say quietly and Alex holds my hand a bit tighter.

'Yes, poor Grandpa,' she repeats and I'm glad she's here with me.

We cross the road and head towards the shopping precinct. There are no houses now, just an empty road. Ahead of us is a bus stop and, as we get nearer, I can see that there's a figure sitting on the bench, hunched up against the wind.

'Alex! Look!' I whisper, pointing towards the bench. She follows my gaze and suddenly lets go of my hand and starts sprinting.

'Grandpa!' I hear her exclaim as she gets nearer and I run as fast as I can, getting to the bus stop just behind her.

Grandpa looks up, but doesn't seem the least bit surprised to see us standing there.

'Hello, girls!' he says, smiling in his lovely, kind Grandpa way that makes me want to snuggle up to him on the bench. I sit down next to him and put my hand on his arm, wanting him to know I'm here.

'I've been waiting for a bus for hours now, but there's been nothing. I don't know how I'm going to get home in time for my tea – Mother is going to be furious!' He chuckles to himself and looks up at the bus timetable on the wall. 'There should be a bus along any minute though – don't you worry.'

I look at Alex for help, but she's moved away slightly and is murmuring into her mobile phone.

When she hangs up, she walks over to where we're sitting.

'Budge up then,' she tells Grandpa, who chuckles a bit more and then moves across so that she can squeeze on to the bench beside him.

'Look at me: a thorn between two roses,' he laughs.

'Grandpa, where were you going?' I ask him. He turns to me and this time he does look surprised.

'Home, of course! I'm going home! Mother will be waiting for me and I'm sure she said it was ham for tea tonight so this bus had better get a move on.'

'Granny's waiting for you, Grandpa,' says Alex gently. 'She's worried about you – she wants you back at home with her.'

But we can both see that he doesn't know what Alex is talking about. I start trying to explain, but Alex shakes her head at me and so we sit, the three of us, huddled together in the cold bus stop until Mum pulls up in the car and leaps out with cries of, 'Oh, Dad!'

Then we help get Grandpa into the back seat and Mum drives us to Granny's. And when we get there Mum gently helps him up the path and inside, and she settles him into his favourite armchair while Granny fusses round him, tucking a blanket over his legs and preparing a tray with tea and cake. And the whole time Grandpa doesn't say a word. He smiles and nods, but he isn't looking at anyone properly. It's like his body is here with us, but his head is somewhere else – maybe sixty years ago when he was a boy going home to his mum and looking forward to some ham for his tea.

When it's time to leave, Mum takes Granny into the kitchen for a hushed conversation. I give Grandpa a hug and, when I straighten up, Alex is there, right beside me. And I don't need to say anything – she can see it in my eyes – and she puts her arms round me and holds me while I cry. And I know that, no matter how hard things get, Alex will always be there to make it better. She will always understand.

Left Foot Blue

I've been practising my violin for ages, but I still sound as screechy and squeaky as I did when I started. I'm dreading my lesson on Thursday; Mr Williams is going to moan at me and say that I have no hope of passing my Grade 3 exam because I have absolutely no musical ability and a baboon could play the violin better than me. Well, he probably won't use those exact words, but that's what he thinks – I can see it in his eyes.

My fingers are aching and I've had enough for one day. Time to have a break. As I pack my violin into its case, I can hear the sound of yelling and laughing coming from downstairs. Alex is home and it sounds like she's brought half the school back with her.

I open my bedroom door and walk downstairs. Mum is in the kitchen, humming along to the radio, and I plonk myself on to a kitchen stool and grab an apple.

'It's sounding good, Izzy,' says Mum, stirring a pan that's bubbling away on the stove. I roll my eyes – I KNOW that it sounded awful and I don't need Mum to pretend that it didn't – but unfortunately Mum turns round and catches me. And if there's one thing Mum can't stand it's eye-rolling.

'It sounded horrible,' I tell her, taking a big bite out of my apple. 'I'm totally going to fail my exam.'

'Don't talk with your mouth full,' Mum says automatically, 'and yes, with an attitude like that you probably WILL fail.'

I make a harrumphing noise; that isn't a very kind thing to say to me when I'm worried. I'm nervous enough already without Mum making it worse.

'What I MEAN is that you have to believe in yourself a bit more. As long as you practise, you'll be fine.'

I'm not convinced by Mum's argument, but I can't be bothered to keep having this conversation. And actually I really love music and playing the violin. I just wish that I was a bit better at it.

There's a loud shout of laughter from the living

room and Mum and I both glance towards the kitchen door. Alex is really popular – she's got loads of friends and they're always hanging out at each other's houses. Not like me. I've got Hannah, but that's it really.

I lean sideways off my stool and try to peer across the hall to see what's going on. It sounds like they're having a lot of fun in there. Mum sees me looking and smiles at me.

'Why don't you go and say hello?' she says. I get off the stool and walk towards the kitchen door. When I look back, Mum nods her head at me and then returns to her cooking.

I stand outside the living room and peep inside. The door is half open so I can watch them without being seen and they're making so much racket that nobody has heard me approach. They're playing Twister, which I thought was a game for little kids, but from the laughter I'm guessing it's just as much fun for big kids too.

Alex's friend Sara is perched on the arm of the sofa and has got the board. She's flicking the spinner with her long pink nails and calling out instructions to Alex, Finn, Stefan and Dylan who are in a tangled mess on the Twister mat.

'Finn – put your right hand on a green spot,'

calls Sara and I watch as Finn tries to move his arm.

'Stop it!' shrieks Alex. 'You're going to push me over!'

'Sorry!' yells Finn, reaching his arm out and over Alex's back, although he doesn't sound very sorry at all.

There's a muffled sound from beneath Stefan who is balanced on his tiptoes, with both arms reaching to different corners of the mat.

'What?' shouts Stefan. 'I can't hear you!'

Dylan's red face emerges from under one of Stefan's legs. 'I SAID, seriously, man – you're going to suffocate me. Could you move your backside just a bit, PLEASE?'

This makes Alex start laughing and suddenly the whole lot of them collapse in a heap on the floor.

'You're all useless,' declares Sara over the noise. 'Nobody won that round.'

I snigger as I watch Dylan trying to escape the pile, wriggling his way out as if he's a caterpillar. Alex hears me and looks up. I've moved slightly forward in an attempt to see a bit better and my head is peering round the door frame. I freeze, hoping that she doesn't yell at me in front of her friends – that would be completely embarrassing.

She doesn't though. Instead, her face splits into a big grin and she pulls herself off the floor and stands up.

'Izzy! Come and join in!'

I take a few steps forward and then stop, unsure about whether she really means it. I know Finn really well, but I've only met Dylan and Stefan a few times when they've been over for band practice with Alex. And Sara has never really paid me much attention; I get the feeling that she thinks little sisters are a pain.

Alex walks over to me and grabs my hand, pulling me into the group.

'OK, we'll play again, only this time Dylan can spin the spinner to stop him moaning!' She smiles at Dylan who looks hugely relieved as he takes the spinner board off Sara and settles on to the sofa. 'Everyone else, do NOT squash my very gorgeous little sister. OK? And be warned: she's a champion Twister player!'

She says this in a funny way that makes Finn and Stefan grin at me and I take my position on the Twister mat, feeling happier than I have all day.

'Izzy – left foot blue,' calls Dylan and I step on to a blue spot.

'Alex – right foot green.'

Alex steps behind me and whispers over my shoulder. 'Let's show them what us Stone sisters are made of! Rock hard, that's us! Unbeatable when we're together!'

I love Alex so much when she's like this. She's the only person in the whole world who can make me feel like I'm the most interesting, special person ever, with just a few words. I mean, I know that Mum loves me, but that's different – she's my mum, she has to love me. Alex makes me feel like she's CHOSEN to love me, and that makes me feel better than anything.

The Colour of Happiness

I am bored, bored, bored. It's Saturday and I've got absolutely nothing to do. Hannah phoned me earlier and asked if I wanted to hang out in town, but I told her I wasn't feeling well and I'd give it a miss.

This isn't totally true. I hate lying to her, but the truth makes me sound really silly and I've had enough of feeling silly to last a lifetime. The reason that I don't want to go to town is that I don't want to see any boys from school. Ever since the day of the basketball disaster, a group of them have been waiting for me on the way home.

It's not like they really do anything to me. Nothing that I could tell Mum or a teacher about. I'd sound completely ridiculous making a fuss about a few rude words and horrid looks. And anyway I've got Alex. She was walking home behind me last week and saw what was going on. She was totally brilliant – telling them exactly what she'd do to them if they gave me any more grief – and Alex in full-blown battle mode is pretty terrifying.

So as long as she's around I know I'm safe. But, if it's just me and Hannah and we bump into them, I don't think they'll leave me alone. It's like the basketball match made people notice me – and not in a good way. I liked it before, when nobody really knew I was even there.

I'm sitting at the kitchen table and wondering if I'm bored enough to join Mum in doing the chores. She's finished the vacuuming and has moved on to cleaning the work surfaces, and I'm just about to offer to help when Alex and Finn tumble through the back door.

'It's freezing out there,' says Alex, shivering dramatically before pulling off her scarf and throwing it on to the table.

'I did tell you to wear a coat,' Mum tuts, but it's a conversation they've had a million times and she knows that nothing she can say will make Alex listen. I don't understand it: being cold is horrible and I don't really see what the problem is with wearing a coat. It's not like it's a fashion crime, surely? Alex won't wear a coat ever, even on a freezing January day like today. It doesn't stop her moaning about being cold though.

I don't actually know how Finn puts up with her. We all love Finn and I think he loves us back, although he loves Alex the most. He virtually lives in our house some days, which is fine with me because Finn is fantastic. He lives across the road and his mum is friends with our mum and they've known each other since Finn and Alex were babies. Mum has got photos of them lying next to each other on a rug in our garden. Sometimes Finn comes over because band practice is at our house and sometimes he comes over for no reason, just because he feels like it. He and Alex spend most of their time together. I think he must be very patient to cope with all her drama.

'Anyway,' continues Alex, as if Mum hasn't spoken, 'we're planning on a musical afternoon, complete with the *West Side Story* DVD and serious amounts of popcorn. Is it OK if we have the living room, Mum?'

Mum nods and squirts the cooker with cleaning spray.

'Sounds fun! I might join you when I've finished these jobs. Granny and Grandpa should be here soon as well.'

'Didn't you tell me your grandpa used to do a lot of singing when he was younger?' Finn asks Alex.

'Yeah,' says Alex. 'He was always singing when I was little.'

'He used to sing in local amateur dramatics performances,' says Mum. 'I loved seeing him up there on stage – everyone always said how handsome he was and when he started singing the room would go silent. He was quite something in those days.'

'Why doesn't he sing any more?' I ask her. I know that Grandpa still loves music because I play my violin for him all the time, but I'm not sure I've ever heard him sing.

'Oh, I don't think he can remember the words to the songs any more,' Mum tells me, a sad look passing over her face for a second. 'I'm not sure he even remembers that he used to sing.'

Alex grabs a large bowl from the cupboard and puts it on the table. Finn pulls two big bags of popcorn out of a carrier that he's been holding and fills the bowl, right to the brim. The sweet smell of popcorn hits me and I wish, for the thousandth time, that I was seventeen and not twelve.

'Come on, Izzy.'

I look up, so busy feeling sorry for myself and thinking about Grandpa and his forgotten voice, that I haven't noticed Finn and Alex walking towards the kitchen door. They're standing there, looking as if they're waiting for me.

'Hurry up, sleepyhead!' says Alex. 'We're ready to start.'

A warm feeling spreads through me, starting at my toes and moving up to my tummy and then down to the ends of my fingers. It might be freezing outside, but in our house it's warm and snug. I follow them through to the living room and then we sit, squashed on to the sofa, with the bowl of popcorn resting on Alex's knees because she's in the middle.

'Watch her, Izzy,' warns Finn. 'She'll take more than her fair share if we're not careful!'

'Cheek!' says Alex, elbowing Finn in the ribs and then grabbing a fistful of popcorn and cramming it into her mouth. 'Ummm – yum, yum, yum, delicious popcorn and it's all for me.'

'You are such a kid,' sighs Finn, sounding like Mum for a moment, which makes Alex screech with laughter.

'And you're SO mature, naturally?' she asks him and then turns to me. 'Don't let him fool you, Izzy. He's the most juvenile person I know. Here – watch this!'

She picks up a piece of popcorn and turns back to Finn.

'Open wide,' she says and he grins before tipping his head back and opening his mouth. Alex throws the popcorn in the air and Finn leans forward and catches it, right in his mouth.

'One of these days you're going to choke doing that,' says Mum, coming into the room and settling into the armchair with a cup of tea. 'Izzy, ignore everything that these two do – they're terrible role models and you should probably do the exact opposite of anything you see them getting up to.'

'Charming!' says Alex. 'I'll have you know that I have many admirable qualities.'

'Yes, you do, my darling,' says Mum. 'Now, are we watching this film or not?'

But before we can begin there's a knock at the door.

'You can start without me,' says Mum, getting up and going out into the hallway. Alex presses play and, as the opening credits roll, Mum comes back into the room with Granny and Grandpa.

'Is there room for a little one?' asks Granny, and Finn leaps up and helps Mum settle Grandpa into the armchair. Granny sits down on the other sofa and Mum sends Alex out to the kitchen to make two more cups of tea. I pause the film and go over to give Granny a hug.

'Mum says you're watching *West Side Story*,' says Granny. 'Grandpa was in a production of this once.'

'Seriously!' I breathe, looking over at Grandpa and trying to imagine him doing something so cool. 'Where was that?'

'Oh, just in the town hall!' laughs Granny. 'But it's hard to imagine a more dashing Tony. I fell in love with him all over again watching him up there onstage.'

'When did he do that?' I ask her.

'Oh, years and years ago. Before your mum was born. But he used to sing all the songs for a long time after. He'd sing them to your mum to get her to go to sleep at night!'

'I remember him doing that!' says Mum, coming over to the sofa. Alex has come back in with the tea so I pass one to Granny and then sit back with Finn and Alex while Mum settles down next to Granny. 'He sang me those songs for years – how could I have forgotten that?'

I hand the remote to Alex and she presses play. We're all quiet, engrossed in the storyline, until the first song where the character of Tony sings. Suddenly, as the actor in the film starts singing, Grandpa opens his mouth and joins in. His voice is croaky, like it's out of practice, but none of us are looking at the screen any more. We're all watching Grandpa, who can't remember where he lives or what he had for breakfast, but, as it turns out, knows the words to *West Side Story* perfectly.

We spend the next few hours watching Grandpa and the film. His voice gets louder and more powerful with each song and I see Granny and Mum looking at each other in amazement, Mum holding on to Granny's hand and squeezing it tightly.

Alex stretches her legs out and rests them on Finn, and occasionally feeds him popcorn when he looks at her in a hungry way. She sings along to some of the songs with Grandpa and we all tease Mum for crying when Tony dies, even though I definitely see Alex wiping her eyes when she thinks nobody's looking.

And sitting on our sofa, with my whole family together, I think I can totally define the colour of happiness.

Izzy

What makes some people
more special
than others?
Don't even try to tell me that this isn't true.
I don't mind.
It's just a fact.

Maybe it's something that you can
get better at.
Like if I practise my violin every day I will
almost definitely
improve.
So perhaps I can work on
being
more
special.

But when I look in the mirror I just see
me.
Not astonishing, not hideous –
just me.
Nothing I can do about that.

I don't *know* what I can do to
change – I don't know what I *need* to do to
change.
I think I'm all right,
I'm just
not
that
special.

I watch the way Finn looks at Alex,
like she is precious
and he can't
lose her.

The way he grasps her hand in his
like she's his
favourite
and he doesn't want to
share her.

The way he protects her like she's a
delicate flower
and he doesn't want to
crush her.

The way she lets him.

And I know
that nobody is bothered about
sharing
losing
crushing
me.

I need to learn her secret –
sparkle, shimmer, flicker, glow.
I need to make myself
more
special.

Got the Blues

'If something interesting doesn't happen around here soon then I'm going to have to make it happen.' Alex flops down on to her bed and sighs. She's in a totally stinking mood today. I haven't got a clue what's wrong with her unless she's got the January blues, so I ignore her moaning and examine my face in her dressing-table mirror. No, it's no good pretending – I am truly terrible at putting on lipstick.

I'm spending this afternoon busy with the task of trying to make myself look older than twelve. It's surprisingly tricky. My eyes are quite big and very brown so they don't look too bad, but it's my hair that always lets me down. It's frizzy. There's no other word for it. Frizzy and not-quite-brown. Mum tells me that it's my unique selling point and makes me stand out, but she's just being kind. I have spent my whole life envying Alex her curly, glossy, almost-black hair, but she doesn't ever seem to realize how lucky she is. Mum's got the same hair as Alex so I'm the odd one out. Apparently, I get my hair from my dad. The one thing he's ever given me. Anyway, I've decided that I can maybe distract people from my hair with clever use of make-up. Alex said I could use her stuff and I thought we'd have fun, but so far all she's done is stare out of the window and whinge about being bored.

I turn to her, pretty sure that one look at my face will make her laugh and snap her out of her miserable mood.

'Ta-dah!' I grin at her, a crazy big smile that makes my bright red lips look even more clown-like.

'You look a complete state, Izzy,' Alex says in a flat voice and rolls over on to her stomach. 'And *you* can stop grimacing at me too, you freaky thing.' She grabs something off her pillow and, stretching her arm back over her head, throws it into the corner of her room. I look to see what's offended her so much.

'Alex! You can't treat Mr Cuddles like that.'

'Give me one good reason why not,' she says, rolling on to her back and staring up at the ceiling.

I'm in shock. Some things are sacred and should not be messed with – Alex has gone too far this time.

'Because he's Mr Cuddles. The same Mr Cuddles that Grandpa gave you the day you were born. The same Mr Cuddles that you've snuggled up to EVERY NIGHT since . . . well, forever. Even when you've been on a sleepover. You can't just chuck him around like he's a bit of rubbish. He's seventeen years old, Alex – you need to look after him.'

'News flash, Izzy. It's a stupid stuffed teddy bear.' Alex has made her voice sound really low and dull, like she thinks I'm incredibly stupid. I don't like how she's making me feel – as if I'm too young to be interesting.

I grab a tissue off her dresser and wipe my mouth, really hard. When most of the lipstick is on the tissue, I drop it into the bin and walk across the room, avoiding the piles of clothes that are lying randomly across the floor. I pick up Mr Cuddles and hold him close to me for a moment. I know that he's just a toy, but Alex has always had him and sometimes the old stuff is the most important. I carefully pick my way across the stack of magazines that are between me and the bed and hand Mr Cuddles back to her.

Alex takes him from me and looks at him closely. She strokes his fur and sniffs his head and then passes him back to me.

'You can have him, if he means that much to you.'

I don't know what to say. The thing is, I've wanted Mr Cuddles ever since I can remember. I've got my own cuddly toys, of course, but none of them seems special. Not like him anyway. He was a 'welcome to the world' present to Alex from Grandpa. Mum was really young when she had Alex, and Grandpa was majorly upset with her until the day Alex was born when (as Mum tells us every year on Alex's birthday) he took one look at his first ever grandchild and fell totally in love with her. He dashed straight from the hospital into town, spent ages choosing a teddy bear that had the nicest face (only the best would do for his granddaughter) and put it in Alex's cot when he went back later to visit. So Mr Cuddles has slept in the same bed as Alex every night since she was born.

By the time I came along, babies weren't such a surprise to our family. I guess the novelty had worn off a little bit. I've got loads of things to cuddle: a rabbit, a hippo, a strange-looking kangaroo glove puppet with a baby in its pouch and quite a few teddy bears. Mum kept a sweet wooden rattle that I was given when I was a baby and a family of plastic ducks that you can pull along on a string. They used to quack, but not any more. I reckon it's just another one of the perks of being the oldest child: people make a bit more of a fuss if you're the first.

This is why I don't know what to do right now. I've longed to have Mr Cuddles snuggled up to me in my bed at night – but not like this. Alex is being cross and confusing and I don't think she really means it.

'You can't give him to me. He's yours. It'd make Grandpa sad if you didn't have him any more.' Alex rolls her eyes at me, but sits up, cross-legged, on her bed. 'And I think you'd be sad without him too.' I say this last bit really quietly, just in case it makes her yell at me again.

Alex reaches out her hand and strokes Mr Cuddles again. Then she looks up at me and smiles, and she looks like my normal, lovely big sister again.

'OK, I guess he can stay.' She takes Mr Cuddles from me and stares him hard in the eye (he's only got one eye left after years of being scrunched and snuggled and slept on by Alex). 'You've been given a stay of execution, Mr Cuddles. Izzy has argued your case. Now what do you say to her?'

'Thank you, Izzy,' growls Mr Cuddles/Alex.

'You're welcome,' I tell him, grinning at Alex, and then navigating across her floor to the door, taking great care not to trample on the piles of school books that are strewn everywhere. I think that I could have a great career ahead of me as a minesweeper, all the practice I get avoiding stepping on Alex's stuff.

Once I'm safely out of her war zone of a room and across the landing, I open my own bedroom door and step inside. My room could not be more different to Alex's. Everything has a place. My homework is stacked tidily on my desk and my clothes drawers are all neatly closed – not half open with underwear and T-shirts flowing out. I'm not weird or anything – I just like everything to be tidy. I like knowing where everything is; it makes me feel calm inside. Alex teases me about it, but Mum says there's nothing wrong with needing to be ordered and that everybody likes to feel in control of something.

I sit down on my bed and twist my mood ring round and round on my finger. I love my mood ring and I wear it all the time. Alex gave it to me for my tenth birthday. She got it from one of the funny little shops that she likes: shops that sell candles and incense and weird statues. I know that it's just supposed to be a bit of fun, but I realized pretty quickly that my mood ring is actually quite accurate. I wouldn't ever tell anybody, but sometimes it feels like it REALLY can tell what's going on in my house, even before I can.

It started one day when I noticed that it had gone an amazing silver colour and when I checked with my mood-ring guide it said that could mean loneliness. And then, the very next day, Betty, my cat who I'd had for eight years, got run over and died, and I felt lonelier than I've ever felt in my whole entire life. It just seemed too much of a coincidence.

Anyway, it's a murky colour at the moment, which means that I must be feeling anxious or scared. I suppose Alex's grumpy mood has made me feel a bit worried so maybe that's it. Then again, we've got that horrible maths test at school tomorrow and I just know that I'm going to fail – I didn't understand a word that Mrs Hardman said when she was teaching us about simple equations.

There was definitely nothing simple about them though, I know that for sure.

Something's making me feel nervous and I don't like it. It's like that feeling you get when there's about to be a big storm: things start to feel wrong. I think I'll distract myself until Mum gets back from work by finishing my homework. Then I might make sure my pencil case has got everything I'll need for tomorrow's test. Best to be prepared, just in case a miracle happens and I actually understand one of the questions. It'd be a shame if that happened and my pen had run out of ink.

All That Glitters Is Not Gold

Some nights I have the same dream. A recurring dream – a dream that you just can't stop, even if you really want to. I dream that I'm sitting in a seat in a theatre. The seat is covered in red velvet and I can tell it's old because of the way that there's a rip on the side and the armrests are worn through and shiny, from the hundreds and thousands of arms that have rested on them over the years. There are rows of seats stretching out in front of me and rows of seats reaching into the distance behind me, but they're all empty. I'm all alone in the theatre, except for one other person.

Alex is on the stage, standing in a single spotlight. She starts to dance, slowly at first, but then faster and faster, until she's whirling and twirling so fast that I forget to breathe – I'm so sure that she'll fall. There's never any music, but it doesn't matter because Alex *is* the music. The way she moves is so beautiful, so everything, that music couldn't compete with her. Definitely not me on my violin.

And then, suddenly, she stops. I clap as loudly as I can – I clap until my hands hurt. I stand up and cheer and call her name.

'Alex! Alex! I'm over here!'

She stands on the stage, eyes sparkling, with the biggest smile I've ever seen. She's breathing deeply, out of breath, and I can feel her excitement and pride; it's radiating out from her in purple waves.

I want to run to her, to hug her and tell her how amazing she is, to tell whoever will listen that this is my big sister. I feel like I'll burst, I'm so proud.

And then something catches Alex's attention and she turns slightly, looking right in my direction. I wave and shout, but she looks straight past me. I spin round to see who's behind me – whose name is on her lips – but there's nobody there.

When I turn back, Alex has gone. This is when I wake up. When the dreams first began, I'd be sweating and crying. Mum would come running in and I'd try to explain why I was so sad. But, after a while, the crying stopped. Now I wake up and lie in the dark, looking up at my glow stars on the ceiling. I wonder why, not once, even though I've been having this dream for over a year, Alex has never looked at me.

Tickled Pink

I'm sitting at the kitchen table struggling over my science homework when I hear the back door open.

'Hi, Finn,' says Mum, without turning round from the stove.

'Hi,' Finn replies, flopping down into a chair. He's wearing a grey sweatshirt that's perfect for him; grey people are reliable people and I'd trust Finn with anything. 'What you working on, Izzy?'

'The rock cycle,' I tell him.

'That's cool! You get way better homework than we did in Year 7. If you want any CDs, just let me know. I've got all the classics and loads of examples – garage rock, indie rock, punk rock, soft rock, hard rock, grunge.' Finn stops to take a breath. 'And then I've got blues rock, psychedelic rock and, obviously, progressive rock.'

'Not *that* kind of rock,' I say. 'I've got to look

at how different rocks are made, like sedimentary rocks and igneous rocks.'

Finn looks disappointed so I rush to reassure him.

'Your kinds of rock are much more interesting than mine,' I tell him. 'I wish my homework *was* about them!'

'Well, I'm not going to be much use to you then – I was rubbish at science. Gave it up the first chance I had.'

I sense Mum turning round behind me.

'But wouldn't you agree, Finn, that science is a very useful subject and Izzy should do her absolute best to finish her homework?' Her voice is friendly, but I know she's raising her eyebrows at Finn in a 'get the hint and agree with me' way.

'Oh yes. I totally agree. Science is very important. I really wish I'd worked a bit harder when I was in Year 7. And just wait till you're in Year 13 – we have so much work to do it isn't funny!'

Mum is satisfied with his answer and turns back to the stove. Finn grins at me and I stifle a groan. Why does Mum have to make me look like such a baby in front of him? I always do my homework; it's not like she has to nag me to do it.

'Here you go, Finn – try one of these.' Mum puts down a plate of biscuits on the table in front of us. 'Careful, they only came out of the oven a few minutes ago so they're piping hot!'

'Thanks, I thought I could smell something good.' Finn grabs a biscuit and then quickly drops it, yelping and shoving his fingers in his mouth.

'I did warn you,' says Mum.

I laugh at the face Finn is pulling and carefully take a biscuit for myself, gently pulling pieces off the sides and blowing on them before I risk eating one.

Today must be a no-reason visit from Finn because there's no band practice. I know this because Alex spends hours and hours getting ready on band nights and I can't ever get anywhere near the bathroom. Not until she's gone out at least. Alex is quiet today – suspiciously quiet actually. Now that I think about it, she's not making any noise whatsoever, which is very unusual. There's no radio blaring from her room, or the sound of her hairdryer at full hair-destroying throttle. Very strange indeed.

Finn has obviously recovered from his burns because he reaches for another biscuit and stuffs it into his mouth, whole.

'Ooobledook Aldrgghhh ergghhh?' he splutters through the crumbs. I really, really like Finn, but I wish that he wasn't such a boy sometimes. There are crumbs all over the table and somebody will have to clear them up and you can bet that it won't be him.

'What?' I ask him. 'I don't speak biscuit language.'

Finn swallows and wipes his mouth.

'That was lush – thanks! I said, is Alex about?'

I look towards the ceiling, which is daft because I don't have X-ray vision.

'Well, I *thought* she was in her room,' I tell him. 'But now I'm not so sure. It's very quiet up there.'

Finn stands up.

'I'll go and have a look,' he says, and saunters off towards the stairs. Mum doesn't say a word, just keeps stirring her pan on the stove. If it was any other boy, she'd have a fit – there's no way that Alex would be allowed to have a boy in her room – but Finn is different. I don't know why, but he just is. It's silly really because he actually still is a boy, even if he's just Finn.

I keep going with my homework, labelling a diagram with erosion and weathering and other confusing things. After a few minutes, I hear heavy footsteps clomping down the stairs and then Finn appears in the kitchen doorway.

'Was she not there?' asks Mum, looking worried for a moment. She likes to keep very close tabs on me and Alex, which is not a problem for me as I have nowhere else to be but home or school, but Alex hates Mum 'constantly going on' about where she'll be and what time she'll be home. They had a whopping argument about it the other night and Alex yelled at Mum that maybe she should just be done with it and make Alex wear a tag like a prisoner – then she could track her location at all times. Mum shouted back that she thought that was a great idea and that when Alex showed she was worthy of trust then she, Mum, would be more than happy to give it to her.

I pretended that I couldn't hear them, which was quite difficult as I was watching TV in the living room and they were standing in the hallway right outside the door. I turned the volume up on the TV to drown them out, but then Alex stormed off and slammed the front door, and Mum marched into the living room and yelled at me for having the sound too loud. So unfair – it was Alex who wound her up, not me.

'She's there,' Finn tells Mum. His voice is

quieter than normal and I look up to see what's wrong. 'She's busy. I'll catch up with her another time.' He walks quickly across the kitchen and opens the back door. 'Thanks for the grub. Good luck with the homework, Izzy.'

'Finn –' starts Mum, but the door has closed and he's gone. Mum looks at me and shrugs. I shrug back. I have no idea what just happened. Finn and Alex are inseparable. It makes me feel a bit left out actually – the way they can spend hours lounging around with each other, totally relaxed and laughing at jokes that only they understand. She's never been too busy for him before. Not ever.

'Maybe she's finally starting to understand the importance of her A levels,' Mum says, drying her hands on a tea towel. She looks quietly pleased, but I don't buy it. Alex is never that predictable.

'Supper's in the oven. You've got about half an hour,' Mum warns me and then she heads towards her study and the mountain of marking that's balanced on her desk. She teaches for three days every week and the rest of the time she's always really busy looking after us and Granny and Grandpa. She doesn't ever really go out with friends, even though Alex has been going on at her to get a social life. She does talk to Granny on the phone for ages every day though, and she pops in to see them virtually every day too, so it's not like she hasn't got anyone to talk to.

I keep going with my rocks for a few minutes, but curiosity overwhelms me and I can't think about sediments and magma until I know what Alex is doing. I creep out of the kitchen, past the closed study door and up the stairs. Alex's room is at the top on the right and her door is slightly open – Finn can't have closed it properly when he left. I'm not an eavesdropper, but surely if I just happen to hear something then that's OK? And if I'm crouched on the floor by Alex's door when I happen to hear something then that's totally explainable and fine. I could be looking for a contact lens or something. Except I don't wear contact lenses so I'd probably be looking for something else small and hard to find. Like a pin. Or a needle. Or maybe a pencil sharpener – I can never find one of those when I need it.

I sink on to the carpet and press my face up against the door. I can hear Alex, but she's not talking in her normal voice. She's speaking really quietly and giggling. Alex doesn't giggle. She laughs – a loud, rumbling laugh that makes everyone who hears it join in. It's totally contagious, Alex's laugh; even if you're completely miserable it makes you start sniggering. But that's not the laugh she's doing now. Now she's making a sweet, tinkling sound, like sleigh bells. It's not a bad laugh – it's just not her laugh. It sounds like a pink laugh, fluffy and sweet. I wonder if she's thinking about choosing a new laugh like she chooses new handwriting styles. I hope not. It wouldn't sound like her.

It's hard to hear what she's saying in this new fairy-princess voice that she's using, but if I press my face against the wall and squint I can see her through one eye. She's lying on her bed and talking on her mobile. I have no idea who she's talking to, but I don't think it's her best friend, Sara, and I know it can't be Finn. Whoever it is must be extremely important for Alex to send Finn away.

I glance down at my mood ring. It's red, which means danger, and I feel a tingle of fear run down my spine.

Izzy

Some things just go
together.
Like toast and peanut butter, or
envelopes and stamps.

You CAN have
one
without the other, but they're
better together.
That's just the way it is.

Like me and
Alex.
Better together.

Without her, I'm OK. Not fantastic, but not
totally useless.

But with her
I can do anything.

Without her, I creep along, shoulders
hunched against the
mean shouts
from the aggro boys,
swallowing their nasty words
so that they swirl and whirl
inside my stomach,
making me feel
jagged and
alone.

Footsteps behind me make me
speed up,
fear prickling my neck like a
miniature hedgehog
crawling along the collar of my school shirt.

My shoulders scrunch into my
ears as a hand
grabs
me.
And a voice calls out and I know that she is
here

and there is not an aggro boy alive who can
stand up to Alex.
She shouts and she tells them what
she will do to them
if they ever
bother
me
again.

Then she drapes her arm round me
and my shoulders sink back down like one of
Mum's cakes when she takes it out of the oven.

And we walk home.
The heaviness of Alex's arm
tethers me to her and I am
safe.
We don't talk about it,
but I know that she is watching out for me,
and I know that
I need her.

And a tiny bit of me wonders,
What would happen to me if
Alex
wasn't here?

Green with Envy

'Izzy!'

Alex is yelling at me from the bathroom. I'm lying on my bed and I've just had a really good idea for a verse I want to write, so I pretend I can't hear her and keep writing. I know I'm probably rubbish at writing poetry and I would never show anybody ANYTHING that I've written, but I like the way it feels when I write the words on the page. It feels like it doesn't matter if nobody ever reads it but me.

'IZZY!' She's not going to give up so I put my pen down and roll sideways off the bed.

'What?' I ask as I open the bathroom door. Alex is lying back in the bath, clouds of bubbles floating right up to the rim and almost overflowing on to the floor. I can never make the bath that bubbly. I think she must use at least half a bottle of bubble bath every time she has a bath. There are candles all along the window sill and green gunk all over Alex's face.

'What IS that?' I ask her.

'Face mask,' mumbles Alex, barely moving her lips.

'Why?'

'Good for the skin. It's got cucumber extract in it. It's very soothing.'

It doesn't look soothing. It looks uncomfortable. It's hardened on Alex's face and makes her look like a zombie.

'Why did you call me?'

'Revision. Mum won't let me go out tonight if I haven't done any work so you're going to test me while I get ready. Kill two birds with one stone. Very efficient.'

'I don't want to kill any birds. And how can I test you? I haven't got a clue about A levels.'

'That's the genius part of my plan,' says Alex, reaching out her foot and turning on the hot tap with her toes. I watch as the bubbles advance. 'Go into my room and get the postcards off my desk. I've written down some questions and the answers are at the bottom. You've just got to read me the questions and see if I get them right.'

I scuff my foot along the bath mat, squishing some of the bubbles that have overflowed.

'I was actually busy,' I tell Alex.

'Aw – come on, Izzy. Help me out. I'll be forever grateful.' Alex puts on her best wheedling voice and I know that I'll do what she's asked. I was really enjoying writing, but it always makes me feel good if Alex wants to do something with me, even if it does mean sitting in the bathroom helping her to revise.

'What did your last slave die of?' I mutter, heading towards the bathroom door.

'Not helping me revise!' Alex calls after me. 'Thanks, Izzy. I'll owe you, I promise!'

I walk into Alex's room, shuddering slightly at the mess. It's obvious that she's got a big night planned because it's even more of a state than usual. Her wardrobe door is open and the wardrobe is bare. That's because every single item of clothing owned by Alex is spread across the floor, her bed, her chair and her desk. She's rubbish at putting her clothes in the wash so her dirty vest tops and a pair of muddy jeans are lying in a sorry pile next to her laundry basket. I mean, what's that all about? It would take just as much effort to put her stuff IN the laundry basket as it does to put them on the floor next to it. It just makes no sense.

Leaping across the room, from one safe zone to another, I finally make it to the desk. I flick some smelly socks off the top of the desk using a pencil and find the postcards. Then I have to repeat the whole manoeuvre backwards until I reach the safety of the landing.

By the time I get back to the bathroom, Alex has washed off the face mask and is busy applying something orange with bits in to her arms.

'Exfoliator,' she explains when she sees me looking. 'Right, hit me with the questions.'

I put the lid down on the toilet and sit on the seat. Glancing at the postcards in my hand, I see that this is English revision. I read the first question.

'How is the theme of love addressed in *Romeo and Juliet*?'

Alex sinks lower in the bath and chews her bottom lip.

'Well, Romeo and Juliet love each other obviously. But they're star-crossed lovers, doomed never to be together.'

'What's a "star-crossed lover"?' I ask her.

'It means their fate was written in the stars –

they would only ever be unlucky if they stayed together,' says Alex with a daft, moony look on her face. 'They were the ultimate romantic couple.' She sighs dramatically and gazes at the hot-water tap like it's something precious. 'Remember *West Side Story*? That's basically the funky version of *Romeo and Juliet*. Same plot, better songs.'

'I thought they both died,' I say. 'That's not very romantic. And anyway the answer you've written here is all about the language of love, the dramatic effects created around the theme of love and the different aspects of love. You've not said anything like that.'

'Yes, well, never mind,' says Alex quickly. 'Ask me the next question.'

I sigh very quietly – in fact, so quietly that the sigh only exists inside my head. I know Alex when she's in this mood and she doesn't really want to revise. She just wants me to listen while she thinks out loud. Alex loves an audience: she hates being on her own. I don't usually mind – I like it when she chooses me. But my poem could have been quite good this time and it won't be the same now I've been interrupted mid-sentence.

'Come on, Izzy. I've got to get ready for my date in a minute.'

This is news. Alex has got loads of friends and she goes out all the time with her big crowd, but I've never heard her talk about a date before. I need to tread carefully if I'm going to get vital information out of her.

'Who's your date with?' I ask casually, shuffling through the postcards and making it seem like I'm looking for a good question.

'Charlie,' says Alex, now vigorously scrubbing her legs with a flannel.

'Charlie? You mean Man-of-the-Match Charlie?'

'I certainly do,' grins Alex, looking up at me.

Wow. I don't know what to say. I might only be in Year 7, but everyone at school knows Man-of-the-Match Charlie. He's a school legend: a demon on the football pitch and totally brilliant at just about everything he does. I heard that he took two A levels one year early and that a famous football team wants to sign him up, but he's already been offered a place at university and he's going to be a doctor. Probably a brain surgeon or something. And not to mention the teeny fact that he's gorgeous. If you like that kind of thing anyway.

'Is he your boyfriend?' I ask Alex. She's a perfect match for Charlie – beautiful and funny and impossible to ignore. I can't help feeling that they would make an unstoppable couple.

'Maybe,' she tells me. 'Now ask me another question.'

I try to focus and read out the next card.

'How is the drama created in Act 3, Scene 1?'

'Don't know. Can't remember what happens in Act 3, Scene 1. Next question.'

'Explain the reason for the conflict between Juliet and her father.'

Alex pulls out the plug and stands up.

'Chuck me the towel.'

I throw it over to her and she wraps herself up tightly, like a caterpillar in a cocoon. Then she stands in front of the mirror and starts swiping at her face with cotton wool.

'OK, Juliet and her dad. Er – I guess they're conflicted because she doesn't do what he wants her to do and that makes him mad. Because dads are bossy and don't want their daughters to live their own lives. Something like that.' She throws the cotton wool in the bin and begins rubbing cream on to her face.

I think for a moment about what she's just said.

'Was our dad bossy?' I ask her.

There's a moment of silence.

'Not really,' Alex says. 'What makes you ask that?'

'I just wondered,' I say. 'That's all.'

Alex is still looking in the mirror, but she catches my eye and looks at me.

'You can always ask Mum about him, you know. She means it when she says you can ask her anything.'

I pick up the toilet roll and start unravelling it.

'I know. I just wish I remembered something for myself. It's not the same, always having to ask. And I don't know what questions I should be asking. I might not be asking the right ones.' I twist the toilet roll back the other way so it's all neat and tidy and put it back on the shelf.

'So ask me,' says Alex, turning to face me and leaning against the sink. 'I might not have all the answers, but I can try.'

I look at the floor and think about what I want to know. Alex was seven when our dad walked out, just a few months after I was born. I heard Mum telling Finn's mum once that I was supposed to be their 'rescue baby', the thing that brought them back together. I really wish I hadn't heard her say that because ever since then, whenever I think about it, I feel like a total failure. Me being born didn't make them love each other again – it made Dad go away. I can't have been a very cute baby if he didn't want to stay with me. Perhaps I cried a lot and it drove him away. Babies can be very annoying.

'I know that he came back to visit a few times,' I say eventually.

'I remember that,' says Alex. 'He played with me in the garden. I used to love him pushing me on the swing. I was always yelling at him to swing me higher and higher!' She smiles at the memory. 'I used to think I could fly when he did that. And then I'd go just a bit too high and my stomach would flip over and I'd be scared – and he'd grab the swing and stop me, and I knew he'd never let anything bad happen to me.'

We've still got that swing in our garden. We always call it Alex's swing because it was hers first. I go on it sometimes, but nobody's ever pushed me until it felt like I was flying.

'Where was I?' I ask her. My voice sounds a bit whiney, like I'm jealous, but I don't think I can be jealous about something I don't remember.

'Oh, in the house with Mum, I guess,' says Alex, turning back to the mirror and her make-up bag.

I'm quiet for a minute, wondering why I wasn't

out in the garden, having fun with my dad. Alex notices the silence and raises her eyebrows at me in the mirror.

'You were a baby, Izzy. It was probably too cold for you in the garden. Or it was time for you to have your bottle or something. Don't worry about it.'

'Sure,' I tell her, standing up. 'Are we done with the revising now?'

'Yeah, no time left,' she says. 'Charlie will be here any second. Will you go down and distract him if I'm not ready? I can live without Mum asking him a million questions about what his intentions are.'

This time I let my groan escape into the bathroom.

'Alex! I've got stuff to do. And I'll feel totally stupid trying to talk to him. What am I supposed to say? Scored any goals lately?'

Alex laughs.

'You'll think of something. Consider it social skills practice. It's good for you – you should be thanking me.'

I squeeze past her and out on to the landing.

'And don't forget to tell Mum that I did some revision!' Alex yells after me.

I go back into my room, leaving the door open so that I can listen out for the front doorbell. I wish we hadn't had that conversation about Dad. I can't stop thinking about him and Alex, laughing and playing outside without me. I might have been a baby, but I bet I had feelings. I bet I minded being left behind. And it's not like he can make it up to me now. According to Mum, he had a longing for freedom and that freedom did not mean timetabling every other weekend so that he could take his daughters to McDonald's. Freedom for Dad meant moving to the other side of the world with promises to write and send photos and money so that we could visit. Maybe his plane crashed on the way there because there's never been a letter or a photograph, and we don't have an address for him so we can't visit him, even if we wanted to.

Which we don't. Mum is all that we need and we don't want anyone else. We've done all right up until now, she says. We're a team of three – Team Stone – and I can't imagine it any other way. Mum, Alex and me against the world. Together forever.

I've just picked up my notebook and read what I've written when the doorbell rings.

'Izzy!' yells Alex.

'Yes, yes, keep your hair on,' I shout, throwing down my pen and running out on to the landing and down the stairs. I can't deny that I'm quite excited. Man-of-the-Match Charlie! Here in our house!

'I've got it!' I yell towards the kitchen and then I stand in front of the door, smooth my hair down, take a deep breath and turn the handle.

'Hello,' I say in my politest voice.

'Is Alex in?' asks Charlie. His voice is quieter than I'd imagined.

'She's just getting ready,' I tell him. We look at each other for a moment before I remember my manners. 'Would you like to come in?'

I hold open the door and Charlie steps into the house. I look at our messy front hall and wonder what he can tell about us – what he thinks about us. My eyes fall on the embarrassing photograph on the wall of me on the beach in only a nappy. I *was* only one year old when it was taken, but still, I can do without Charlie seeing it.

'Would you like to sit down while you wait?' I ask him quickly, trying to steer him towards the living room, but he doesn't move.

'No thanks,' he says.

We stand in silence for a bit, me shifting from foot to foot. This is really awkward and I'm not sure what to do. It's not like this when Finn comes over. I never have to think about what to say to him, it just happens. I can feel myself starting to blush and know that I have approximately two seconds before my face is bright red and giving off enough heat to fry a sausage. I need to break the silence – start up a conversation.

I think back to what Alex has told me about boys. Occasionally, after a night out, she'll come into my room and sit on my bed, imparting some bits of wisdom, and I try to file them away in my mind for a time when they'll be useful. This is exactly that time and thankfully a helpful nugget pops into my brain. Alex says that boys are only good at talking about things that they like doing. Charlie is standing here, in our front hall, and if I want to engage him in a bit of casual chit-chat then I need to ask him about something he's interested in.

'So,' I say, trying to sound relaxed, 'scored any goals recently?'

Charlie looks at me in surprise, but before I can go any redder I hear Alex coming down the stairs. She isn't clomping down in her huge boots, making the photographs on the wall rattle until they nearly fall off. Neither is she yelling at the top of her voice as if everyone else is hard of hearing. She's not doing any of the things that she normally does when she's leaving the house. Instead, she's tottering down each step in a pair of sparkly silver shoes with the highest heel I've ever seen. And she's wearing a dress. Without jeans underneath or a massive chunky cardigan on top. She almost looks ladylike and I have to clasp my hand over my mouth to muffle the gasp that's threatening to come out. Luckily, Charlie isn't looking at me. He can't take his eyes off Alex and I don't blame him. She looks utterly gorgeous.

I've never seen Alex wear the colour silver before and I think about what it means. Silver stands for glamour and mystery and feminine strength – which I think is a bit like girl power. I like collecting phrases that are linked to colours, but the only one I can think of right now is 'every cloud has a silver lining', which means that even when something bad happens, there'll be something good in there too. I don't know how that's connected to Alex choosing silver high heels.

Mum comes out from the kitchen and says hello to Charlie. He manages to stop drooling over Alex for long enough to speak to Mum, but I catch a steely glint in Mum's eye when she's looking at him, as if she knows exactly what he's thinking.

'Back by eleven,' Mum tells Alex.

'No problem,' Alex replies sweetly, gazing at Charlie like he's her Romeo.

Charlie holds out his hand and Alex takes it and they walk down the hall. I scamper ahead of them and open the door, and they glide past me and down the garden path, neither of them giving me or Mum another glance. I watch them go and then close the door, turning to see Mum looking out of the living room window. I go and stand next to her and together we watch Charlie open his car door and help Alex into the passenger seat.

'She didn't get mad when you told her to be home on time,' I tell Mum. 'That's good.'

'Hmmm,' she says, still watching until the car pulls away from the kerb. I can tell by her voice that she's not happy. I'm not sure why, but my heart is beating a bit too fast and my skin feels all shivery. I consult my mood ring and it's green. Green for jealousy. Is that why I'm feeling like this – because Alex has got someone who looks at her like she's the most special person on earth?

But as I twiddle my ring it changes colour and suddenly it's red again. Danger. I wonder if it was Charlie that Alex was talking to on the phone the other day, the day when she sent Finn away. My mood ring went red that day too.

I might only be in Year 7 and have never had a boyfriend and know nothing about any of this stuff, but there's definitely something dangerous about Alex and Charlie. And I think it's the way that they looked at each other as if nobody else existed. As if the only thing that made any sense was *them*. I remember that silver stands for something else too: loneliness, like when Betty the cat died. I think about what Alex told me about star-crossed lovers being doomed, that they could only bring bad luck to each other. And I really, really wish that Alex hadn't gone out with Charlie tonight.

Purple with Rage

It's been six weeks since Alex went on her first date with Charlie. Six weeks since everything started to feel a bit different. I can't quite work out *how* things have changed, but my mood ring is orange all the time, which proves that there's something going on. According to my mood-ring guide, orange indicates 'mixed emotions'. That definitely describes Alex's mood at the moment. One minute she's the normal Alex – loud, bossy, impossible to ignore – and then it's like she's had a personality transplant and the next minute she's quiet and moody, staring out of the window and twiddling her hair. Alex can't *stand* hair-twiddlers; she always says they do it because they think it makes them look cute, but I don't think she even realizes she's doing it.

Then, when it's nearly time for her to meet

Charlie (which she's doing A LOT), she locks herself in the bathroom and when she comes out she doesn't look anything like Alex. She's started straightening her hair when before it was always twisted up in a mad pile on top of her head and held together with whatever she could find, like pencils or chopsticks. The other evening I'm sure I spotted streaks of glitter across her cheeks. Alex HATES girly, sparkly stuff. It's all incredibly confusing.

I haven't managed to have a proper conversation with Charlie yet. He's really good at standing in our hallway and he's always polite to Mum, but I don't think he's very good at making small talk. It makes me wonder what he and Alex chat about when they're together because Alex loves talking. If talking was an Olympic sport then she'd bring home the gold medal every time. That's one of the reasons she spends so much time with Finn: they talk and talk, and half the time I haven't got a clue what they're on about and I get bored with listening. I would've thought they'd get fed up with talking so much and that their mouths would ache, but they never stop. So I'm really not sure how Alex is managing to cope with Strong-but-Silent Charlie. He seriously never seems to have anything to say. I suppose he might be a really good listener though. Alex would like that.

She's not seeing Charlie tonight. Mum is out at Granny and Grandpa's having a crisis meeting because Grandpa wandered off again today – Mum says he's getting worse. Tonight it's band practice and they're all meeting at our house so Alex can babysit me. I HATE that word. I've been trying for ages to get Mum and Alex to stop using it. It makes me feel utterly pathetic, like I'm a little child who can't look after herself. I don't need anybody to look after me, and I've told Mum that time and time again, but every time I mention it she just says, 'Remember the night of the tapping tree?'

It's so unfair. I'm going to be judged for the rest of my life because of one stupid mistake. And it was a completely easy mistake to make too – anyone else would have done what I did.

Mum was going to be late home because she had a meeting at school and Alex was supposed to be going to the cinema with Sara. Mum asked Alex to cancel her plans so she could stay at home with me, but Alex moaned and complained so much that I begged Mum to let me stay at home on my own. I didn't want Alex to hate me for spoiling her evening. Miraculously, Mum agreed and everything was fine until it got dark and I heard someone knocking on the window. I might have freaked out a *tiny* bit, but I tried to be brave and I stood by the window and shouted out to ask who was there. The tapping carried on and then I thought I heard someone groaning and it sounded menacing, full of threat and death.

My mind was totally full of murderers and dead bodies and 'me-next' thoughts so I did what any reasonable person would do. I phoned 999. I might have been crying a little bit when I spoke to the operator (not howling hysterically, which is what Alex says when she retells the story) and before I knew what was going on there were two police cars screeching on to our drive, followed by an ambulance. The flashing lights and screaming sirens alerted Finn's mum and she rang Mum's mobile before dashing across the road in her slippers.

It turns out that I might *possibly* have mentioned dead bodies and murderous groans when the nice lady operator was trying to calm me down, and apparently that moves you to the top of the priority list. Mum arrived home and nearly crashed into one of the police cars because she was driving at about eighty miles an hour. (She was lucky not to end up with a speeding ticket because we live on a residential street and the limit is thirty miles an hour.)

Unfortunately for me, Alex turned up just as the police were doing a search of our flower beds. She raced into the living room where Mum was cuddling me and started crying, saying that she'd never leave me alone again, and she was sorry that she'd gone to the cinema instead of staying with me and that the film was rubbish anyway. I started to feel all good and relaxed until, suddenly, I heard it again. I sat bolt upright and screamed.

'There it is!' I yelled. 'That's the noise I heard. He's still out there!'

The police officer who was standing by the window pulled the curtains apart and we all looked out. I had my hands in front of my face, peeking through my fingers – which, as it turned out was not necessary, as the only thing out there was a branch from the apple tree on our front lawn, blowing in the wind and brushing against the window.

'That was the noise you heard?' asked the police officer.

I nodded and burrowed my head in Mum's

armpit so that nobody could see my very red face. Mum and the police officer muttered a few words to each other and then he went outside to call off the dogs (not literally, they hadn't actually got the dogs in by then, thank goodness). Alex stopped sobbing very abruptly and said that I was an idiot, which I felt was a bit harsh because the tapping had sounded very scary and how was I supposed to know that it was a very windy night? The ambulance left and then the police all got into their cars, but not before one of them had suggested to Mum that I shouldn't be left home alone again for a while. Possibly until I'm thirty-five. Well, he probably didn't say that, but Alex did and, since that night, Mum has NEVER left me on my own at night, not for one single second.

So tonight band practice is in our living room. Stefan arrived earlier, his dad helping him drag his drum kit out of the car and into the house. I tried to keep out of their way, but everywhere I went ended up being where they needed to go. I said sorry to Stefan's dad, but he just smiled at me and said something that I didn't understand. Stefan's parents moved here from Poland when Stefan was a baby. His mum speaks pretty amazing English, but his dad doesn't speak a word. Stefan told me once that his dad can read English and understands everything that you say to him – he just can't speak it. It doesn't seem to bother him though and he's always smiling. I think he's really proud of Stefan because he helps him take his drums everywhere and he never seems to get cross or grumpy about it.

I'm sitting in the kitchen and trying to finish my homework because once they start practising I'll never get anything done. On the Rocks is a very loud band. I can hear that Dylan has arrived because the floor has started vibrating with the buzz coming from his bass guitar and I put my head nearer to the page, desperately finishing the last part of my story before it's too loud to think straight.

I'm just closing my book when Finn dashes in through the back door, his guitar slung across his back.

'Coming in to listen, Izzy?' he asks me, ruffling my hair as he speeds past. I pretend to scowl at him and press my hands down on my head, trying to straighten my hair.

'Maybe,' I tease, but I'm already getting up from the table. I love it when the band rehearses at our house. Going into the living room, I head towards my favourite spot. Curling up on the armchair, surrounded by guitar cases and amplifiers and leads, I watch as Finn quickly tunes his guitar and Stefan adjusts his drum stool until he's found a position that he likes. Dylan stands to one side, plucking out a steady rhythm and looking into the distance. Dylan is really shy, but you'd never know that when he starts playing – he totally comes to life when he's got his guitar in his hands. I have a secret wish that one day, when I'm good enough, I'll get an electric violin and Alex will let me join On the Rocks. I think about this every time I do violin practice and it makes me work extra hard.

Then Alex steps up to the microphone that's standing in the middle of the room. She nods at Stefan and he hits his drumsticks together four times before they all launch into their first song. On the Rocks perform covers of other songs and some of their own. This is a cover song that I know really well and I find myself tapping along to the beat as Alex starts to sing.

Alex is exactly the sort of person who should be on *Britain's Got Talent*. If I'm totally honest, I'm not sure that she's the best singer in the whole world, but something happens to her when she starts singing and it means that you literally cannot take your eyes off her. She can't stay still and the way she moves, as if she's feeling every single part of the music flowing through her, makes you believe that she could probably do anything.

They've done the first verse and, as they move into the chorus, Finn steps up to the microphone. He sings the backing vocals next to Alex and their voices dip and dive round the melody so perfectly that suddenly my arms are cold and I can feel goosebumps. Alex glances at Finn and sings the lyrics to him and, as she sings the words about love and friendship and hope, I see Finn gaze at her as if she's his entire world. And then Alex stops singing and spins round to glare at Stefan.

'What are you *doing*?' she shouts at him and everything crashes to a halt. Stefan shrugs at Alex.

'What are you on about? Why did you stop?'

Alex sighs – a huge over-the-top sigh that blows all of the happy feelings right out of the room.

'I stopped because you played it wrong. We agreed that you'd lose that drum fill at the end of the chorus and go straight into the second verse.'

Stefan shrugs again, this time in the direction of Dylan who is suddenly busying himself with a guitar string.

'I just thought I'd see how it sounded. Me and

Dylan practised something new last week and we thought we'd surprise you tonight – see what you thought.'

'Well, I *thought* it sounded awful. Like you're trying to get all the attention.' Alex has got her hands on her hips and she's really cross now, her lips pressed tightly together and lines criss-crossing her forehead.

'No chance of that with you about,' mutters Stefan.

'WHAT DID YOU SAY?' yells Alex, and I shift uneasily in my armchair. This is not what band practice is meant to be like. Normally they play a few songs and then listen to any new stuff they've all been working on, and then they lounge about for ages, listening to music and eating crisps. The room feels heavy, as if something horrible is about to happen, and, sure enough, my mood ring has gone a murky colour.

'Steady on, Alex,' says Finn, putting his hand on her arm, but she brushes him off and acts like he hasn't even spoken to her. She stands very still, glaring furiously at Stefan, not seeming to notice the energy that's fizzing about the room.

'How dare you suggest that it's all about me!'

she screeches. 'I am NOT always trying to get attention. I just want us to be good. IS THAT A CRIME?'

I am utterly transfixed by Alex. This is not like her at all. Not the shouting – that's exactly like her – but she doesn't normally shout in a properly angry way. Mostly when she shouts she's being funny or tantrummy. This doesn't feel like either of those. A movement in the corner catches my attention and I turn to see Dylan hurriedly packing his guitar into its case. Finn walks across to speak to him quietly and then Dylan picks up his guitar and amp and walks quickly out of the room without looking back. I don't think he likes confrontation. I've never once seen him have an argument with anyone.

Finn walks back towards Alex who's still standing in the middle of the room.

'Look, Alex –' starts Stefan, but then he stops, his face registering surprise, before hurriedly turning away and starting to dismantle his kit. I wonder what he's seen and why he isn't shouting back at Alex for being in such a grouchy mood.

Finn reaches Alex, but she turns away from him before he can touch her, which means that she's facing me. Tears are running down her cheeks and, as I look, her face seems to crumple in on itself. It's a very strange thing to watch. One moment her face is all screwed up in total anger and the next it's as if all her features have collapsed – as if she's too upset to keep her face in its normal position. I reach towards her, but she ignores me and, as she rushes from the room, I hear huge heart-breaking sobs gasping out from her mouth.

I don't know what to do. I start to stand up, but Finn stops me.

'Wait a minute, Izzy. I'll just go and check on her.' He races out of the room and Stefan and I listen as we hear two pairs of footsteps pounding up the stairs. Then a door slams hard and a minute later Finn appears back in the doorway. He doesn't look at me and the feeling of fear that started in my stomach when Alex began yelling spreads to my chest.

'Might as well call it a day,' he tells Stefan, who nods and then picks up his phone to ring his dad. I don't know what he says to his dad, but I bet it's the Polish for 'a crazy girl has just ruined our evening and you need to come and collect me before she totally loses the plot'.

'He's on his way,' he tells Finn, hanging up the phone. 'Sooner I get a car of my own the better.'

Together, they pack up the drums and take

them out to our front hall. Stefan keeps glancing nervously towards the stairs, but Alex doesn't appear. I stay in the armchair and I think they've forgotten that I'm there until Stefan's dad has arrived and Finn has helped load up the car. Then Finn comes back into the living room and stands over me.

'You going to be OK until your mum gets back?' he asks me.

I glance at the clock on the mantelpiece. It's totally disgusting – a huge, wooden, swirly thing with a very annoying tick. It was a wedding present to Mum and Dad and Mum hates it. I asked her once why we've still got it and she looked surprised and said that she had no idea, but she still didn't get rid of it. Alex tried to put it in a bag of stuff to go to my school jumble sale once, but it somehow found its way back on to the mantelpiece and has stayed there ever since. We're stuck with it.

'I'll be fine,' I say to Finn. 'Mum'll be home soon.'

Actually, I have no idea when she'll be home, and Alex is obviously going to be rubbish company. I can feel my skin starting to feel prickly and itchy because I've lied to Finn, and if there's one thing I try really hard not to do it's to lie. That's not because I'm a goody-goody or anything – it just makes me feel really horrible inside if I lie so I mostly tell the truth because it's easier. If I was being honest, I'd ask Finn to stay and we could get our game of Scrabble out from the cupboard under the TV and sit at the kitchen table, eating biscuits and laughing about who can make up the most bizarre word. I like words: knowing what they mean and the power that they have makes me feel a bit more in control.

I don't want Finn to think that I need looking after though, so I don't say any of this and he leaves, this time without ruffling my hair or giving me a high five.

I plod upstairs and knock on Alex's door. No harm in trying, I suppose.

'Go away,' she shouts.

'It's me! Izzy,' I call back, worried that she might think it's Finn or Stefan come to annoy her.

'I know. Go away.'

I can hear her start to cry again and wish, with every bit of me, that I knew what to do. That I had some good words to make her feel better. I stand outside her door for a little while, but no words come to me, so I trudge across the landing and go into my own room. I've done my homework and I finished my book yesterday, so I have absolutely nothing to do. I wonder for a minute if I should make Alex some hot chocolate, but then I remember how she sounded and decide that an early night would probably be a good idea.

I clean my teeth and put my pink pyjamas on. I'm not mad keen on pink, but it's a calm, caring colour and I could use a bit of that right now. Then I turn out my lamp and sink into bed, hoping that tomorrow Alex will laugh about her daft mood and this will all just be a silly misunderstanding.

Darkness-destroyer

Alex and I walk home from school together most days at the moment. We've never really made actual plans to meet up, but by the time I get to the school gates she's usually there, chatting to people and laughing. Waiting for me. The aggro boys won't come anywhere near when she's with me. They sometimes shoot me nasty looks in PE lessons, but I try to keep out of their way and I'm hoping they'll get bored of the whole thing. They're bound to move on to terrorizing someone else before too long anyway.

Today the sun is shining and it feels quite warm, even though it's only the end of March. Alex is moaning though.

'This country is so ridiculous,' she says. 'It's hot now when we'd all totally accept it being wet and cold and then it'll get to August and we'll all be shivering in our winter woollies.'

I laugh. 'Yeah, someone should do something about it! Maybe it's the government's fault.'

Alex sighs. 'I just wish it'd make its mind up. Imagine living somewhere that had real weather.'

'What's not real about our weather?' I ask her. 'It feels pretty real to me.'

'Oh, you know what I mean,' she says, waving her hand dismissively at the sky. 'Snow in the winter, sun in the summer. Crisp autumn days with red falling leaves and fresh spring mornings with flowers and birds singing.'

'We have singing birds,' I point out. 'There are some pigeons living in the tree in our garden. I think they might be building a nest.'

'Don't you mean the "pigeon of peace"?' teases Alex, and I feel myself blushing. One Christmas, when I was little, I saw a Christmas card with a dove on the front and Mum told me that it was a bird that meant peace. A few months later, I got really excited when I saw a pigeon and loudly told everyone that it was the pigeon of peace. Alex has been calling them that ever since, even though it's not even funny any more. 'And pigeons don't count,' she adds.

I can't even pretend to know why she's suddenly so cross with the weather, especially when it's actually nice today. She's been like this for a while though – funny and brilliant one minute and then grouchy and complaining the next. I wish her exams were sooner and then she could stop stressing out. It's hard work not knowing which Alex is going to come down to breakfast every morning.

We get home and Alex opens the front door.

'Hi, girls,' Mum calls from her study. 'Did you have good days?'

'Hi, Mum, my day was OK,' I yell back, hanging up my school bag on a hook in the hall.

'How about you, Alex? Good day?'

'Just peachy,' mutters Alex, throwing her bag on to the floor and walking through to the kitchen. I follow her, stepping over her bag and sticking my head round the study door to see Mum.

'What's up with her?' asks Mum, nodding in the direction of the kitchen.

'The usual,' I tell her. 'Grouchy, grumpy, illogical.'

'Ah,' smiles Mum. 'Nothing to worry about then!'

Then she raises her voice and calls towards the door.

'I baked! Don't faint in surprise! Cut yourselves a nice large piece and I'm in here if you need me.'

'Thanks, Mum – I'm fine,' Alex calls back, sounding a bit happier.

'The magic of cake!' Mum mouths at me and I giggle. She's pretty good at dealing with Alex, which is a good job because I haven't got a clue what to say to her when she's in a bad mood.

I walk into the kitchen in time to see Alex cutting two huge wedges of cake, the buttercream oozing out of the middle like lava. My tummy rumbles and I suddenly realize that I'm starving. Alex hands me a plate and opens the back door.

'Coming out?' she asks, grabbing one of the pairs of wellies that are hanging on the welly-tree outside the back door, her plate balanced precariously in one hand. When she's out of the way, I follow her, although my sense of balance isn't as good as Alex's so I have to put my plate down on the step while I tug on my wellies. Then I pick it up and walk across the lawn to where Alex is settling on to the swing.

'So how was your day really?' she asks me. I look at her and she's staring at me, looking right in my eyes and giving me her full attention. She does this: when she's busy with something else, it almost feels like she's forgotten about me, but when she turns her laser focus on to me I feel as if nothing in the universe is more important to Alex than I am.

I sit down gingerly on the grass, patting at it with my hands to check it isn't soaking wet and I'm not going to stand up in a minute with a drenched backside. It's surprisingly dry though, so I relax and start munching on Mum's cake.

'It was OK,' I say through a mouthful of vanilla sponge. Mum's cakes might look a bit odd, but they taste delicious.

'What about those boys?'

'Oh, they're not a problem! They won't come anywhere near me while you're around!' I grin up at Alex, expecting her to smile back. But she doesn't. She's swinging gently and frowning – she looks worried. 'Really, Alex, they're terrified of you! You don't need to worry about me.'

There's silence for a few minutes while we eat our cake and then Alex puts her plate down on the grass.

'You need to be able to stand up for yourself, Izzy,' she says.

I laugh. 'Why? Nobody's going to bother me while I've got a darkness-destroying, monster-menacing ninja of a big sister, are they?' This is a joke we've had since I was tiny and afraid of the dark. Alex would creep into my room and shout at the monsters who I was sure were lurking in my wardrobe. Then she'd lie down next to me and tell me stories – always stories where the dark ended up being a good thing. Mum used to find us when she came up to bed, all snuggled up and fast asleep, with Alex's arms wrapped tightly round me.

'I won't always be around to rescue you, Izzy,' Alex says in a quiet voice. I look at her, feeling puzzled. We're a family – of course she'll always be here.

Then I remember. I've done such a good job of pretending that it isn't going to happen that I've actually managed to forget about it. University. In September Alex will pack her bags and Mum will put them in the car and then they'll drive for hours and hours. And then Mum will come back with an empty car and no Alex.

I stare at the tree in our garden, trying to imagine our house without Alex. It will be so QUIET. I don't think it'll feel like home at all. School will be different too, knowing that there's no chance of bumping into her in the corridors or the library; well, actually, to be totally honest there's absolutely no chance of bumping into Alex in the library NOW because she never goes there. I'm not sure she even knows where it is. And Grandpa – I need Alex to help me be strong for him.

'But you'll be fine, Izzy.' Alex is talking to me and I can tell she's trying to cheer me up. 'You just need to stand up to boys like that. Tell them where to go.'

And where's that? I want to ask her. The library? But I don't really feel like making a joke of it. Not having Alex to watch out for me is no laughing matter, especially not now when I seem to have become public enemy number one.

'And tell Mum if it gets worse,' she adds. This time I do laugh – loudly and right at her.

'I can't believe you said that!' I tell her. 'When have you ever got Mum to sort out your problems? Never – that's when!'

Alex finally smiles. 'Yes, but you're not me,' she says, pushing off from the ground with both feet and swinging high into the air.

And just like that I feel terrible. Because Alex has said exactly what I've always known. I'm not her. I'm nothing like her. I'm the person who needs other people to fight my battles because I've never been a battle-fighter. Nor am I a monster-menacer or a darkness-destroyer. It's a good job that Mum didn't have any more children after me because I would have been a rubbish big sister.

I get to my feet and gather up both our plates.

'I'm going in,' I tell Alex.

'OK,' she says, and I walk inside, leaving Alex swinging higher and higher in the garden as the air gets colder and the sky turns overcast and grey.

Red Herrings

I'm late for school, which is something that I really, really hate. I'm not sure how it happened, but when my alarm clock went off I just hit the snooze button and rolled over and went back to sleep. I NEVER do that. Now I've got no time to sort my hair out properly and for some reason I don't seem to have any clean pairs of socks so I've had to wear one brown sock and one black sock, and that's going to make me feel fidgety all day because they're the complete opposite of each other.

I've managed to eat some cereal, but my bowl will have to stay in the sink until I get home later. Mum left earlier – I have a vague memory of her calling goodbye up the stairs – and there's no sign of Alex. She was out really late last night and told Mum that she was studying at Sara's house, although I saw her when she left and she wasn't dressed like she was going to spend the night reading a textbook. She put her finger to her lips though when she tiptoed down the stairs and when I went into my room she'd left a note on my bed, asking me to tell Mum that I'd heard her and Sara planning their revision timetable.

This has been going on for a few weeks. Ever since that awful band practice actually. She's never home and I keep finding notes, written in violet ink, asking me to cover for her with Mum. I don't know what's going on, but it doesn't feel like it's anything good.

She must be around somewhere. There's no time to look for her though and, as I run upstairs, two at a time, I wish that our house didn't seem quite so empty.

I push open the bathroom door and race inside, only to screech to a standstill as Alex spins round, grabbing a towel and holding it in front of herself.

'Get out!' she yells, sounding really angry.

'I just need to clean my teeth,' I tell her, reaching for the toothpaste.

'I SAID get out, Izzy. I mean it. Leave.' Alex's voice is hissy and I look at her in surprise. She's clutching the towel tightly as if she doesn't want me to see a single millimetre of her body. This is weird because she's normally got no problem with sharing the bathroom with me.

I don't want to make her mad, but I really am late and the thought of having to walk into my maths class alone makes me brave.

'I'll be thirty seconds,' I plead with her, squeezing the toothpaste on to my brush. I normally brush my teeth for a full two minutes – I really don't want to get any fillings – but I suppose I can make an exception this morning. I'll just have to add the time on tonight and brush for longer.

I shove the brush in my mouth and brush frantically, ignoring the fierce glares that I can see Alex shooting me in the mirror. As soon as I can feel minty freshness flooding through all parts of my mouth, I rinse my toothbrush and put it back in the cup on the sink.

'I'm going now,' I tell Alex.

'Good,' she mutters, looking out of the window.

'Aren't you going to school?' I ask her, suddenly curious about why she's still not dressed.

'Back off, Izzy!' she explodes, rounding on me. 'It's got exactly NOTHING to do with you so get lost. For your information, I feel really sick so, if it's OK with you, I'll be staying at home today. ALL RIGHT?'

I can feel tears springing up behind my eyes and I blink furiously in an attempt to stop them. Why is Alex being so mean to me? Have I done something wrong and forgotten about it? Quietly I turn round and walk out of the bathroom, but as soon as I reach the landing I start running – down the stairs, through the hall, pausing only to grab my school bag, out of the front door, slamming it hard behind me and out on to our drive. I only stop running when I reach the school gates and then I walk in with the last of the stragglers, making it to registration by the skin of my teeth. I'm sweating and panting for breath, but even that isn't enough to get the memory out of my head – the memory of Alex looking at me like she hates me.

Now I'm sitting in my worst lesson of the week – citizenship. There are some things that you really shouldn't be forced to talk about with other people and anything to do with personal, social or health issues is definitely included in that category. Hannah and I sit as near to the back as humanly possible and spend most of the lesson praying that we won't be forced to say anything. Last term my report for citizenship said: 'Izzy could improve her Attitude to Learning scores if she would make an effort to contribute in class discussions.' That is NEVER going to happen.

Today we're learning about drugs. I have absolutely no intention of ever taking an illegal substance. I hate the idea of not being in control of what I'm doing – why would anyone want to feel like that? Mrs Wallis is showing us a PowerPoint presentation about people who take drugs. We're supposed to be working out which of the people on the display are drug users. The first picture is of a homeless man sitting in the street with a mangy-looking dog curled up next to him.

'It's Simon's dad!' calls out Matthew and everyone sniggers. Simon goes bright red and thumps Matthew on the arm, and then Mrs Wallis tells us all to be quiet or she'll make us write an essay on why drugs are harmful. That shuts everyone up and she goes on to the next slide.

I feel bad for Simon. We were at primary school together and I remember him in Year 3 when his dad left home. He came into school and cried in the role-play area every day for half a term. Then he stopped crying and just got on with it, but I've never forgotten the sight of him sitting on a tiny chair in our pretend cafe, surrounded by cups and plates and plastic food, and sobbing on his own. Matthew didn't go to our primary school so I guess he doesn't know about Simon's dad.

The next picture is of a hippy-looking student with long, dreadlocked hair. This is followed by a picture of a man in an office, a teenager on a bike, a nice-looking nurse and an old man digging his garden.

'So, which of these people uses drugs?' asks Mrs Wallis, turning off the projector and putting the lights back on.

We're given a few minutes to talk to our partners.

'Definitely the homeless man,' says Hannah to me.

I think about it for a moment. 'Did she say we could choose more than one? Because that student looked like she'd take drugs, don't you reckon?'

'Maybe,' Hannah says. 'D'you think I should get my hair cut? Really short, I mean – something totally different.'

'I'm not sure,' I tell her, putting my head on one side and squinting, trying to imagine her with short hair. Hannah has got the longest hair of anyone I know and I'm not sure she'd look like *her* if she cut it. I don't really like it when things change too much so I'm about to tell her that long hair suits her much better when Mrs Wallis calls us all to stop talking and face the front.

'So,' she says, once the boys have finally turned back to their desks. 'What do you think? Who are the drug users?'

A few people at the front of the class put their hands up and suggest the same pictures that we thought. The homeless man. The student with dreadlocks. Mrs Wallis smiles, like we've said exactly what she expected us to say.

'What would you say if I told you that they ALL use drugs?' she asks us and the classroom buzzes with surprise. 'All kinds of people use drugs,' she says and for the first time this term she has the complete attention of the whole class.

'Even that old man in the garden?' asks a girl sitting a few rows in front of me.

'Why not?' says Mrs Wallis. 'You can't make assumptions about people based on their appearance or age. People use drugs for different reasons. And today we're thinking about the effects that taking illegal drugs can have. Does anyone know how to spot signs of drug abuse?'

'Drugs make you high!' shouts out Matthew and everyone laughs again.

Mrs Wallis claps her hands to make us all be quiet. 'Yes, that's one effect and it's one of the reasons that people take drugs in the first place. Certain drugs make you feel happy and like you can do anything – for a little while. But then the effect wears off and you're left feeling miserable and unwell. So you take more drugs to feel happy again; that's where the addiction part comes in.'

She perches on the front of her desk and looks at us. 'But how can we tell if someone's taking drugs?'

We're all quiet for a moment, not really sure of the answer. Then Simon puts up his hand.

'They might start to look pale and get sick,' he says and Mrs Wallis beams at him.

'Well done, Simon. Yes, drug users don't tend to look particularly healthy. The drugs might make them sick and they might lose a lot of weight. Drugs can affect your appetite too, so someone on drugs might change their eating habits.'

'Drugs make you moody!' calls someone else.

'Excellent!' praises Mrs Wallis. 'Mood swings are a major effect of drug use. Happy and cheerful one minute, depressed and angry the next. Anything else?'

'Being secretive cos they're scared of being found out!'

'Drug stuff in their bag!'

'Doing badly at school or bunking off!'

'Spending loads of time in their room!'

The class is on a roll and I sit quietly, listening to what they're saying. And with every new suggestion my stomach folds in on itself a little bit more. Moody, secretive, sick. Pale, angry, missing school. The class is describing my sister. The more I think about it, the more I know it must be true.

Alex has started taking drugs. That would explain why she got so cross with Stefan at band practice and why she hasn't gone to a single band practice since then. It would explain why she shouts at Mum and me all the time and why she wasn't going to school this morning. With a thudding heart, I realize that she didn't want me to come into the bathroom this morning because she didn't want me to see her body. Maybe it's all wasted and thin or maybe she didn't want me to see her arms. I start to feel dizzy and put my head down on my desk, imagining Alex injecting drugs into her body with a needle. I think I might actually be sick and I've never felt so scared in my life.

'Izzy? Are you OK?' whispers Hannah, but I can't answer her. I don't want to talk to anyone, but she's prodding me in the side and when I don't respond she calls Mrs Wallis.

'Mrs Wallis? I think Izzy feels ill.'

I want to tell her to be quiet, but my head is thumping and my heart is racing, and I don't think I can look up. I hear footsteps and then Mrs Wallis is speaking into my ear.

'Izzy? What's wrong?'

The bell rings and twenty-five chairs scrape across the floor.

'Leave quietly!' calls Mrs Wallis although nobody seems to hear her. I keep my head down and hope that she'll leave me alone. 'You can go to your next class,' she tells Hannah, who I can sense hovering nervously behind me. 'I'll send Izzy along when she's ready.'

I hear Hannah leave and then it's just Mrs Wallis and me.

'Are you unwell?' she asks. I shake my head as much as I dare. 'No, I thought not,' she says. 'Try to sit up, Izzy – you'll be fine.'

Her voice is kind but firm and I carefully raise my head until I'm sitting up in my seat. I don't look at Mrs Wallis though. I don't know what to say to her and I don't want to lie.

'Was it the lesson that upset you?' she says.

'Yes,' I whisper.

'Don't worry, Izzy, it's an upsetting subject and hearing about all of that can have a funny effect on people – particularly at your age. It's nothing to worry about, but next lesson try to focus more on the mechanics of what we're learning. Think of it like science instead of something emotional. That might help a little bit.'

She smiles at me and she's being so kind that for a second I nearly tell her. I nearly betray my own sister. But then I take a deep breath and hold it in. I smile back at Mrs Wallis and tell her that I'll get a drink of water before I go to my next lesson and that yes, I'm actually fine now and I feel a bit silly. I don't tell her that my big sister is addicted to drugs and that I'm the only person who knows. I don't tell her that this will tear my family apart and that nothing will ever be the same again. I don't tell her that I'm more scared than I've ever been – and that I'm worried that if I don't get home soon then Alex will have done something really stupid. People die from taking drugs, don't they?

I don't tell her any of this. Instead, I get up, calmly push my chair under the table and walk out of the room, looking on the outside like I'm perfectly in control, but feeling on the inside like my whole world has just collapsed.

The day drags on and on. Hannah tries to ask me about what is wrong, but I fob her off. I check my mood ring every few minutes and every time it's turquoise. It's NEVER been turquoise since Alex bought it for me. At lunchtime I race into the library and use one of the computers to Google colour meanings. Turquoise represents secrecy, unreliability and deception. I know that I have to get home as soon as possible and the minute the final bell rings I'm racing out of the door, sprinting as fast as I can for the second time today.

I race through the front door of our house, half desperate to see Alex and half terrified about what state she might be in. As the day has gone on, I've been imagining worse and worse things, and now I'm about ready to call 999 again and get Alex the medical attention she so obviously needs.

'Alex?' I call, throwing my bag into the corner. Homework is going to have to wait today.

A grunting sound comes from the living room and, with my heart in my mouth, I tiptoe towards the door. The TV is on and Alex is lying on the sofa, looking bored. I walk over to her and squeeze on to the edge of the sofa so that I can look at her properly.

'Are you OK?' I ask her.

'Uhhm,' she says, which doesn't tell me very much. She reaches down and takes a handful of crisps out of the king-size packet lying on the sofa. I sniff and wrinkle my nose in disgust. Cheese and onion? Alex and I have always been in perfect agreement that cheese and onion flavour crisps are the work of the devil and not fit for human consumption. We even play a game called 'Cheese and Onion Snog' where one of us will suggest a name and the other has to decide if they would kiss that person EVEN if they'd been eating cheese and onion crisps. So far, we've not found a single boy we'd want to kiss – although I haven't asked her about Charlie yet.

I try to focus and put crisp flavours out of my mind. They're not important at the moment. I need Alex to confess to her addiction and then we can work out how to tell Mum.

'It's OK, Alex,' I tell her, rubbing her leg in what I hope is a relaxing way.

She ignores me, although she shifts her leg away from my hand.

'You can talk to me, you know,' I say.

Alex is still staring at the rubbish daytime talk show on the TV and I wonder if she's had some kind of mental breakdown. I think hard about what to say. I need to get it right – let her know that she can trust me.

'I know what's going on,' I say. 'I know why you felt sick this morning.'

This finally gets her attention. She sits up so quickly that the packet of crisps falls off the sofa and spills foul crumbs all over the carpet. Bet Alex won't clean that up and I'll end up doing it.

'What are you on about?' she snaps, glaring at me.

I sit up a bit straighter and try to look mature and trustworthy.

'You can talk to me about what's going on. I can help you.'

Alex laughs, a hard, short laugh that has nothing funny about it.

'How can YOU help ME? You're just a kid. You can't do anything.'

This hurts. I've spent all day worrying myself silly about Alex and the least she can do is be civil to me. She doesn't actually have to be rude.

'You've got to tell Mum, Alex. You need help.'

Alex grabs my arm so hard that I wince.

'Don't you dare say a thing to Mum,' she snarls. 'I mean it, Izzy – I'll never forgive you if you tell her.'

I'm too shocked to say anything so I just look at Alex. Her eyes look tired, but they still have enough energy to scowl at me, making it clear that she means what she says. Suddenly I feel frightened – I don't recognize this Alex.

'It's got nothing to do with you,' she says, letting go of me and slumping back against the cushions. She closes her eyes and I feel a rush of anger buzzing through me. Standing up, I lean over her and let the anger out.

'How can you say that?' I shout at her and Alex opens her eyes, shock registering on her face. 'It's got everything to do with me! This is my house too and if you're bringing that stuff here then you're making it something to do with me.'

Alex opens her mouth as if she's going to ask me a question, but I race on, desperate to tell her how I feel.

'You're my sister, Alex, and I'll always love you, no matter what you do. But please, please stop doing this to yourself. It's too dangerous. I know you think that I don't know anything, but we've learnt all about it in citizenship and drugs can hurt you, Alex. They can kill you. And I don't want you to die!'

Having made my point, I burst into tears, and I stand there feeling furious with myself for acting like a child, but unable to stop the tsunami of tears that are overwhelming me.

Alex stands up and wraps her arms round me.

'What did you just say?' she whispers in my ear.

'I know you're taking drugs,' I sob back, gulping in huge breaths in between each word. I sound pathetic, but I don't care now – Alex is hugging me. I did it; she can admit her problem and we can solve it together. Alex needs me and she knows I'm here for her.

I feel her body start to shake and I stop crying, holding on to her tightly.

'It's OK,' I tell her. 'It's going to be OK.'

For one moment I feel totally powerful. I hold Alex in my arms and imagine her confiding in me. Then I hear a completely unexpected sound – the sound of Alex laughing. Properly laughing. And I realize that her shaking is not a result of her being overcome with emotion, but a result of her being unable to stop sniggering hysterically.

I pull away from her and watch as she wipes her eyes.

'Oh, Izzy, you are funny,' she says, straightening her shirt and turning back to the sofa. This is not what I expected.

'I'm not funny. This isn't funny,' I tell her. 'You need to admit it, Alex.'

She flops back on to the sofa again.

'I'm not on drugs, Izzy,' she says.

'You ARE!' I say, a little bit louder than I meant to, but I'm feeling desperate. 'You must be. It explains everything.'

'Well, I'm sorry to disappoint you, but I'm really not. So if that's all you've got to tell me then I'll get back to my afternoon.'

I stamp my foot in frustration before realizing that Alex is not going to take me seriously and confide in me if I behave like a toddler.

'Well, you can talk to me when you're ready,' I say, but she doesn't look away from the TV. 'Alex? Did you hear me?'

'It's hard not to hear you,' she mutters. 'Are there any other revelations you've had about me and would like to share?'

'No,' I whisper.

'Then, in that case, please leave me in peace. I

can totally reassure you that I will not be taking drugs of any kind while you do your homework.' She turns up the volume on the TV and I give up.

I walk into the hall and retrieve my bag and then sit down at the kitchen table, but I'm too upset to think about my history homework. Life in Victorian Britain might have been grim, but life in the Stone house is no picnic right now. Alex is obviously in denial and I'm just going to have to find hard evidence and confront her with it. I will not let her destroy her life. This is all Cheese-and-Onion Charlie's fault, I bet. There wasn't a problem until he came along. Maybe he's the one who has introduced Alex to drugs, just like he must have encouraged her to eat those disgusting crisps. I just need to find proof, and then I can show Mum and we can help Alex do the right thing.

Not Everything Is Black Or White

'Izzy, have you seen Alex?' asks Mum, running into the kitchen. 'And where's my bag?'

I put down my science book (all I ever seem to do these days is schoolwork) and look blearily up at Mum. I don't know why she's asking me. She knows I've been sitting here for the last hour.

'No,' I tell her.

'No to which one?' she says, bending down and dragging her bag out from under the kitchen table. 'How on earth did it get there?'

'No to both. I haven't seen Alex and I didn't know where your bag was until you just found it.'

'You were virtually sitting on top of it,' mutters Mum, sounding grumpy. 'Are you sure you haven't seen Alex?'

'Yes, Mum,' I say, closing my book. I'm feeling

completely distracted now and I've done enough for today anyway. Hannah's coming over in a while and we're going to start working on our history assignment.

'What time's Hannah getting here?' asks Mum, looking at her watch. 'Will you be OK on your own until she arrives?'

'Mum! Stop worrying. She'll be here in about half an hour. I'm going to read my book while I wait for her.'

I give Mum a quick hug and head upstairs.

'Tell Alex to hurry up if she's up there,' Mum calls after me. 'Mr Fanley won't wait if we're late.'

Alex hates going to the orthodontist. She calls him 'Mr Fanger' and moans like mad when she's got an appointment. She says it's embarrassing and that she's the only girl in her year with braces (except she calls them train tracks). Mum tells her that she'll be glad she had the chance to make her teeth perfect and that she wishes she'd had this opportunity when she was younger. I think Alex has got lovely teeth, even with the braces. They're sparkling white and all neat and even. She's got film-star teeth.

Not like me – mine are all clumped together in a muddly crowd, some hiding behind the others.

Mum says not to worry and that I'm still growing. She says that my mouth is too small for my teeth at the moment, but that it'll grow. Alex moans when she hears Mum say that and says that I talk too much as it is. I'm on the waiting list to see Mr Fanley, but I'm not sure that's a good thing. Alex always makes such a fuss about it that maybe I'd be better off with crooked teeth.

I walk into my bedroom and pick up my notebook from the window ledge. Glancing out of the window, I see Alex, sitting on her swing and swaying to and fro in the April sunshine. I'm about to bang on the window to get her attention, but stop when she pulls her mobile out of her pocket. She reads something on the screen and then her face screws up. For a second she looks angry and I watch as she throws her phone across the flower beds and towards the garden shed, as if it's said something nasty. The angry look disappears and is replaced by a different emotion – maybe sadness or worry or fear. I'm too far away to tell and, before I can decide whether to call to her, I see Mum appear on the lawn below me. She shouts to Alex and then goes back into the house.

Alex gets off the swing and walks towards the

back door. She looks slow and ill, like something is really wrong.

Mum calls goodbye to me and then I hear the front door slam as they leave. This is it: my chance to find the evidence I need to confront Alex. She's not OK, that's really obvious. I'm just surprised that Mum hasn't spotted that there's a problem. If I can find proof that Alex is taking drugs then I can show Mum and she can deal with it.

I throw my notebook on my bed, race out of my room and then stop, my hand on the handle of Alex's door. It feels wrong, like snooping. I know she'd hate the idea of me spying on her things, but I have to do this. It's for her own good. Taking a deep breath, I open the door and walk inside, closing it quietly behind me.

It's hard to know where to start. Alex's room is a mess as usual. My other *slight* problem is that I don't really know what I'm looking for. Drug stuff. That's what they said in that citizenship lesson. Finding drug stuff in their bag or bedroom. I know that some people use needles to take drugs, but I can't really imagine Alex doing that. She hates needles. She makes a really big fuss if she ever has to have an injection and once she even fainted. Also, she cares a lot about her appearance and I don't think she'd like having lots of little holes in her arms.

So I'm going to have to keep an open mind. I'm looking for anything suspicious – anything that shouldn't be here. I start under Alex's bed, but I'm sneezing so much after thirty seconds that I have to stop. It doesn't look like anything's been moved under here since the last millennium so I don't think her secret stash can be kept here. Next I try the bottom of her wardrobe; that doesn't take long because most of her clothes are on the floor. Nothing in there.

I stand in the middle of her room and look around. If I was Alex, where would I put something that I didn't want anyone else to find? I close my eyes and try to think like her, but it's no good. I'm nothing like Alex and I just can't imagine things like she does. I wouldn't be any good at hiding something secret, not like her. I suddenly feel really stupid. What was I thinking, imagining that I could second-guess Alex? Imagining that I could help her, be cleverer than her. She's always going to be older and more exciting and more *everything* than me. If Alex doesn't want me to know something then I won't know it – not until she decides to tell me.

The thought makes me feel pathetic and small. It also makes me feel like I have no control: I just have to wait until other people choose to fill me in. I'm suddenly angry. It's totally unfair. I'm a part of this family too and I should be listened to. I kick something lying on the floor by my foot and watch as it sails across the room, landing behind the empty laundry basket. Mr Cuddles!

Hurrying across the room, I pull the basket out a bit further and reach down behind it to retrieve poor Mr Cuddles.

'I'm sorry,' I tell him as I stretch my arm down into the gap. 'It's not you I'm mad at.'

My hand brushes against his soft, furry head and I pull him out. As I do, I catch sight of Alex's T-shirt lying in a crumpled heap on the floor and, in an attempt to make up for invading her privacy, I pick it up and open the lid of the laundry basket. But there, at the bottom of the very empty basket, is something that doesn't belong there. I reach down and pull out a wooden box.

Heart racing, I drop Mr Cuddles on the floor and sink down next to him. Could this be it? The evidence I'm looking for? Now it's in my hands I'm not sure if I actually want to open it, but then I remember Alex, sitting on the swing and looking so utterly unhappy. I can do this for her. I can show her that I'm here for her – that she can rely on me, even if I am only twelve.

The box is really beautiful. I've never seen it before. It's got swirly silver patterns across the top and it latches shut with a tiny little clasp on the front. It's the right size to rest on my knees as I kneel on the floor, and it smells like Alex's favourite patchouli incense sticks.

As my fingers fumble with the clasp, I have a sudden moment of wondering. I wonder if I'll always remember this second – if I'll be glad that I opened the box or if I'll forever regret finding it. I think about a Greek myth that we heard at school, about a girl called Pandora and a box that she was given by Zeus, the King of the Gods. He told her to look after the box and to never, ever open it. In my opinion, that was a stupid thing to say to her. It's like telling someone NOT to think about elephants or NOT to look behind them: it's virtually impossible not to do it. If Zeus didn't want the box opened then he shouldn't have made such a big deal about it – he just made Pandora curious. Anyway, she opened the box (no surprises there) and inside were all the evils of the world. They all flew out and spread round the world and it's why bad things happen now apparently. The only thing left inside the box was hope, which I suppose means that, even when awful things are going on, good stuff can still happen. Or something.

I remember our English teacher telling us that there are only a few different story plots in the whole, entire world – quests and adventures; forbidden love and escape; rescues and riddles; growing up and sacrifice. I wonder if it's true and I wonder if I'll share my story with Pandora. It seems a bit strange that I, a normal, boring girl from England, could have anything in common with a beautiful woman from Greek mythology. I really, really hope that I don't end up like her, with all the evils of the world being unleashed in Alex's bedroom.

The clasp gives way and I lift up the lid. Inside the box is not what I expected. It doesn't look like anything to do with drugs and it doesn't look particularly evil either. It looks like envelopes. Lots of envelopes with my name written on the front in violet ink.

I tip the box upside down and empty the envelopes on to the floor. I don't know what to think about this. I hesitate for only a second because that's MY name written on the front and if something's addressed to you then it's fine to open it. I'm sure that's the rule at the Royal Mail anyway.

Grabbing the nearest envelope, I carefully ease the flap open, just in case I need to reseal it later. Inside is a letter, written to me.

6th April
Dear Izzy,

I'm sorry I haven't spent much time with you lately. I really want to, but you know now why I've needed to have a bit of space. I just need time to get my head round all of this. I'm sorry if that sounds selfish – I know you're worried about me.

I THINK I'll be fine. I'm not a hundred per cent sure about that, but people usually are fine, aren't they? It's what we always say, 'Yeah, fine thanks', when someone asks how we are. That's why I don't bother asking. What's the point? Everyone says the same – that they're fine, even when they're shrivelling up and dying on the inside.

I have to believe that I'll be fine. That things can go back to how they were. That my whole world isn't about to cave in. I lie in bed at night and send myself to sleep chanting the same thing over and over again.

This isn't happening. This isn't happening. This isn't happening.

Only it is.

Love you forever,
Alex xx

I put the letter down and then straight away pick it back up and read it again. I don't understand. What's wrong with Alex? What doesn't she want to happen? Why would she say that I know NOW why she needs some space? None of it makes any sense.

Grabbing another envelope, I rip it open, not bothering to try to keep it neat this time. I scan the top for the date and realize that this one was written before the last one. They're not in any kind of order so I'll just need to read them all to work out what's going on.

15th March

Dear Izzy,

Why does everyone assume, just because I've got a big mouth, that it means I've got no feelings? I'm really sick of it — people acting like they can say anything to me and it won't matter.

Stefan really wound me up tonight at band practice. I can't believe he thinks I'm only interested in getting all the attention. I've only ever been interested in what's best for On the Rocks. And, to be honest, I'm totally over being the centre of attention. Which is a shame because, when everyone finds out, I'm going to be the closest thing to a celebrity that anyone has ever seen around here. For all the wrong reasons.

I don't know what's going to happen to the band when I've gone. Maybe they'll replace me. That'd be awful — I don't think I could bear it. What if they got another singer and she's prettier and better than me? Maybe everyone will say that I'd held them all back and they were lucky I was gone. I think that's why I got so upset with Stefan — I just want it to be perfect while I'm still a part of it. I suppose I'll have to apologize to him.

I'm probably done with the band anyway. I feel so ill right now and I just want to sleep all the time. I'm scared that people are going to start talking about me. Funny — that's never bothered me before.

Love you forever,
Alex xx

The doorbell rings, startling me back into right now. For a minute I panic, thinking that Alex and Mum are back, but then I remember that they've got a key and wouldn't need to ring the doorbell. I look at my watch and realize that it's probably Hannah, come to work on our history assignment. Nothing could be less important to me right now so I stay sitting on the floor, while she rings the doorbell, and then listen as she gives up and walks away.

My legs are aching so I uncurl them and sit down properly, stretching them out and then crossing them in front of me. I sweep the pile of letters on to one side so that I can keep track of which ones I've read. My brain is whirring and I can feel little prickles of sweat under my armpits. These letters are not good. I'm starting to think that I was wrong about Alex – I don't think she's on drugs at all. I think it's a whole lot worse than that and I'm not sure I've got the strength to read the rest of the letters. But I must. Because Alex is using these letters to tell me something that she just can't tell me in person. Alex had to be strong to write these words and I need to be strong enough to read them.

I think about what she's written – about feeling ill and tired; about everyone talking about her. She's written about being replaced when she's gone. And it's suddenly shockingly obvious to me what's going on. Alex isn't on drugs: she's dying. My big sister is dying and she can't bring herself to tell me.

I'm not a person who cries very often. I don't like the way it makes me feel so usually the worst that happens when I'm upset is a few tears prickling at the back of my eyes. It feels strange and unwanted to have tears flowing uncontrollably down my face, but there's not one thing that I can do about it. I have to read the rest of the letters. I need to find the letter where she tells me WHY. I need to know what Alex is facing so that I can be prepared, so that I can help her and be brave for her. The thing is, I'm only twelve. Alex is right when she says I'm just a kid. I'm not sure I can be brave enough to watch her disappear in front of me. I don't want to see her wither and shrink and become frail and pale. Alex is the big sister for a reason – she's braver and funnier and better than me. I don't know if I can be big for her.

At some point I've picked up Mr Cuddles and I hold him tightly to me now as I choose the next envelope and open it, pulling out the single piece of paper with as much fear as if it WAS all the evils of the world coming out of Pandora's box.

14th April
Dear Izzy,

Please don't tell Mum. I know that this is a terrible thing to ask you, but it's really, really important to me that she doesn't find out just yet. I'll try to explain why and I know that I can't stop you from telling, but at least hear me out before you make any decisions.

Mum has got so many hopes for us – for you and for me. She wants us to BE someone, to do something with our lives. She had me when she was really young and life was tough for her for ages. She's always told me that she wants ar lives to be easier than that. Most of all, she wants us to be happy. Finding out about me is going to destroy her. And she's got enough to worry about with Granny and Grandpa at the moment. She doesn't need me adding to her stress.

I want to give her as much time as possible before she knows the truth. I bet you're thinking it's because I'm scared. Well, you're right. I am scared – more scared than I've ever been in my life. And maybe I'm being selfish, but I want some time for me too – time to deal with this before I have to deal with it for Mum. This is not what she'll be expecting. Not one little bit. I need to know how I feel about it before I tell her. Does that make sense?

I promise I'll tell her when the time is right. I won't leave it too late, but I'm just not strong enough to cope with her unhappiness right now. I know she'll be scared for me and I know she'll be disappointed. I WILL tell her, Izzy.

Love you forever,
Alex xx

This is awful. Mum doesn't know? I skim the letter again, trying to make my brain work a bit quicker. It's true that Mum wants the best for us; she was really excited when Alex got offered a place at university (we all went out for a special celebratory meal and she even let us order a pudding, which NEVER happens). The most confusing part of the letter is at the end though. Why would Mum be disappointed? That's a really weird thing to say. I can understand her being scared and sad and miserable, but I'm not sure that people get 'disappointed' about someone dying. That makes no sense.

I reach for another letter, hoping that this one will help me work out exactly what's going on.

29th March
Dear Izzy,

I know you're not sure about Charlie, but it's not his fault. Not all his fault anyway. He's trying really hard to cope with this — but, like he says, it wasn't exactly what he signed up for. Well, I tell him, it wasn't what I signed up for either, but it's what's happening, so we've got to deal with it.

He came with me to the doctor's when I made the first appointment. We had a bit of an argument about it actually because I didn't know he had a football match after school and the appointment was right in the middle of the match. When I first told him, he said that there was no way he could miss the match so I told him that it was fine. I said that Sara could always come with me. Unfortunately I started crying before I'd finished saying how fine it was that he was happy to put a stupid pig's bladder game before me, his girlfriend, which ruined my independent woman vibe quite a lot.

I tried to march off, but he caught up with me and said that if it mattered that much to me then he'd see if Dev would stand in for him. He said it like there was only a slim chance of it happening, but I know for a fact that Dev is desperate to get a chance to play. I told him that it wasn't about it mattering to ME — it should matter to HIM. He went a bit red then and put his arm round me and said that of course he'd come with me. And after school he bought me some cheese and onion crisps from the corner shop — I'm totally addicted to them, which is weird when you think about how much we've always hated them! So he is trying, Izzy.

The appointment with the doctor was terrible. I was so scared that I couldn't stop shaking, even though she was lovely. She asked me a load of questions and then confirmed what I was pretty sure I already knew. I'd done loads of research on the Internet so I was fairly sure of what she was going to say. Hearing the words made it seem so real though. Charlie went pale and started tapping his foot on the floor, totally irritatingly. The doctor was really kind and gave him some water. I think he'd thought I was making it up to be honest. She suggested I take Mum to the next appointment — said that Mum was going to need to know soon and it was better to have her support early on. She said I was going to need lots of support.

I asked Charlie if he wants to be there when

I tell Mum, but he just shook his head. He doesn't say much about how he's feeling. I never noticed that before.

Love you forever,
Alex xx

I can't believe she's trying to defend Charlie. I mean, what sort of person puts a football match before supporting their girlfriend? I don't understand why she didn't talk to Mum first though, when she started to suspect that something was wrong. Surely Mum would have been far better than Football-Before-Friends Charlie?

I glance at the time again and realize that I haven't got long – Mum and Alex will be home soon. I open another envelope and read the date. This one was only written a few days ago.

23rd April
Dear Izzy,

I haven't given you any of the letters that I've been writing. I know that this makes my letter-writing completely pointless — that communication is a two-way process and it only works if I actually let you read what I've written.

The thing is, it's YOU that I'm most scared about telling. That sounds utterly ridiculous even as I write it – you're twelve years old and probably the least frightening person I have ever met in my entire life. You are loving and trusting and I know that when you look at me you think you're looking at the best big sister in the world. I know that you think you want to be like me.

That's why I can't tell you. I don't want to be the person who spoils all of that. You're so innocent – I wish I'd been as innocent as you when I was your age. You wish you were older and more sophisticated, but that's what makes you so special.

I'm sorry, Izzy, more sorry than I can ever put down in words. I'm not going to be around for you in the way that you need me. I'm a useless big sister and you deserve so much better. Thank you for always believing the best about me. Knowing how much you look up to me has helped me to be a bit of a nicer person (only a bit, obviously – I'm not THAT nice . . .!!).

I'm mostly sorry that I'm not brave enough to tell you myself. Mum will do a much better job of it than I would anyway. She'll help you to make sense of it. I wish I could make sense of it, but I suppose I will eventually.

Love you forever,
Alex xxx

And that's it. No more envelopes. She isn't going to tell me. This is so typically Alex: create a big drama and then walk out halfway through.

I gaze round her room, hoping that more answers might throw themselves at me, but the only things I can see are signs that Alex left her room in a rush as usual. I sit for a few minutes, unable to move, while I think about everything I've just read. I feel like I've lived my whole life in the last thirty minutes – forced to face things that I never even imagined I would have to consider until I was a grown-up.

I know that I need to move, but it isn't until I hear a key in the front door that I spring into action. Stuffing the letters back into the envelopes, I bundle them all back into the box and then I hide the box back down inside the laundry basket. I race out of Alex's room and into my own room just in time. I can hear Mum coming upstairs.

'We're home, Izzy,' she calls, heading into the bathroom. 'Everything OK?'

'Fine!' I shout back, collapsing down on to my window ledge, adrenalin coursing through my body and making me feel like giggling. Except nothing is funny any more and Mum has no idea.

I hear the back door open and watch as Alex walks across the lawn. The sound of the shower turning on comes through my bedroom wall and I know that Mum won't be out of the bathroom for at least fifteen minutes. Alex heads towards the flower beds and bends down, parting the leaves of the plants with her hands. Searching for something. I think about how Alex looked when she was sitting on the swing earlier and I suddenly remember her mobile phone. She threw it into the flower bed and I'm pretty sure she didn't pick it up again before she left for the orthodontist.

She doesn't find it though and I see her start to move faster, trampling on some of the plants as she moves further towards the shed. At one point she straightens up and turns to face the house, peering up at the windows. For some reason I find myself moving behind the curtain, making sure that she can't see me spying on her. I don't even know why I do this; normally I'd wave at her and try to get her attention, hoping that she'd beckon me down to chat to her while she lounged about on the swing. I remember the day a few weeks ago when we sat out there together and Alex told me that she wouldn't always be around to look out for me. This must be what she meant and I had no idea.

The shower is turned off and I can hear Mum clattering about in the bathroom. She'll be out in a minute – Alex hasn't got long. As if she senses it out in the garden, Alex leaves the flower bed and walks across to the swing. She sits down and pretends to throw something and I realize that she's trying to repeat her earlier action when she threw the phone away. She gets up again and starts searching the long grass on the lawn on her hands and knees, but I know for a fact that she's looking in the wrong place. I definitely saw her phone fly across the flower beds and disappear next to the shed. My bet is on it rolling into the little gap between the shed and the big fir tree where we used to have a den. Alex has probably forgotten all about that place, but I haven't. We used to spend hours in there, hiding from everyone and talking about the cafe that we were going to own when we were both grown up.

I could bang on the window and tell Alex where I think her phone is. Or I could stand here in the shadows, watching her get more and more frantic as she looks in all the wrong places. It's a new feeling for me, being the person who knows. I think I like it. It makes a change from always being the last to find out.

Mum leaves the bathroom and goes downstairs, shouting at me to wash my hands and come and help set the table for supper. I wait for just a moment more though, until I hear the back door open and Mum yelling to Alex that she needs to come inside. The door closes and Alex casts one more longing look in the direction of the flower beds before trudging towards the house, the sun sinking lower and lower in the sky with every step she takes, so that when she reaches the back door the garden is cast into a sudden darkness that makes me shiver.

Black of Night

I'm lying in bed, but I can't sleep. Alex is filling my mind, crowding out every other thought. I've tried counting sheep and imagining lots of cute little lambs leaping pointlessly over a farm gate, but the image of Alex in a shepherdess costume, screaming at the sheep to leave her alone, spoilt it. I've tried to be rational – maybe I've made a mistake – but then I think about those letters, written but not delivered, and I know that I'm right.

It's the same problem as always. I know something, but I don't really know. And now that I know (or don't know) then I need to know it all. I'm completely out of control, dependent on when Alex chooses to fill me in on the whole story. And the not knowing is actually going to make me go mad. Unless I do something about it.

I sit up in bed, my mind spiralling round and round. Everyone thinks it doesn't matter about me. They think I don't understand and that I can wait until THEY think it's the right time to tell me stuff. This is what happened with Dad – nobody actually told me that he was never coming back, I just kind of worked it out for myself. Not this time though. I'm not just going to sit here letting my mind run wild, imagining one hundred and one things that might be killing Alex. And now I know (or sort of know) I can't just act like there's nothing going on.

I swing my legs out of bed and reach across for my dressing gown. Mum and Alex went to bed hours ago, but I don't want to risk waking them so I open the drawer on my bedside table and take out my In-Case-of-Emergencies torch. Turning it on, I quickly check my mood ring; it glows a brilliant gold. Gold is for strength and I know that I can do this. I'm strong enough to find out the truth.

I turn off the torch and pad quietly across my carpet to the door. Our house is old with lots of creaks, but I make it to the bottom of the stairs without hearing a sound from Mum's or Alex's room. At the bottom I speed up and walk quickly into the kitchen. Opening the back door, I grab my wellies from the welly-tree and step out into the garden, heading straight to where I saw Alex throw the phone.

It's really strange being out in the garden at night. There's a full moon and it makes the night seem almost like day, except the shadows are all wrong and there's an eerie glow around the edges of the lawn that makes it hard to see beyond. I turn in fright when something makes a weird snuffling noise behind me, freezing as still as a statue until I see a hedgehog shuffling its way across the lawn. I wish that darkness-destroying Alex was with me.

Heading across the grass, I avoid the flower bed and step on to the little path that leads to the shed. I can hear something rustling inside the shed and hope that it's a rat or a mouse and not an axe-wielding madman. I half jog past the shed door and then stop and turn back to face the garden. I'm looking straight at Alex's swing and the direction that she threw the phone, and I know I'm in the right place.

Sliding along the side of the shed, I push through

the branches of the fir tree and I'm inside our den. There's an old wooden crate turned upside down that we used to use as a seat and I sit down on it now, my eyes adjusting to the darkness. The branches completely hide me from view – nobody would even know I was here.

I can feel my heart starting to slow down and return to its normal rhythm. Now I'm here, safe in the den, it feels quite beautiful to be out at night. It's not that cold and I can hear the wind trickling through the branches of the fir tree. It reminds me of a book that Mum used to read to me when I was little, about three children who lived near an enchanted wood with a magic tree. The part of that story that I loved the most was the other trees in the wood – the way they went *wisha, wisha, wisha* and told each other all the secrets of the wood. I can almost imagine that happening now; that the trees around our old den are whispering the secrets and promises that Alex and I told each other when we came here.

Maybe they're talking about what Alex would tell me about boys – that they aren't to be trusted and they'll never be as important as your family. Or the day that she made me swear we'd never have any secrets from each other – that sisters tell each other EVERYTHING. Maybe they remember our plans for our cafe – the brightly painted walls and the shelves stuffed with books that our customers could look at while they ate our delicious cakes. We spent hours trying to think of a name and agreed that everyone would be welcome; it wouldn't matter if you couldn't eat a particular food, you'd always find something good on our menu.

Alex won't be around to run a cafe with me now. If I need any boy advice then I'll have to ask Mum, which just won't be the same. And Alex is keeping the worst possible secret from me right now, which is why I'm out here in the middle of the night, the cold, damp rubber of my wellies feeling utterly disgusting against my bare feet. I have to know what Alex is facing so that I can help her.

I look round the floor of the den. There are a few leaves and twigs, but I can't see a mobile phone. Then I spot something tucked against the roots of the tree. It's too big to be Alex's phone, but I know instantly what it is. I pick it up and put it on my knees. It takes me a moment to prise the lid off because it's rusted from all the rain, but then I manage to pull up one corner and the rest comes away easily. It's our old tin – the tin we used to pass messages to each other.

I get my torch out of my pocket and turn it on, shining it into the tin. The inside is dry and, while the pieces of paper are crumpled and the writing's a bit faded, it's still possible to read what we've written. I pull out a note that I wrote in indigo felt tip when I was probably about eight – even then indigo was my favourite colour although I didn't know then that it means being responsible and faithful. Indigo people like life to be structured and are very organized; that definitely describes me so I suppose I picked indigo because it's such a good match for me. It's very nearly violet, without the dramatic bits.

Hi Alex,

I hate school. Let's run away together and never go to school again.

Love Izzy xxxxxxx

Nothing much has changed there then – that still sounds like a good idea to me. I find a note written by Alex.

Izzy,
Meet me here after supper tonight. I have
chocolate and some hilarious gossip from
school!

Love you forever,
Alex x

I slip this note into my pocket, remembering how
special I felt when Alex treated me like that – like
I was someone worth talking to. I don't feel like
reading the rest of the notes and I put the lid
back on, slipping the tin into its hiding place by
the tree. As I do, I see something strange – a weird
light flashing on and off behind the trunk of the
tree. Alex's phone! I turn off my torch and stretch
my arm as far as it will go and just manage to
grasp it, pulling it across the dirt and leaves
until it's firmly in my hands. The screen is flashing
with unread text messages and I stuff the phone
deep into the pocket of my dressing gown, worried
that the unearthly glow will get me seen if
someone just happens to be glancing out of the
window.

Finding the phone brings me back to reality

and I remember why I'm out here. Suddenly the den feels creepy and unfriendly, and I start to feel anxious and scared. I bend down low to avoid the branches and duck out of the den, running past the shed and across the lawn until I'm at the back door.

Once inside, I shake off the wellies and creep upstairs. Back in the safety of my room I feel overwhelmingly tired and like I might fall asleep standing up if I don't get into bed this very instant. But Alex's phone can't wait. I've got it now and I can find out the whole truth. Suddenly I'm not at all certain that the truth is what I actually want to know.

I'm not sure what I'm expecting to find. I know what I'm doing is wrong and that I'm invading Alex's privacy in the worst way, but I just can't cope with a single second more of not knowing. I never knew that half knowing something is so totally awful. The truth surely can't be as bad as some of the things that I'm imagining?

I find the last text that has been read – the text that upset Alex so much, and press open. For a moment my eyes look everywhere but at the phone. There's still time to change what I'm doing.

I could turn off the phone and put it back in the den. I remember Pandora again and how a single action can change everything. And then I make my choice.

Bolt From the Blue

I wake up late the next day, my night adventures feeling more like a bad dream than anything real. Reaching my hand under my pillow makes everything zoom into focus pretty quickly though. Alex's phone is still there, filled with secrets and truths and goodness-knows-what-else. I have to make sure that I won't be discovered with it. Alex would go mad if she knew what I've done.

It's Saturday, so as soon as we've finished breakfast I'm going to be free. Mum tells Alex that she needs new clothes and that she thought they'd go into town for the morning. Alex didn't react like she normally would though; any other time she'd have almost bitten Mum's arm off in her enthusiasm for a shopping trip, but today she just snarls a bit and says that she can't be bothered. That makes Mum get cross and she tells Alex that she can't keep wearing clothes that are too small for her – and has Alex looked in the mirror lately and seen her shirt buttons straining to stay closed? It's not decent, Mum says.

'Are you calling me fat?' Alex suddenly shouts at Mum and the atmosphere at the breakfast table drops into white, arctic temperatures. I look hard at my cornflakes, hoping that my face isn't going red. I should have stayed in bed this morning; it's too hard having to be around Mum and Alex, knowing what I know.

'Don't be so ridiculous, Alex,' says Mum. 'I'm just pointing out that you're still growing and it's time you had some new clothes. It was supposed to be a *nice* thing for goodness' sake!'

'Well, I'm sorry that I don't want to go shopping with someone who thinks I'm FAT,' says Alex, and she and Mum glare at each other across the box of cornflakes.

'You can buy me some new clothes,' I say in an attempt to lighten the mood and distract Mum from Alex. 'I don't mind.'

'Shut up, Izzy,' mutters Alex viciously. 'I can live without your "perfect daughter" routine this morning.'

'Alex!' snaps Mum. 'That's quite enough. We're

going out and that's the end of it. No more arguing.' She gets up and starts slamming the breakfast dishes into the sink, so hard that I'm amazed nothing smashes. 'Be ready to go by quarter past.'

Alex slouches out of the kitchen without looking at me. Mum turns round when she's gone.

'Do you want to come with us?' she asks me, her voice sounding much gentler than it did when she was talking to Alex.

'I'd rather stay here,' I say, hoping that she'll let me. 'I've got homework to do and Alex is in such a grouchy mood.'

That does the trick. Mum nods at me and dries her hands on a tea towel.

'No, it probably won't be a fun morning,' she murmurs, half to herself. 'If you're sure you'll be OK then you can stay here, but don't open the door to anyone except Finn and call me if you get even a little bit worried.' She walks past me, stopping to drop a kiss on top of my head. 'She won't stay grumpy forever, you know,' she tells me and then she goes to get ready. I'm not actually sure that's true – now I've read her text message I think it's entirely possible that Alex could stay in a foul mood for the rest of her life. But I can't go shopping this morning. I need to figure out what to do about Alex and her problem.

When Alex and Mum have gone, I run upstairs and retrieve the phone from under my pillow. Then I go back downstairs and head into the garden. It looks totally different this morning to the way it looked last night – not frightening at all. I walk towards Alex's swing and sit down, pushing off with my feet so that I'm swaying to and fro. I do this for a few minutes and then I turn on the phone and scroll through the menu until I find the recent messages. I can see that there are a few unread messages, but it's not them that I'm interested in. I want to read the message that I read last night because part of me can hardly believe that it's true. Maybe there's still a chance that I read it wrong?

I read the message again several times just to be certain. That's not because it's got difficult words. It's because my brain is refusing to accept that what I read last night was correct. Because in all of my wildest imaginings I was absolutely, categorically NOT imagining this.

Caught Red-handed

Alex's phone has a new home. It's been at the back of my sock drawer for the last three days. I keep expecting her to ask me if I've seen it, but she hasn't said a word. Mum asked her where it was yesterday and Alex just shrugged and said that she'd lost it. This is not unusual: she's not managed to keep hold of the same phone for longer than about six months EVER – hardly surprising if she goes round throwing them in flower beds when she doesn't like her text messages. Mum got cross with her and said that she has no respect for her belongings and that she, Mum, is fed up with constantly bailing her out. Alex just shrugged again and said that she didn't want a new phone anyway.

I keep getting her phone out to check for any updates. It's giving me something to do and distracting me from the utter terror that is swirling round the pit of my stomach. Alex gets a lot of text messages, mostly from Sara and Finn, but also some from Charlie. The one that upset her that day in the garden was from him.

I've read it approximately eighty times so far. To begin with I hoped that rereading it would let me see that I'd made some sort of terrible mistake. Jumped to conclusions. I'm not actually the sort of person who does that – I prefer to gather in all the evidence before I make a decision about something – but I thought that this time maybe I'd got it really wrong. Because that obviously happens, even to people like me who double-check everything. People like me who look twice before they leap.

I have to keep reminding myself of the good news. Alex is not dying. Under normal circumstances this would make me very happy. I've not really had time to celebrate though because there's also some bad news. Isn't there always? I've never really understood that phrase about giving with one hand and taking away with the other, but I sort of get it now.

After a while, I couldn't pretend that I'd got Charlie's text message wrong. So then I started rereading it in the hope that I'd be able to work out what to do about it. Because Alex doesn't seem to be doing anything at all, and I feel like I'm living a complete lie.

We've just finished supper and I've escaped to my room. Mum's still mad at Alex about the phone, Alex is barely talking at all and I'm too scared to open my mouth in case everything I know comes pouring out. I'm so worried that I'll make all of this even worse – that I'll say something wrong and nobody will ever forgive anybody else ever again. That's why Alex has to do something soon, before she messes up our family for good.

I lift up my pillow and slide her phone out from its hiding place. It's on silent: it'd be a bit of a giveaway if it started buzzing every time a text came through. I turn it on and read THE message for the eighty-first time.

Sorry about b4. Don't know wot 2 tell u xcept i don't want a baby. Not now. Not ever. Sorry. Charlie

Alex is pregnant. Even if it wasn't utterly obvious from this text and the way she's behaving – being sick, moody, hiding her body and wearing baggy clothes – then the texts she's received since this one make it totally clear.

Sara sent this one a few hours after the one from Charlie:

> Wot's up babe? Where r u? Leaving now – c u at the pub. S xx

Followed by this one:

> OMG Alex! Just saw Charlie. Is it true? R u pregnant? Y u not picking up phone? Call me NOW. S xx

This one came the next day:

> R u OK? Worried about u. How long u known? Y didn't u tell me? Wot r u going 2 do about it? Are you keeping it? S xx

Alex is obviously avoiding Sara and hasn't told her that her phone is missing. Sara sends about ten texts a day, each one getting more and more insistent. She sounds desperate to find out what's going on – I never knew that she was so nosy. No wonder Alex isn't bothered about getting a new phone.

Finn, on the other hand, has sent two texts. One of them is checking that Alex would be at band practice that night (she wouldn't – she's barely leaving the house; she's not even been to school this week, although Mum doesn't know that). The other text was sent the day after and just asked Alex if she was all right. So I'm pretty sure that Finn has no idea about what's going on. I'd have thought that it'd make me feel good, not being the last to find out as per usual, but actually it doesn't. I just feel a bit horrible inside.

I badly want to talk to Alex, but she isn't talking to me. She's not NOT talking to me – at suppertime she asked me to pass the ketchup – but whenever I try to have a conversation with her she cuts me off and disappears into her room. I asked Mum if she'd noticed anything different about Alex – I think I was hoping that she might start to get suspicious and realize that there's a problem – but she just gave me a hug and said that Alex is under lots of pressure with her exams and that we all have to accept that she's growing up and getting ready to leave us.

Mum's pottering around in the garden and I'm thinking that this is my chance to talk to Alex. I heard her go downstairs a few minutes ago and the sound of water running, so I can catch her in the kitchen while she makes a cup of tea. I've got to make her listen to me. I feel like I'm going to burst if I don't talk about it soon. Everything I know is swirling around inside me like a tornado, growing bigger and bigger, and I'm scared that soon it'll be so big that it'll spill out of my mouth and I won't be able to keep quiet any more.

I put Alex's phone in my pocket and tiptoe downstairs so that she won't hear me coming. As I walk into the kitchen, I see Alex reaching up for a new box of teabags; her shirt rides up and I see the gentle swell of her stomach over the top of her jeans. Even though I know she's pregnant, it makes me stand still in shock. There's an actual baby growing inside Alex. A real, living baby that's making Alex sick and pale and causing all this trouble. I hate it.

I must make a sound because Alex swings round and looks at me, yanking her shirt down at the same time.

'Crikey, Izzy, you scared me!' she says. I just keep looking at her stomach, trying to imagine what she'll look like when it's all swollen and fat. She won't look like Alex, that's for sure.

'Izzy?' she says, sounding worried. She should

sound worried. She should have told Mum straight away, not waited until now. 'Are you OK?'

I've waited for days to have this conversation, but now it's time I can't think of a single thing to say. It's not something I've ever thought about before. Plus, I don't really know what I want Alex to say to me. I'm not sure how I feel about her right now. I know that I'm scared about what's going to happen to her and I'm worried about what Mum's going to say, but I realize as I stand in the doorway that I'm angry too – angry with Alex.

In the end, with the silence stretching between us like the Sahara Desert, I choose actions instead of words. Reaching into my pocket, I thrust Alex's mobile phone towards her. She looks confused for a second and then surprised – and then she rearranges her face to try and look pleased.

'Oh great, you found my phone! Where was it?'

'In our den,' I tell her, feeling amazed that she's still going to try and pretend to me.

'Weird,' she says, reaching out and taking it from me. 'I wonder how it got there.'

'It's where it landed when you threw it there,' I say, my voice sounding flat. I can't be bothered with pretending any more. Alex looks up from her phone where she's been frantically searching her messages, finally registering that something is wrong.

'Izzy?'

'I read your texts,' I tell her, feeling surprisingly empty. Her face contorts with anger, but I'm ready for this.

'How dare –' she starts, but I don't let her finish.

'And I read my letters,' I say. 'The letters you wrote to me, but didn't have the courage to actually give me.'

Alex slumps into the nearest chair, her eyes never leaving mine.

'I can't believe you snooped in my room. And stole my phone. Why would you do that, Izzy?'

She sounds completely hurt, like I'VE betrayed HER, and it's too much for me to deal with. All the fear and worry and nervousness of the last few days come pouring out and I glare at Alex, pinning her to the spot with my anger.

'Why would I do that? Let me see – because you've been acting completely weird and you scared me, and I've had to deal with thinking you were on drugs, and then thinking that you were going to die. And now this! All on my own, Alex.'

'It's got nothing to do with you,' she mutters,

but I can tell that her heart isn't in it because I can barely hear her.

'So why were you writing letters to ME!' I yell at her. 'And why haven't you told Mum? You have to tell her, Alex, or I will!'

Alex sits up straighter in the chair.

'No, Izzy! I'm totally serious about this. You cannot tell her. I'll never forgive you if you do, not for the rest of my life! And keep your voice down for goodness' sake – Mum could walk in at any minute.'

I gulp in a deep breath and look at Alex in amazement. She has never spoken like that to me before, not ever.

'Think about the sister code, Izzy. This is exactly the time that I need you to remember what we promised.' Alex is looking at me pleadingly and I feel my anger start to disappear.

Alex introduced the sister code when I was about ten and she was fifteen. It started with not telling Mum when the other one had done something wrong – like the time that her favourite mug got broken. I was washing up and Alex was drying and I thought it'd be funny to splash her with the soapsuds. Unfortunately I was a little too enthusiastic with my splashing and I managed to break the handle on the mug. Alex told me about the sister code and hid the broken mug in with the rubbish. When Mum couldn't find it, Alex didn't say a word, but on Mum's birthday she helped me choose a new mug for Mum. The sister code stopped me getting told off and helped me to make something wrong right again.

Since then we've used it for loads of things. I cover for Alex when she's sneaking out to the pub or going clubbing – Mum seems more likely to believe her if I say that I've heard her making plans for studying with Sara. As Alex says, it helps her to get some much-needed relaxation so that she can work even harder at school and that Mum is already stressed with her own job and worrying about Grandpa – she doesn't need to be worrying about Alex. In return, Alex lets me stay up late when Mum goes out and she always tells Mum that I was in bed on time.

The sister code means putting your sister first and keeping her safe, even if it makes you feel a bit uncomfortable at the time. It means trusting your sister to do the right thing, even if you've lost almost all faith in her. The sister code means that if your sister asks you to do something then you do it because your sister is the only person who can know you almost as much as you know yourself.

Alex has invoked the sister code and I need to show her that I'm worthy. The sister code doesn't recognize big sisters or little sisters: it only knows that we are sisters and always will be. I need to be brave for Alex and trust her.

'I won't tell her. I promise,' I whisper to Alex and her face crumples in relief. 'But I think she needs to know.'

'She does and I promise I'll tell her,' says Alex, getting up and walking across to me. 'But I need to wait until the time is right, Izzy, or it'll just make it worse.'

I'm not sure that this is true but, as Alex hugs me, I decide to go with what she says. She knows far more about this than I do after all, and maybe she's right. Maybe there will be a good time for her to tell Mum. But, as I feel her rounded tummy pressing against me, I wonder how long she thinks she can wait until even Mum can't ignore the evidence in front of her.

'You've just got to keep it a secret for a little while longer, just until I get everything sorted,' says Alex, giving me a final squeeze.

'Keep what a secret?' says a voice and we spring apart, both looking totally guilty and red-faced.

Finn is standing at our back door, leaning against the door frame. I have no idea how long he's been standing there, but by the look on his face it was long enough.

Alex strolls over to the kettle and switches it back on.

'Perfect timing, I'm just making a cup of tea. Want one? Come in and close the back door.' She doesn't look at Finn, but he can't tear his eyes away from her. I feel awkward, but there's no way I'm leaving Alex now so I sit down quietly on the stool by the fridge and hope they'll forget I'm here.

Alex busies herself with the kettle, pouring boiling water into two cups. I reach across and open the fridge door, bending down to pull out the milk and passing it to her when she walks over to me.

'You didn't come to band practice,' says Finn. It's a statement, not a question, and Alex doesn't reply. 'What's going on, Alex?'

'Nothing,' she says, pouring the milk into the cups and putting one on the table for Finn. 'Drink your tea.' I see her looking anxiously out of the window and I follow her gaze, but it's OK. Mum is moving around near the shed and doesn't seem to have any idea of the clouds that are gathering over our house.

Finn looks at the tea, but doesn't move. He likes his tea as strong as possible, so strong that 'you could stand a spoon up in it' Mum always says. It's something that he and Alex have in common, and they moan on and on if anyone ever makes either of them a weak cup of pale tea. The cup of tea that Alex has made looks more like warm milk than tea; there's no way that Finn will drink it and I don't blame him. The storm that's brewing in our kitchen is stronger than Finn's cup of tea.

'Alex.' His voice is firm, like he's not leaving here without answers, and I feel cold inside when I see what's about to happen.

'Finn.' She's trying to make a joke of it, distract him by being silly, but as she still won't look at him it's not going to work.

'What's wrong, Al? What's the big secret?'

Alex shakes her head and starts opening and closing cupboard doors.

'Where's the sugar? It's got to be here somewhere.'

I want to remind her that she doesn't have

sugar in her tea, but then I think better of it. This is definitely between Finn and Alex and I don't think she's really looking for the sugar anyway, not when I can see it in the sugar bowl, right in front of her on the kitchen counter.

'Is it true?' asks Finn in a quiet voice.

Alex stills, one hand reaching into the cupboard and closing round a tin of baked beans.

'Is what true?' she whispers.

'Is it true that you're –' Finn doesn't seem able to say the word and Alex turns round slowly, looking down at the floor. Finn tries again. 'Is it true that you and Charlie are –' But he doesn't need to say any more because Alex has raised her head and is looking at him, and he can see the answer written all over her face. It's like she wants him to know – that or she just can't hide the truth from Finn like she could hide it from me and Mum.

'Oh God,' groans Finn, running his hand through his floppy hair. I think how ridiculous this all looks: Finn with tufts of hair sticking up at weird angles and Alex clutching a tin of baked beans like it's going to save her. It's not how these things happen on the TV anyway. There's absolutely nothing glamorous or exciting about this moment. It all just seems a bit scary, and a bit messy, and a huge mistake – like we've stumbled into somebody else's story for a while.

'Finn –' starts Alex, but he puts his hand up, like he doesn't want to hear her. 'I don't know what to do,' she finishes, ignoring his hand and slumping against the kitchen counter.

There's silence for a few seconds and then Finn looks at Alex.

'What did your mum say?' he asks her. Alex doesn't answer and, for the first time since he walked into the room, Finn looks over at me.

'That's the big secret, isn't it?' he says and I nod, not looking at Alex in case she's mad with me. Finn sighs really loudly and turns back to Alex. 'You've got to tell her, Alex. Now.'

'I can't.'

'You can. You have to. What if she finds out from someone else?'

'She won't, will she?' Alex's voice has a warning in it that I can hear all the way over here by the fridge.

Finn slams his hand against the door frame and I jump in surprise.

'So what are you going to do? Wait until she notices? Or have you got other plans?' He's angry, but I don't know why. It's not his baby after all, so it doesn't really affect him.

'Charlie's sorting something out. I'm just waiting for him to tell me what we're doing.' Alex doesn't sound like her normal self – her voice is wavering and quiet, like she's unsure about what she's saying. 'He doesn't want me to tell Mum until we've got all the details sorted.'

'Is that what he's doing now, while you're sitting here on your own?' Finn asks her, his voice getting louder with each word.

I feel a bit hurt by this. Alex isn't exactly on her own, is she? She's got me and I'm working quite hard to deal with all of this, which isn't being made any easier by her and Finn having an argument in the middle of our kitchen.

'Yes, it is,' Alex tells him. 'He's getting everything sorted.' She sounds trusting, like she truly believes that Charlie is going to save the day, and it's too much for Finn.

'Right, so that wasn't Charlie I just saw in the pub with the rest of his football team?' he explodes. Alex's face goes red, but she stays silent.

'That was Charlie "getting everything sorted", was it? Because it looked to me like he was bragging about scoring a goal and laughing at some stupid joke made by an equally stupid girl.'

Tears bubble up in Alex's eyes, but she grips her tin of baked beans even harder and stares at Finn.

'Come on, Alex! Wake up! Lover boy is NOT going to do the right thing. You know it. Time to deal with that and start figuring out what YOU are going to do. If you wait for him, you'll be waiting forever!'

'Maybe he's worth waiting for – forever,' Alex says quietly, looking at Finn until he looks away, shaking his head in disgust.

I think this is probably the most romantic thing I've ever heard anybody say. It's the sort of thing I expect Juliet said about Romeo when the Montagues and Capulets were fighting and yelling at them, and forcing them to stay away from each other. It just seems a bit sad that Alex has said it about Charlie though because I'm sure he's an OK kind of person really, but I'm not at all convinced that he's Alex's 'forever' person.

'Then you don't need me then, do you?' Finn asks Alex. This time it really does sound like a question, hovering in the air above the kitchen table. They look at each other for a moment, but then Alex is the first to look away, not answering.

'You know where I am,' Finn tells her. 'Where I'll always be.' And then he turns and leaves, and it feels like he's walking out of much more than our kitchen, and Alex leans her head on the kitchen cupboard and cries and cries and cries until I think that she must have no tears left inside her.

Red Sky in the Morning, Shepherd's Warning

If I thought not knowing a secret was hard then I had absolutely no idea how difficult it is to keep one. Since that awful night in the kitchen two weeks ago, I've barely spoken to Mum because I'm so terrified that it'll all come pouring out of me in one long, guilty flow of words. Fortunately it's a really busy time for her at school so she's working extra hard, and then at suppertimes, if everyone's quiet, Mum thinks it's because we're tired.

Alex has gone back to school. She's not going to get away with not telling Mum for very long and I've told her that, but she doesn't seem particularly bothered. She's started sitting on her own in the library at lunchtimes. Well, she was alone to start with, but one day I saw Finn in the school canteen and he asked me where she was.

He laughed a bit when I told him and muttered something about how he'd never have looked for her there in a month of sunny days. Now they sit there, heads together and talking quietly. She's not doing any revision even though her exams are about to start any minute now. I suppose she's got more important things to think about other than school. Like growing a baby, for starters.

I snuck into the IT room at lunchtime last week and looked up babies on the Internet. I could have done it at home, but Mum checks our search history every now and again and I don't want to make her suspicious. I know that the baby was thirteen weeks old when I talked to Alex that night because I read it on one of her texts from Sara – Charlie told her. So right now her baby is about fifteen weeks old and the size of an orange. It can hiccup and it's starting to hear sounds. That seems extremely weird, like a mini alien has made its home inside Alex.

Apparently, she should be 'glowing' now too, whatever that's supposed to mean. When I read that, it made me think about Alex all lit up, a neon green light radiating out from her body, but I know it doesn't mean that really and it's a good job too because that would be an instant giveaway that she's pregnant. There's no way she could hide from Mum looking like a human glow stick.

I haven't been hanging around with Hannah much recently. I'm finding it quite hard to think about anything other than Alex and everything else seems so unimportant and childish.

We're sitting in citizenship again. Our topic today is dilemmas and Mrs Wallis is running through a list of different scenarios that apparently we might encounter in our daily lives. I'm not really listening, but then Hannah nudges my arm.

'What do you think?' she asks me. I have no idea what the question was so I just look at her blankly and she grins. 'Where were *you*, Izzy? Somewhere better than this rubbish lesson, I hope?' I smile back at her and she repeats the question.

'What is a dilemma?'

'What do you mean?' I ask her.

'What's the definition of a dilemma? Mrs Wallis has given us two minutes to work it out.'

'That's easy,' I tell her. 'Something where there's no right answer. Where you absolutely, totally and utterly will never get it right for everyone.'

'Fantastic, Izzy!' says Mrs Wallis from behind me. I didn't realize she was prowling the room, listening in to the discussions, and I feel my face go red. 'Everyone listen to Izzy's definition of a dilemma.'

I look at her in disbelief – I don't DO speaking in citizenship – but she nods encouragingly at me and somehow I manage to stutter my way through my definition again, Hannah looking at me in amazement.

Then Mrs Wallis returns to the front and I sink as far down in my chair as is humanly possible.

'Bad luck,' murmurs Hannah to me and I grimace in her direction, determined to keep my mouth closed for the rest of the lesson.

The next task is based on choosing how we would deal with a dilemma. There are four choices. We can choose to consider the point of view of everyone involved; go with our gut instinct; ask someone for advice; or toss a coin. I sit quietly, listening while the people on the front row get all enthusiastic about which is the best option. I bet none of them have ever had a proper, genuine, grown-up dilemma to deal with in their entire lives.

Mrs Wallis shows a picture of three people tied to a train track – like one of those old black-and-white silent movie clips where everyone runs about flapping and has a huge moustache. She tells us that a madman has tied them down and a train is coming. She asks us to imagine that we're the first person to discover the scene. Luckily for the three people there's a handy switch that we can flip that will divert the train to another track and miss squishing them. But it's like everything: just when you think there's a bit of good news, you get slapped in the face with disappointment. On the other track there is one person, tied down by the same madman.

So what should we do? Should we flip the switch and save three lives but allow one person to die? Or should we do nothing and let the train continue on its regular track? Will we save three lives or one life? Are we responsible because we can DO something? Just because we CAN do something, does that mean that we SHOULD? Or should we just leave it to chance or fate or whatever you believe in?

The questions are coming thick and fast and I sit in the middle of the classroom while all around me people excitedly discuss the problem. It's like they get a kick out of having so much power, even when it's pretend. I think about the options and I think about my dilemma.

Something is going wrong with Alex. Even more than it already was. She won't talk to me and I heard her whispering on the phone in the hall yesterday. She shooed me away when she saw me, but I know that something's up. She still hasn't told Mum and I'm starting to think that she isn't going to. This morning at breakfast she was totally different – all chattery and bubbly – and when Mum left for work Alex actually got up and gave her a hug. It wasn't a very big hug, probably because she didn't want Mum to feel the ever-growing bump pressed against her, but it was more than she's done for ages and I could tell that Mum was pleased.

I look at my mood ring and it's turned blue. Blue is for truth and trust, confidence and loyalty. I feel totally confused about what I should be doing for the best. Should I be loyal to Alex and not tell her secret? Or is it better for everyone if I tell the truth? Just because I CAN, does that mean I SHOULD? Alex isn't just Alex any more, she's two people, and the baby inside her can't make its own choices.

I looked it up online and found a website that said that women should have choices when they get pregnant – that some people don't even think it's a proper baby until it's actually born, so it doesn't really matter what happens to it because it's not like it can cry or eat or even think anything properly. I hate what this baby is doing to Alex, but I still think someone should be thinking about what *it* might want to happen. And I can't be sure WHAT is going through Alex's head at the moment. It's just like when I didn't get a chance to play with Dad when he used to visit: nobody thinks about what babies want.

Alex told me that it'd hurt Mum really badly if she found out about the baby. But I think that Mum is stronger than Alex realizes and I'm starting to wonder if Alex and her baby need Mum to help them. Surely it's better to save two lives and risk upsetting one?

Matthew is yelling that he'd just toss a coin so that who got hurt wasn't his responsibility. One of the girls tells him that he's totally irresponsible and pathetic – that the only fair thing to do would be to get the opinion of all four people tied to the train track. That makes all the boys howl with laughter.

'Not a very practical solution,' shouts one of them.

'And who's going to say "save the others – I'll

die for them"?' asks Matthew. 'Everyone would just look out for themselves – that's how it works!'

'Can't you think of a single person who would sacrifice themselves for others?' asks Mrs Wallis. She actually sounds interested, like she really wants to hear what we've got to say.

I feel my hand rising in the air and sense Hannah looking at me in horror. Mrs Wallis looks over at me and nods her head.

'Izzy?'

'You'd want the other person to live if you really loved them,' I tell her.

'Oooohhhh,' says Matthew in a sing-song voice, but Mrs Wallis shushes him by waving her hand in his direction and miraculously he shuts up.

'Go on, Izzy,' she says to me.

I think that my report this term had better be fantastic for citizenship after all this contributing that I seem to be doing. My face is a bit red, but it suddenly feels really important that I say this.

'It's not about people being tied to train tracks really, is it, Miss?' I say. 'It's about being brave enough to do the right thing even when you haven't got a clue what the right thing is.' I take a deep breath. 'So I think the answer is different every time. Sometimes it's better to ask for help.

Sometimes you might just have to guess, which is a bit like flipping a coin. And other times – most of the time actually – you just have to do what feels right and know that, even if you get it wrong, you did what you thought was the best thing.'

The class has gone quiet and everyone's looking at me. This is probably because I've just said more in thirty seconds than I've ever said in Year 7. I shuffle awkwardly in my chair.

'That's just what I think anyway,' I mutter.

The bell rings and the silence is broken by everyone leaping up and grabbing their bags. I join in, but as I walk past Mrs Wallis's desk she puts out her hand and stops me.

'Can I have a second, Izzy?' she asks. She waits until everyone has gone and then gestures to a chair in the front row. I sit down and she perches in front of me on her desk.

'That was a really great answer that you gave there,' she says, smiling at me.

'Thanks,' I say. I realize that I like Mrs Wallis; she treats everyone like they're worth listening to.

'How's your sister these days?' she asks me and I look at her in surprise. 'I haven't seen much of her recently and I used to like our little chats.'

'She's fine,' I say, trying to shake off the feeling

that Mrs Wallis is searching my face for the truth. I'm getting very good at lying, considering that I've had very little practice over the last twelve years.

'Tell her I was asking about her,' she says and I nod. 'She's always welcome to come and see me any time.' I wonder if Mrs Wallis knows. Surely she can't know – there's no way Alex would have told her. Then again, Mrs Wallis has a way of looking at you like she can see right into your brain. I wouldn't be surprised if she'd guessed all on her own. Not that she can do anything about it. Alex is seventeen and can do what she wants. And apparently this is what she wants.

'Izzy?'

I realize that Mrs Wallis has asked me a question and I blush.

'That goes for you too,' she repeats. 'Any time you need some advice then my door is open. The same with your other teachers; if we can help you then we will.'

Yeah, right, I can just imagine Mrs Hardman listening to me while I tell her every single thing that's wrong with my life. She'd have got bored and nipped off to the staffroom for a coffee hours before I'd finished.

'Thanks, Miss,' I say.

'You'd better get to your next class,' she says, standing up and putting the books on her desk into a neat pile. I pick up my bag and walk towards the door, but as I open it I hear Mrs Wallis call my name.

I turn to look at her. She's looking out of the window at the huge tree near the car park and for a moment I think I've misheard. But then she speaks, without looking at me.

'Trust yourself, Izzy. You were completely right with your answer today. Every situation is different and you just have to do your best. Sometimes you have to guess what to do and other times it's too big for you alone and you need to ask for help. And that takes a bravery that I know you have.'

She carries on looking out of the window and I walk through the door, closing it quietly behind me. I know what I need to do and it's the right thing for Alex and her baby and for me and for Mum.

Violet Ink

There's only one lesson left after citizenship and it's PE. Since that disastrous day when I humiliated myself in basketball, I have tried to keep a very low profile in PE lessons. Today I'm going to exceed my previous attempts by not even turning up. There's forty-five minutes until the end of school and hardly anybody will even notice that I'm not there. Even if they do notice they'll probably think I'm ill and have just gone home.

Which is exactly where I'm going. I know that Alex didn't come to school again today so I'm going to go home and give her one more chance to tell Mum. And if she won't tell her then I will. This has gone on long enough: Mum needs to know. Alex will thank me when all the drama is done, when she can talk to Mum properly and know that Mum still loves her. Because there's nothing that Alex could do that would make Mum stop loving her – I know that a hundred per cent for sure.

I creep out of the school gates feeling like I'm on some sort of mission and I run as much of the way home as I can. Now though I'm having to walk up our road. I really do want to get home as quickly as possible, but my bag is ridiculously heavy and my legs are aching and my lungs feel like they're about to burst. Also, I'm a little bit scared about what I'm about to do. I'm not sure Alex is going to particularly appreciate my ultimatum and I don't want to make her angry. It's probably not good for the baby if she starts screaming and shouting, especially as it can hear things now.

I can see our front door and I slow down even more. Alex is in there somewhere, making plans and decisions that she thinks have nothing to do with us. My mood ring is turquoise again: yet more secrets and deception. Well, I've had enough of all this sneaking around; it's time Family Stone dealt with this situation like a proper team. Alex needs to understand that we're all a part of this. It's not just about her.

As I walk down the path, I look up at the house.

It's the same, but something about it seems not quite right. I feel a sudden tingle of fear run down my spine and I quicken my steps, reaching in my pocket for my key at the same time. I reach the front door and fumble with the key, dropping it on the step. I'm being completely useless and I haven't even spoken to Alex yet. How on earth am I going to persuade her to listen to me if I can't even get into the house like a normal person?

I pick up the key, turn it in the lock and push the door open. Taking a deep breath, I step inside, noticing that the post is still lying on the doormat. I step over it and put my bag on the floor, kicking my shoes off into the corner. Then I go looking for Alex.

I creep into the living room, but she isn't in there. A glance through the kitchen door shows me that the room is empty so I walk quietly upstairs and check the bathroom. Empty. Her bedroom door is wide open and I can tell straight away that something is horribly wrong.

'Alex!' I shout, turning round on the landing, all attempts at taking her by surprise forgotten.

There's no reply and I shout her name again, louder this time. Maybe she's gone out for a walk. Except that's a ludicrous suggestion; Alex has never voluntarily gone for a walk in her entire life, unless it's walking from the car to the shops.

Maybe she's outside, on her swing? I laugh at myself for getting so wound up about nothing, but the sound of my laughter in the empty house is odd and makes me feel even more worried about where Alex might be. I run downstairs, swinging round the stair post at the bottom, and race across the kitchen. I can see through the window that she's not on her swing, but that doesn't stop me from yanking open the latch that locks the back door, ramming my feet into wellies and running outside into the sunshine.

I check the whole area around her swing, but there's no evidence at all that Alex has even been out here today. I look on the path that leads to the front of the house, but she's not there. I even search behind the shed and in our den, just in case she's gone in there for old times' sake. But Alex is nowhere to be found and miserably I walk back to the house, all the time telling myself that there's a perfectly reasonable explanation for why she's not here.

By the time I've taken off the wellies and poured myself a glass of orange juice from the fridge, I'm starting to calm down. Alex probably went into school after I did. She'll be back later and I won't tell her how worried I was about her. I'm probably going to end up with a detention for skiving off PE and all for nothing. I'll just have to find a good time to talk to Alex later, before Mum gets home from work.

I'm feeling a bit daft now, like I let myself get all stressed out about nothing. I was just so ready to talk to Alex – I suppose I'm a bit disappointed that I'll have to psych myself up all over again.

I pull out a chair and sit down at the kitchen table, plonking my glass of juice down in front of me. And that's when I see it. An envelope, leaning against a jar of peanut butter. An envelope with my name written on the front in violet ink.

I slowly reach across and look at it, carefully turning it over and over in my hands. It feels like everything is in slow motion, and all I can think about is that Alex obviously had peanut butter on her toast for breakfast and didn't bother to clear her things away. I don't feel like I really want to open this letter; the last envelope I opened that looked like this had nothing good to tell me. But it's from Alex and she's not here and she's written to me, so there's no way I can ignore this.

I peel the envelope apart very carefully and pull out the piece of paper inside. Then I sit at the kitchen table with sun streaming through the window and read what my big sister has decided to share with me.

Dear Izzy

I want to start by saying sorry. I've made a complete mess of all of this and you've been caught up in the middle. I never meant for that to happen. I never meant to make you have to choose.

It's been really hard to know what to do over the last few months. I think I thought I could make it go away if I pretended it wasn't happening. That didn't work out too well for me though. Because it is happening. This baby is happening and I'm starting to think that I'm glad.

Charlie and I have talked for hours and hours and we've decided that we can do this. It isn't what we chose, but it's what we've got so we need to make it work. We think that we can be a family — him, me and our baby. Like Granny always tells us — you don't get to choose and then moan. I guess, by doing what we did, we kind of chose this baby.

We don't want to hurt anyone though and we want to give ourselves a good chance — that's why we have to leave. If we stay then Mum will always have to see how much I messed up. If I go then maybe she can start to forget. And if we stay at home then I'll always just be yet another stupid teenager that got pregnant. And I don't want my baby to have a mum who is looked at like that.

That's why we're going to start a whole new life. It's going to be a new everything, Izzy! New home, new sensible me, new country. Charlie's Uncle Robert owns a hotel in Switzerland, right in the Alps. He's told Charlie that he'll give him a job. I'm going to have to improve my French cos that's mostly what they speak where we're going (wish I'd concentrated a bit more in lessons!) but Charlie's really good and he says I'll get better really quickly. Well, I'll have to, won't I! By the time you read this letter, we'll be on the train — the 3.45 to London first, then another train that will take us to Dover and finally the night ferry to France. It doesn't leave until late so we'll be sailing in the dark! Then we'll get a train all the way to Switzerland. It's so exciting!

I really hope you and Mum will come and visit us when we get settled. And of course I want the baby to know its awesome Aunty Izzy.

Don't be mad at me. I know that this isn't what you want to happen, but I truly can't stay and face what everyone will think of me. It'll be different when the baby's born. Everyone will love it and they'll forget all about this time when things seem difficult and a mess.

You're a fab little sister. I'm really, really sorry for dragging you into this.

Love you forever,

Alex xxxxx

PS Mum still doesn't know. I think it's best if you tell her at suppertime when we're well on our way. A xxxxx

She's gone. Run away. Abandoned us. However I say it, I can't make it sound any better. I sit for a moment, stunned by Alex's letter. I never thought she'd do this, not for a second. And she's leaving me to tell Mum? That's not fair.

I roll my head round on my shoulders, trying to think and make sense of everything. My eyes catch sight of the clock and I sit up straight, calculating times desperately. It's only five past three now. Alex wasn't expecting me to come home for ages, but because of my skiving I've got some time. Her train hasn't even left yet – I can still stop her!

I stand up and start pacing round the kitchen. The train station is about twenty minutes in the car from here. I could phone for a taxi, but it might take a while to arrive. There's no way I can get the bus; I'd have to walk into town first which would take too long. For a second I debate running, but then sink back down at the table when I realize that, even if I could make it there, I can't stop Alex from leaving. She's utterly determined and me asking her to stay is not going to change the slightest thing.

Defeated, I pick up her letter and read it again, feeling sadder and more frightened than I've ever felt. The PS at the end makes me feel something different though. It makes me feel furious. How dare Alex get me to do her dirty work? Has she given any thought whatsoever to how it's going to make Mum feel? The very least she could have done was leave Mum a note – that's if she was too cowardly to tell her and give Mum the chance to say goodbye properly.

And there it is: the answer to my dilemma. The same answer that it's always been – I just let Alex convince me otherwise. Mum. She can stop Alex doing this and Alex knows it. If Mum can get to the train station before Alex leaves then she can talk to her, let her know that it's OK to stay – that running away is only going to make it worse.

I look at the clock again. Ten past three. Mum will still be teaching and she's always told us that she can only leave school for complete and utter emergencies. The time I felt a bit sick because I used a dodgy pooter in science and sucked up a woodlouse did NOT, apparently, constitute an emergency. But this totally does. It's a desperate time and I need to be brave and make the right decisions.

Running over to the phone, I check the list of important numbers written on the noticeboard next to it. I ring Mum's school, my hands shaking, but knowing that I need to make Mum come home NOW.

The line starts ringing and I force myself to focus.

'Good afternoon. Darnfield Primary School. How can I help you?' says the nice lady in the office. I think her name is Margaret, but I'm not completely sure and now is not the time for trying to be polite.

'Er – hi, it's Izzy Stone. Mrs Stone's daughter,' I stutter.

'Oh, hello, Izzy,' says Possibly-Called-Margaret. 'What can I do for you?'

'I need my mum,' I blurt out. 'At home. Now. It's definitely an emergency. Can she come?'

'Oh my goodness!' She sounds worried, which is a good thing because I need her to tell Mum straight away. 'Is everything OK, Izzy?'

'No!' I tell her. 'It really isn't. And it's going to get even worse if Mum isn't home very soon. Please! Can you tell her I need her right now?'

'Of course I will, dear.' Possibly-Called-Margaret has swung into brisk, school-office mode. 'Don't worry – I'll go and get her now.'

'Thank you,' I say, and hang up the phone. I really hope Mum isn't going to be cross with me for calling her out of school, but she's our only hope if we're going to get to Alex before it's too late.

I grab Alex's letter and put it in my pocket and then I go into the hall and find my shoes. It'll be quickest if I wait for Mum outside, I think, so I find my key and slam the front door behind me, walking down the path to wait for Mum at the kerb.

Her school is less than a ten-minute drive away, but I know it'll take her a few minutes to find someone else to look after her class and gather up all her bags. The day of the pooter incident, it took her about twenty minutes to get to my school; I really hope she's a bit quicker today. A glance at my watch shows me that there's absolutely no time to lose. It's already 3.15 p.m.

The next ten minutes are the longest minutes of my whole life. Every time I hear a car turn down our road my heart does a triple somersault, but it's always someone else. And a weird thing is happening. You know the saying that a watched pot never boils? Well, normally it's true: when you're desperately waiting for something to happen then time seems to move really slowly. Today, when I want the clock to slow down and give us time to get to Alex, the opposite is happening. Every time I look at my watch it seems to have leapt on another two or three minutes. I feel like I've entered an alternate universe where the space-time continuum has totally different rules to our world.

By the time Mum comes screeching round the corner, virtually on two wheels, it's 3.25 p.m. If she steps on it, there's just a chance that we can get to the station before the train leaves. She pulls over next to me and I yank open the door and leap into the passenger seat.

'Go!' I shout at her, but she pulls on the handbrake and just looks at me. 'Come ON!' I yell. 'We've got to hurry!'

'What's going on, Izzy?' Mum asks, leaning across and holding on to my arm. 'Are you OK? What's happening?'

I look at her and my heart stops its mad somersaults and thuds heavily into my stomach. With all of the stress that we won't make it to Alex on time, I had somehow forgotten two very important facts. Mum doesn't know that Alex is running away. And Mum doesn't know that Alex is pregnant.

I look at the car clock – 3.27 p.m. There's no time.

'Mum, I promise I'll tell you, but you need to start driving. We've got to get to the train station,' I say, begging her with my eyes to listen to me.

But she doesn't. Instead, she turns off the ignition and looks at me hard.

'I want to know NOW, Izzy,' she says. 'You rang school, scared poor Margaret half to death with your frantic phone call and made me leave the classroom before the end of school. Now I need to know what's going on, please.'

I take a deep breath and grab hold of Mum's hand.

'If we sit here any longer then it'll be too late. Please, Mum – just trust me this one time!'

Mum strokes my hand and looks at me thoughtfully.

'Are you hurt?' she asks. I shake my head, trying to stop myself from screaming at her. 'Are you in trouble?' I shake my head again: 3.28 p.m.

I have no idea what Mum is going to do and I can feel Alex drifting further and further away. I flop back against the car seat and imagine the train pulling out of the station, taking Alex away forever. I close my eyes in an attempt to blot out the image, but open them quickly when I feel the car rumble to life beneath me.

'The train station?' asks Mum, checking her mirrors and pulling out into the traffic.

'Yes!' I say, sitting up straight. 'If we really hurry, we might get to her in time.'

'Get to who?' asks Mum, turning on to the main road and starting to pick up speed.

'Alex,' I tell her, hoping that the rest of her questions can wait until we get there.

Mum turns to me in surprise. 'Why is Alex at the station?' she asks. I'm quiet and she reaches over for my hand again, giving it a squeeze. 'Izzy, I'm prepared to trust you, but I need to know what's happening here.'

A car brakes suddenly in front of us as a cat dashes across the road.

'Mum!' I shout and she looks back at the road just in time, slamming on the brakes and making the car behind us honk its horn. Mum pushes her hair off her face and breathes out a huge sigh.

'Why is Alex at the train station, Izzy?'

I realize that if we're to have the tiniest chance of getting there in time then Mum is going to need to know.

'She's running away with Charlie,' I say quietly, trying not to spook Mum and cause a multiple pile-up.

'What!' says Mum. She doesn't scream it like I thought she would. It sounds more like a long groan, the way the word comes out of her mouth. 'For goodness' sake, Izzy! Why didn't you tell me?' Her voice is getting louder with each word. 'Silly, silly girl.'

'I'm sorry, Mum,' I say, trying not to cry.

'Oh, not you!' she says, indicating left and pulling off the main road on to a quieter street. 'Alex! She's behaving ridiculously. Where on earth do they think they're going to go?'

I'm quiet now, not wanting to be the one to tell Mum about Alex's plans to go to Switzerland. Maybe we'll get there in time and Mum will never need to find out.

She puts her foot down and we weave round a cyclist. We drive in silence for a while and then Mum starts speaking.

'I told her that they're just exams – that I'll be proud of her whatever her results,' she says, but I think she's talking to herself so I don't say anything. We're past the worst of the town traffic now, but it's cost us ten whole minutes. I lean over to watch the speedometer creeping up, up, up. We're driving fast now and I think we've got a chance.

'And everyone gets nervous about university,' Mum continues, shooting through the traffic lights as they turn amber. 'She's lucky to have the opportunities she's got. I'd have loved the chance to do the things she's going to be doing at her age.'

I stay silent and mentally will the clock to slow down. Surely we'll make it? This happens all the time in films. Just when you think the hero can't possibly get to the heroine in time to rescue her, he leaps in and saves the day. I imagine me and Mum sprinting down the platform, spotting Alex in the distance. I'll call her name and she'll turn and see us, and in that instant she'll see how daft she's been. She'll drop her bags and run towards us, and Mum will hold her in a big hug, and then Alex will scoop me up and we'll all be hugging and laughing and crying, and the train will leave and we'll bring Alex home where she belongs.

The car suddenly swerves round a corner and I fall against the door, banging my shoulder. Pain shoots down my arm, but I don't care because we're here. We've made it! Mum doesn't even bother to find a parking space; she just screeches to a halt in front of the main entrance and together we leap out of the car and race towards the station.

As we fly out on to platform 1, I see the station

clock overhead: 3.44 p.m. One minute to find Alex and make this better. It's totally possible. Then I see that platform 1 is empty. Mum has already started running towards the steps that go over the train tracks and down to platform 2. Platform 2, where a train is waiting.

I race after Mum and start up the steps. A train announcement is blaring all around me, but I can't make any sense of what it's actually announcing. I just know that I need to run faster than I've ever run before. As we reach the end of the bridge, I overtake Mum and hurl myself down the steps and on to the platform. Pushing through all the people who are trying to leave the station, I search desperately for Alex. There's a flash of violet in the crowd up ahead and it looks to me like Alex's favourite coat so I head towards it, not caring about how many people I shove and elbow to get past.

Then I've suddenly broken through the crowd and the platform ahead is empty. I start to run, casting my eyes to the right and looking into the carriages to check that she isn't there. Then a whistle blows and the doors shut and Mum is behind me and we're too late. I turn to Mum in disbelief. How can we have come so far only to fail at the last minute? Mum isn't looking at me though. She's gazing over my shoulder towards the train and as I turn I know what I'm going to see.

There is Alex, pressed up against the window of the train. Her face looks surprised or shocked or unhappy – I can't work out which one – but it's pretty obvious that she wasn't expecting to see us standing here. I take a few steps forward until I'm standing right in front of her, close enough to see the tears that are streaming down her face.

'Alex!' shouts Mum from just behind me. 'Get off the train!' But Alex can't hear her and she can't get off anyway; the doors are closed and they won't open until they get to the next station.

Alex looks at me and puts her hand against the window, her fingers spread apart. I copy her and match my smaller hand against hers and for one moment we're together, separated only by a piece of dirty glass. I know that I'm crying and I can hear Mum calling to Alex, loud cries that carry her worry and fear all the way up the platform, but I ignore everything, looking only at my sister. She mouths something to me through the window and it looks like 'Love you. Forever'.

'I love you too,' I tell her. And then the train is moving and I'm walking alongside, trying to keep my hand on Alex's. I feel it pick up speed and I start to run, desperate to keep her, and then Mum is pulling me away to safety and holding on to me, and I watch as the train moves away, keeping my eyes focused on a tiny flash of violet until I can't see it any more.

Even then we stand on the platform and wait until the train has disappeared from sight. Then Mum turns me round and looks me in the eye.

'Izzy?' she says. It's all she needs to say. She knows there's more to this than she's been told and she knows that I know. She wants answers. 'IZZY!' She raises her voice and gives my shoulders a little shake. And I have no idea where to begin. I'm completely exhausted and I don't want to have to be the one to shatter Mum's dreams. It's too much to ask of me.

Mum seems to realize that I'm incapable of speech at the moment and she suddenly takes off, racing back down the platform and over the bridge to the ticket office. I follow her and catch up just as she gets to the desk.

'Where was that train going?' she demands, startling the sleepy ticket man inside the office.

'Which train?' he asks her, looking up from his newspaper.

'The one that left platform two about a minute ago!' says Mum, the annoyance in her voice obvious.

I could tell her myself. I know exactly where that train is going. But Mum looks so angry and upset that she doesn't seem like my normal mum right now. I'm a bit scared by Furious Mum and I don't want to be the one who breaks the bad news to her.

'Well now, let me see.' He gets up and slowly walks over to the desk. 'Platform two, you say? Leaving at three forty-five p.m?'

'Yes,' says Mum and it sounds like her teeth are clamped tightly together. 'I can't believe it's nearly four o'clock already,' says the ticket man, looking up at the clock and then back at us. 'I've been rushed off my feet today – the time has flown by! It's been so busy. I had a gentleman in earlier who wanted to buy a ticket to Edinburgh, but going via Norwich of all places!' He raises his eyebrows at us in amazement, as if this is the daftest thing he's ever heard. Maybe it is, if you spend all day stuck inside a ticket office. I can feel Mum tense beside me; it's a good job there's a thick glass screen between him and us because otherwise I think she might reach through and give him a good shaking.

'The train?' she asks him.

'Oh yes – well, that train is headed to London, madam,' he tells her. 'Do you want to know all the stations it stops at?'

'No,' says Mum abruptly. 'Just tell me the departure time for the next train to London.'

The man looks at the clock again and then back at Mum sadly.

'That's the last one for today, I'm afraid. Got here a bit late, did you? Just like my wife. She can never get anywhere on time either. I have to tell her we're leaving the house at least ten minutes before we actually need to go – only way to get her to leave punctually. And I do think that punctuality is a good characteristic.' He chuckles to himself and Mum explodes.

'That is completely insane! It's not even four p.m! How can that possibly be the last train to London TODAY?'

She's shouting now, not caring who hears her, and I see the ticket man look sympathetically at me. He probably thinks I come from a broken home and I wonder for a second if he's right: if Alex running away makes us a dysfunctional family.

'I'm very sorry, madam, but there's some works being done on the line so we're running a limited service for the next few days. The next train to London leaves tomorrow at six forty-five a.m. Would you like me to book you a ticket?'

Mum looks at him blankly and I can tell that she suddenly doesn't know what to do. She shakes her head and then takes my hand and together we walk out of the ticket office.

We walk back to the car and I give Mum the letter that Alex left for me. Alex can tell Mum herself, even if she didn't intend to. I sit in the passenger seat and lean my head back on the headrest. I close my eyes and try not to listen as Mum reads the letter and sobs. Then she gets her mobile phone out of her bag and dials Alex's number. Alex doesn't answer on the first call, or the second call or the eighth call. After the eleventh call, Mum leaves a voicemail message, asking Alex to get off the train at the next station and to ring Mum straight away. And she tells Alex's voicemail that she just wants to help and that she loves Alex very, very much.

And, after that, we sit for a really long time, waiting for Alex to ring back. Mum checks the time every thirty seconds and, after an hour, when the ticket man has knocked on the window and told Mum that she can't park here, she wipes her eyes and we drive home very, very slowly. Mum stops the car on the drive and we sit in the car for a bit longer, not saying anything, but neither of us wanting to go into the empty house.

Eventually I start to feel cold so I open my car door and get out. Mum copies me, almost like she's glad that someone has suggested what she should do next. So I open the front door and put the kettle on, and Mum sits at the table in the kitchen while I make a cup of tea. I melt some cheese on toast and put it on a plate in front of her, and then we both sit, looking at the jar of peanut butter, letting our toast go cold.

After about ten minutes of sitting in silence, Mum suddenly leaps to her feet.

'What time did Alex say they were catching the ferry?' she asks me, her voice sounding frantic and something else, but I'm not sure what.

'I can't remember,' I tell her. 'I know Alex was excited about sailing in the dark so it must be quite late.'

Mum plunges her hand into her pocket and brings out Alex's letter. When we were in the car, she spent ages folding it up really carefully, a bit like someone arranging a posh napkin for a wedding, although not in the shape of a swan. Now she unfolds it just as carefully and skim-reads through the letter until she finds what she's looking for.

'She doesn't say a time!' she says and I realize that the other sound in her voice is hope. 'Quick, there's a chance we can get to her before she leaves the country.'

Mum races out of the room and for the second time today I sprint after her. She rushes into the study and turns on the computer, bouncing from foot to foot and frowning as it takes ages to load.

'Come on, come on,' she mutters and then launches forward the second the screen is on. 'Izzy, run and pack a bag and get ready to leave.'

'Why?' I ask her, a bit stupidly. I'm finding it hard to keep up with her and I'm tired. Today has been too much.

'We're going after Alex!' Mum says, wriggling the computer mouse and clicking furiously.

'What should I pack?' I say.

'Oh, I don't know! Anything! We'll need something to eat too. Grab some fruit and cereal bars.'

I walk into the kitchen slowly. I know I should be rushing, that every minute we delay is another minute where Alex has got further away from us, but I can't help thinking that this isn't what she wanted. She didn't want to say goodbye to Mum because she didn't want to give Mum the chance of doing this. Making a fuss and a drama. Alex only likes drama if she's the one creating it.

Just as I've emptied out my school bag on to the table and repacked it with a couple of apples and some crisps, there's a thud from the study and a few seconds later Mum comes hurtling through the door.

'Right, I've looked at the route to Dover and I think we've got a chance of making it on time. You'll have to read the map – can you do that, Izzy?'

She looks at me doubtfully and I nod my head, even though I'm terrible with directions. Last year I even got lost on our school orienteering course and they had to send a search party out to find me. It's not just basketball I'm rubbish at.

'I KNEW I should have bought that satnav when it was on offer,' moans Mum. 'Well, never mind – we'll just have to do the best we can. OK, are you ready? Do you need to use the bathroom because I don't want us to have to stop?'

I shake my head. I don't know what to make of this new Manic Mum. She's freaking me out a tiny bit. She picks my bag up off the table and starts walking towards the door. I go after her, starting to feel a tiny prickle of excitement in my stomach. Maybe we can still make this better. If we can just get to Alex before she boards the ferry, it'll all be OK.

Mum opens the front door and I step outside. She's just pulling it closed when the phone in the hall starts ringing. Mum stops, hesitating.

'Leave it, Mum!' I cry. 'We've got to go!'

'I can't,' Mum tells me, pushing the door open again and stepping back into the hall. 'It might be Alex!'

She rushes over to the phone and picks it up.

'Hello?' she says. 'Oh, Mum – I thought you were Alex.'

It's not Alex at all, only Granny. I pick up the bag that Mum has dropped and walk over to the car. Mum will tell Granny that she can't chat now and it'll be best if I'm waiting in the car, all ready to leave the instant she comes outside. The car is unlocked so I stash my bag on the back seat and sit down in the front.

Mum takes ages. I've had a chance to look at our road atlas and work out which direction we need to go in to get to Dover. I've opened the glove compartment to check if there are any sweets hidden in there, but I think we must have eaten them all up because the only thing I can find is a disgusting Fisherman's Friend. Those sweets are nasty. The first (and last) time I had one I thought it must be some kind of trick sweet: they taste disgusting and totally burn your mouth. Grandpa loves them though; this one must have been left over from the last time Mum took him out in our car.

Finally Mum comes outside. She closes the front door after her and gets into the driver's seat. Then she rests her head on the steering wheel and makes strange shuddering sounds.

'Mum!' I cry, reaching across and patting her on the shoulder. 'What's wrong?' Manic Mum was weird, but Sad Mum is truly awful.

She cries for a bit and I try to hold on to her, feeling awkward. I love my Mum, but I'm not used to being the person who tries to make her feel better; she usually does that for me. After a little while, she lifts her head and wipes her eyes.

'I'm sorry, Izzy. This is so difficult for you.'

'No!' I tell her, desperate to make her happy. 'It's not difficult. It's fine!'

'No, it isn't fine,' she says. 'That was Granny on the phone. Grandpa has gone missing again. He's been gone for ages. Granny thought he was pottering about in the garden shed, but when she went to tell him it was teatime he wasn't there. There's no telling how long he's been gone. He could be anywhere. She's already phoned the police.'

I look at her in horror. This can't all be happening at the same time. Surely there's a limit to the amount of bad stuff that can happen to a family in one day?

'We have to help find Grandpa,' I whisper.

'But I can't just let Alex run off!' cries Mum. She looks at the clock and makes a weird moaning sound. 'Look at the time! We've got no idea what ferry she's leaving on. There's no certainty that we're even going to find them and, if we do, I can hardly drag Alex back here like she's three years old, can I?'

I had been wondering about that. Alex is the same size as Mum and if she was determined to go with Charlie there's no way that Mum could persuade her to stay.

'And I can't abandon Granny and Grandpa,' Mum continues, looking over at me with exhausted eyes. 'They need me here. There's no knowing where Grandpa might be – he could have gone miles by now. There's just nobody else to help.'

She starts crying properly now and I don't know what to do.

'There's me!' I tell her. 'I'll help, Mum.'

That just makes her cry even harder and I sit there, rubbing her shoulders, with tears running silently down my face. When I woke up this morning, I had absolutely no idea that a day could be so terrible.

Eventually Mum stops crying and sits up straighter.

'I'm sorry, Izzy.' She brushes the hair back off her face and smiles at me, although it isn't a very happy smile. 'What would I do without you, hey? You're a fantastic, thoughtful, caring daughter.'

Well, you need one of your daughters to be, I think to myself, and the voice inside my head sounds mean and spiteful and not like me at all.

'I'm going to send Alex a text,' Mum says, picking up her phone. 'Perhaps if she knows what's going on she might change her mind and come home.'

I think Mum has completely lost the plot if she thinks Alex is going to just turn round and come back to us. That wouldn't be very dramatic at all and Alex is all about the big entrance and exit; slinking back quietly after a few hours isn't her style. I sit silently while Mum sends her text, wondering where Alex is now and hoping that Grandpa is somewhere safe. It's starting to get dark and I hate the thought of him out there, all alone. I think about the aggro boys, prowling the streets and looking for trouble, and my skin starts to feel horrible, all itchy and tight. We need to stop worrying about Alex – she chose to leave when she didn't have to – and start focusing on Grandpa who can't help getting confused sometimes. It's not his fault.

I'm just starting to wonder how long we're going to sit here, helping nobody, when Mum's phone rings. Her ringtone is the 'Crazy Frog' tune – Alex downloaded it for a laugh a few months ago and Mum has never got round to changing it. It sounds really wrong now, totally inappropriate. Mum snatches up the phone.

'Alex!' she cries. 'Where are you?'

I can't hear what Alex says in reply, but Mum listens for a second and then starts talking non-stop into the phone.

'Don't worry about that now, we can sort it all out. Alex? Alex – you need to listen to me, sweetheart. You need to get off the train. Running away is NOT the answer. Uh-huh. Yes. Yes, I understand you were scared. Right, yes, I realize that.'

Mum's voice sounds worried and I can tell that she's being really careful about what she says. I know she wants to persuade Alex to come home, but I'm not sure she needs to talk to Alex like she's about to jump off a cliff. Alex will do what she wants to do, whatever Mum says to her. She always does.

Mum is still talking. 'Yes, that's right. Grandpa. I know, I know – it's all happening at once. It's OK, Alex, don't cry. Just tell me the name of the last station you stopped at.'

She's quiet for a moment and I imagine Alex sitting on the train, watching the fields and the houses whizz past as she moves further and further away from us.

'OK, I understand. No, it's all right – just get off the train at the next station and ring me. I'll come and collect you.'

She's quiet again and I can just make out the tinny sound of Alex's voice coming through the phone, although I can't hear the words.

'Of course you do,' Mum is telling Alex. 'OK, OK, we'll head over to Granny now and you ring me when you're off the train. And Alex, I love you. Alex? Alex?'

Mum turns to me, looking scared. 'I think she lost signal. Her phone just cut out.'

'Is she coming home?' I ask.

'Yes!' Mum breathes out, a great big whoosh that sounds like a steam train. 'They're getting off at the next station, although she's got no idea where they are. They must be somewhere near London by now though. Thank goodness *something* has gone right today.'

Her phone makes a pinging sound and she looks down.

'She's sent me a text. Look.' Mum shows me the phone and I read Alex's text.

Next stop is in 30 mins. Charlie's mum will collect us. Don't worry. Find Grandpa. See u soon. LYF, Alex xxx

Mum starts the car.

'Let's go and find Grandpa. Hopefully Alex will be back by the time we get home.'

The next three hours are horrible. We get to Granny's house and she's really upset. The police have arrived. They tell Granny that they normally wouldn't go looking for someone when they've been gone such a short time, but she tells them all about Grandpa and the way he gets so confused, and they say that they'll send out a radio message telling other police officers to look out for him. Then they say they'll have a drive around and they ask Granny what he was wearing, and would he have gone down to the river?

That just makes Granny cry even harder. When the police have gone, Mum tells me to stay with Granny and she'll go looking for Grandpa. I sit with Granny for ages and listen to her saying that it's all her fault and that she should never have left him alone for so long, but she thought he was happy in the garden. I try to tell her that she couldn't have known he'd wander off, but it's like she can't hear me, so in the end I give up and make her a cup of tea instead.

By the time Mum walks back in the front door with Grandpa, we're all exhausted. She found him outside the garden centre, waiting for it to open. When she asked him what he was doing, he told her that it was time to sort out his summer bedding and that he needed to buy some plants. Apparently, this couldn't wait until the morning.

Mum phones the police to tell them that Grandpa's home and then leaves him to Granny, with promises to return tomorrow. Then we race to the car and drive back to our house. Mum hasn't heard anything else from Alex, even though she sent her a text to let her know that Grandpa was safe, and, as we approach our house, I can feel the atmosphere in the car get heavier and heavier.

'Surely she must be home by now,' mutters Mum as she pulls into our road. As we go round the corner, I lean forward to get a glimpse of our house; I can see straight away that it's in darkness. There's nobody inside.

We pull into the driveway and, right on cue, Mum's phone beeps.

'Quick, Izzy, get my phone out of my bag!' she tells me, pulling on the handbrake and turning off the engine. I pass it to her and watch. It's easy enough to tell what the text says by the way her face sags when she reads it, but I'm still shocked when Mum silently passes me the phone.

We r not coming. On ferry. Didn't want to make u choose b/tween me & Grandpa. So glad u found him. Sorry. Will call u l8ter. LYF, Alex xxx

'She lied to me,' whispers Mum. 'She never had any intention of coming home. She just wanted to stop me coming to get her.'

I don't know what to say so I don't say anything. It feels safer that way. Mum seems to have changed from sad to scared to really, really angry and I think it's probably a good idea if I try to keep a low profile right now.

We get out of the car and Mum lets us into the dark house. She makes us both some hot chocolate and we sit together at the table, although I notice that she doesn't drink any of hers. Our house doesn't feel like home without Alex. I can't help wondering if she has any idea what she's done to us. If she cares about us at all.

When I've finished my drink, Mum sends me off to bed, telling me that she needs to make a few phone calls. I go upstairs and peer through the door at Alex's room. It looks completely different. There are no clothes strewn across the floor and the bed is neatly made. The window is open and a summer breeze is floating through the room on the night air, blowing away any sign that Alex was ever here.

Completely miserable, I clean my teeth and head to my room. I'm too tired to put my clothes away properly so I just throw them in a pile on the floor – I can deal with them tomorrow. I pull on my pyjamas and get ready to flop into bed, beyond glad that today is finally finished.

But it's not over quite yet. There, sitting on my pillow, is Mr Cuddles. He stares at me mournfully with his one eye, guarding a note that is propped in front of him.

> Look after him for me. I don't think I need him any more.
>
> Love you forever,
> Alex xxx

I pick up Mr Cuddles and sniff his head. He smells of patchouli incense sticks and vanilla candles and Alex. I snuggle down under the covers and try not to think about Alex's face as the train pulled away. I try to believe that she's doing the right thing. And I'm glad to have Mr Cuddles with me in bed; it feels like she left a little bit of herself here with me, that she hasn't abandoned me completely.

Once in a Blue Moon

I don't think I ever knew just how much of the noise in our house was made by Alex. With only Mum and me here, it's really quiet. Mum has been getting home as early as she can on her workdays and we both sit together in the kitchen, me doing my homework and her planning her lessons. The house has become beige – calm and simple.

When I woke up the day after Alex left, I wasn't sure what to expect. I didn't know if Mum was going to be angry or sad or disappointed or confused. It turns out that she was all of those things multiplied by about one thousand. She told me over breakfast that she'd managed to get hold of Charlie's parents on the phone and that they were just as upset as she was. They said they'd contacted Charlie's uncle as soon as they read the letter that Charlie had left them and he was expecting them. They told Mum that he'd look after them until everything got sorted.

Mum also told me that she'd tried to ring Alex last night, about fifty billion times on her mobile, but Alex wasn't answering. I said that maybe her phone didn't work abroad, but Mum just pulled a weird face and didn't say anything.

When I got back from school that day, Granny and Grandpa were here. Granny gave me a big hug and told me not to worry, that it'd all come out in the wash. I think that means that it'll all be OK in the end but I don't really see how that can happen, to be honest. She and Mum had a huge conversation about whether Mum should travel to Switzerland to get Alex. Mum got all upset again and said that she couldn't have the time off work and, anyway, who would help look after Grandpa? They both looked at Grandpa when she said that, but he was busy unpacking and then repacking Granny's handbag over and over again and didn't notice.

Granny told Mum that they'd be fine and she mustn't worry about them, but even I could see the relief in her face when Mum told her not to be so daft and that she wouldn't leave them. That she'd speak to Alex and decide what to do from there.

Alex phoned Mum when they arrived in Switzerland to let her know that they'd got there safely. I don't know what they said to each other in their conversation, but Mum was very quiet when she got off the phone and later that night she told me that we definitely wouldn't be going after Alex – that she'd agreed to give Alex some time to decide what she wants to do. She said all this like she wasn't at all sure that she'd made the right decision.

Mealtimes and weekends are the worst. We just don't seem to be able to think of anything to talk about that isn't Alex. Mum gets really upset, but that doesn't stop her wanting to talk about what has happened over and over again. Most of the time I don't even have to say anything back: I just chew my food and listen while she asks what she did wrong. At the beginning I tried to tell her that it wasn't her fault – that Alex did this, not Mum – but she didn't seem able to hear me. She just keeps going on about history repeating itself and did she put too much pressure on Alex and it was only that she wanted the best for her and on and on and on.

On Day Five I got home from school and there was a letter on the doormat. It was addressed to Mum, but I knew straight away that it was from Alex – the violet ink was a complete giveaway. I put it on the kitchen table and Mum read it when she got home. She cried a bit while she read it and then she tucked it down the side of the mug that she uses to keep all her pens and pencils in. Alex gave her the mug a few years ago – not for a birthday or anything, but just because. I think they might have had an argument or something, but when Alex came home with the mug it made Mum laugh and pull a face and give Alex a huge hug. She said that she wasn't sure the mug should strictly be given to her because she's always making mistakes and messing up being our mum, but Alex said that was rubbish and she'd chosen a 'Best Mum in the World' mug because Mum really is.

Anyway, when Mum went off to do her marking, I had a look at the letter. I've kind of given up worrying about whether I'm doing the right thing or not these days. I think it's much more important to know what's going on, which everybody is incredibly slow to tell me. So it's really not my fault if I have to find out for myself. I think it shows that I have initiative.

I have no idea why Mum cried when she read the letter though. I couldn't find anything sad in it at all.

Dear Mum,

I'm writing to you from sunny Switzerland! We got here eventually, although at times I thought we never would. The journey took forever — I had absolutely no idea how far away this place is. Part of me really wanted to get off the train when I saw you and Izzy standing on the platform. I still don't understand how you got there?! I hope you understand why I didn't. I needed to do this and I didn't want you to come after me when you could be looking for Grandpa.

This place is so totally beautiful — I wish you were here to see it. The mountains are real, live Alps with snow on the tops — they look like something from a film. It's really hot and sunny too. At breakfast time today it was warm enough to sit outside and we saw two lizards sunbathing on a rock. And get this — the cows actually DO wear bells around their necks!!

The hotel is really pretty with shutters at the windows. I'm sending you a postcard with this letter so that you can see what I'm talking about.

Charlie's Uncle Rob is brilliant. He's totally fine about me and Charlie and the baby, which is a bit of a relief because I wasn't sure how much Charlie had told him before we arrived. The first thing he did when we got here was ring Charlie's parents so that they wouldn't be worried. I don't know what he said, but when he got off the phone he told Charlie that it was OK for now. His wife, Monique, is lovely too. It was her who suggested I ring you to let you know we'd got here safely, which was nice of her.

Charlie's job is to keep the hotel garden from looking too shabby and to help out in the kitchens. I'm going to do some work in the laundry and other bits and pieces. Yesterday I helped clean the rooms and make the beds, which was surprisingly good fun. I bet you never thought you'd hear me say that!

There are lots of complications with getting work permits apparently so for now Uncle Rob is just going to pay us in cash. We've got a tiny little chalet all of our own to live in — it's just like a doll's house, but I'll tell you more about that next time I write. Anyway, we've got somewhere to stay and Charlie brings our food back from the kitchens so it's not like we actually need a lot of money.

It feels like a free holiday really! Everyone is so kind and won't let me do much work because of the baby, so I've spent most of this week just sitting in the sunshine and wondering what you and Izzy are doing!

Well, I'd better go now — it's nearly time for supper. Please try not to worry about me. Everything is working out brilliantly and, although I'm missing you both a lot, I am happy.

Anyway, write back if you want to and tell me how you are. I can get emails here. I miss you.

Love you forever,
Alex xxxx

PS Tell Izzy I had coffee and croissants for breakfast. Delicious!

I asked Mum to show me on the map where exactly Alex and Charlie have gone, and at lunchtimes I go into the library and use the computer to Google images of where they are. I've seen pictures of mountains with snow and cows with bells around their necks, and Alex is right, it does all look really beautiful and amazing. It just doesn't look very 'Alex', that's all. I try and try, but I cannot imagine her there.

Mum had a chat with me a few days after Alex had gone. She said that what Alex had done wasn't fair: it wasn't fair on Mum or the baby, but it particularly wasn't fair on me. She said Alex had put me in an impossible situation and that she was proud of the way I dealt with it. I don't think she really understands how much I knew though, or how long I knew it. When I lie awake in bed at night, I ask myself that question a lot: would this all have been different if I'd just told Mum as soon as I knew? If I'd spoken out as soon as I read the text from Charlie about not wanting a baby? And I know the answer, but I wish I could un-know it because it's a hundred per cent YES. If I'd told Mum then she would have spoken to Alex and Alex would never have run away. I'm not stupid enough to think this is all my fault – it wasn't me that got pregnant after all – but I do know, deep down, that I'm not as sensible and responsible as Mum thinks I am.

On Day Ten I got home from school to find my own letter lying on the doormat. I took it up to my bedroom so that I could really enjoy it and maybe feel, for just a few minutes, that Alex was here chatting to me like old times.

Dear Izzy,

I can't believe I'm here in this awesome place – you really have never seen anything like it in your life! Hardly anyone speaks English, but I'm working really hard on my French and Charlie translates for me – when he's around that is! His Uncle Rob has him working really hard. I hardly get to see him at the moment. It's all worth it though, to be here together. Anyway, it's going to have to be a choice of learning French or stopping talking, so which do you think I'll choose?!

Our little chalet is the best place ever. It's all made out of wood and it smells amazing. We've got our own teeny bathroom with just enough room for a sink, toilet and shower. No bath, which is a shame, because the baby suddenly seems to have grown massive overnight and my back gets quite achy by the end of the day after lugging it around! I miss soaking in a long, deep bubble bath while you chat to me.

There are some shelves on one wall in our room and today I picked some flowers and put them in a jam jar. I have no idea what they are, but they make the place look really cosy. The walls are a bit bare, but I might have a go at drawing the view so that we've got a picture to put up.

It would be so fantastic if you and Mum could come here one day — I know you'd love it. There's a gorgeous little church in the village. I joked with Charlie the other day that it'd be an amazing place to get married. He didn't say a lot, but he did give me a big grin, so you never know! Never say never! Watch this space!!!

We're so happy to be here that it hardly seems like real life! And you should see what

Charlie has bought for the baby — a totally gorgeous (and a bit funny-looking, but don't tell him I said that!) stuffed toy zebra called Stripy!

The weather is completely different to back home (writing that sentence makes me feel totally British!). When it's sunny, it is BOILING HOT, but when it rains it's like standing under a shower. It feels like everything is MORE here — not grey and bleak like at home.

There's so much I want to tell you and I'm sure I haven't said half of it. It's brilliant that it's all working out so well and that Charlie and I are so happy together. I wish I could share all of this with you and Mum as well though. I'm having all the good things while you're both probably a bit worried about me.

Don't worry and try not to miss me too much. I'm really, really happy here!

Love you forever,
Alex xxx

I read her letter over and over again, but in the end I gave up. I couldn't find it, no matter how hard I tried. Alex's letter told me all about the great weather and the growing baby and how happy she is – but nowhere can I find the bit that makes me think she's missing me. Or that she's sorry for what has happened. And the weather isn't THAT bad here actually. It's quite nice, the best summer we've had for years apparently, so it's just bad luck for Alex that she's missing it.

Izzy

Mum won't stop
crying.
She has so many tears that I imagine
the kitchen
flooding
and me having to row across to the kettle
in a rubber dinghy,
just to make her
a cup of tea.

Mum won't stop
talking.
So many words that they fill the air,
skirmishing and jostling and clogging up
my head.
Angry is a strong word.
He elbows his way to the

top spot a lot.
'How could she do this to me?'
'What have I done to deserve this?'
'What was she thinking?'
Angry likes to ask a lot of
questions,
but isn't really interested in the
answers.

Sometimes
Guilty
sneaks
her
way
in.

Guilty is sly and she doesn't come
alone.
Sometimes she brings
Sad
with her.
Sometimes Confused likes to join
the party.
And Guilty has a twin sister.
Her name is
Memories.

'If only I hadn't behaved that way.'
'Do you remember the day I said that?'
'I should have been better.'
'It's all my fault.'

Guilty turns happy memories into
nightmares.
She rewrites the story so that times you
thought were
good times
suddenly have their skin peeled back and a
rotten core
stares back at you.

I
hate
Guilty
most of all.

True Colours

It's the last week of term and everyone is excited. Nobody is getting any work done and even the teachers seem to have given up. Most of our lessons involve watching a film or having a discussion. This suits Hannah and me: we just hide in a quiet corner and chat about the summer holidays.

I've told her about Alex – it seemed silly not to when the news was spreading round school like a fire. Most of the sixth form came and asked me if it was true in those first few days. I suppose it gave them something else to think about instead of stressing over their exams. And it's not every day that the sixth form heart-throb runs away with the popular, dramatic, pretty girl. The worst part was the whole-school assembly we had a week after they'd gone. Our head teacher managed to avoid saying Alex or Charlie's names, but he didn't need to bother trying to be subtle: everyone knew why we were suddenly being lectured on keeping ourselves safe and making the right choices, and him going on and on about where we could get confidential advice if there was anything worrying us.

I spent the entire assembly looking at the floor and avoiding eye contact with anyone. I could feel people looking at me and nudging each other; it reminded me of the basketball incident, but about fifty times worse.

Now, though, it's starting to become old news at school. I wonder how Alex would feel about this if she knew. I know that she wrote in her letters that she didn't want people talking about her, but part of me thinks she'd be a lot more upset to think that people had stopped talking about her. Moved on.

Exams are over and the sixth form has mostly left. I've seen Sara a few times and she always smiles and waves at me, but she's getting ready to go to university and she's got no reason to talk to me. I didn't even like her very much when she was Alex's friend, but I wouldn't mind a chat with her now and then, just to help me remember what it used to be like.

I'm sort of dreading the holidays. It'll just be Mum and me for six long weeks and I'm not sure how we're going to fill our time. Talking about Alex probably. Mum wondered for a while if we could go on holiday to Switzerland and I got really excited. I thought we could show Alex how much we love her and then she'd want to come back with us at the end of the holiday. But it can't happen; it costs too much money for one thing and we can't leave Granny and Grandpa for another.

Granny's getting a carer in to help out with Grandpa. Mum was furious when she found out, but Granny told her she's putting her foot down and that if Mum doesn't have a rest soon then she's going to go mental. Or words to that effect. Granny thought she was doing Mum a favour, but Mum explained to me that the carer will only come for five days and that by the time we got to Switzerland we'd have to come back again. She said she'd spoken to Alex about it and Alex isn't ready to see us yet anyway. Mum phones about three times a week and speaks to her for ages, but I don't think they really talk about any of the things that actually matter. I hear Mum telling Alex about our week and asking her what she's up to, but it never sounds like they're talking properly – not like they used to.

I heard Mum on the phone the other day to Charlie's mum. She didn't know I was listening, but I was just walking past and, when I realized who she was talking to, I couldn't just walk away. So I hid on the top stair where I was out of sight, but could still hear Mum's side of the conversation. It was a bit hard to piece together what they were saying, but Mum didn't sound angry with Charlie's mum, which I thought was surprising because I reckon it's mostly his fault that this is all happening in the first place. I did manage to work out that they've got a plan though. Mum told Charlie's mum that she's being firm but fair with Alex. She said that she phones several times a week, but that she isn't going to force Alex to take her help – that 'those kids need to take responsibility for their actions'. Then she did a lot of 'uh-huhing' and 'yes, I know' while Charlie's mum did the talking.

Mum was really quiet when she came off the phone. I asked her later on when we were peeling potatoes for supper if she hated Alex. She threw down her peeler and looked at me in total horror.

'I could never hate Alex,' she told me. 'Or you. I thought you girls knew that?'

'So why won't you help her?' I asked. I didn't want to upset her or make the evening horrible, but I couldn't help feeling that Mum had abandoned Alex.

'I will help her, but she has to be ready to take my help,' Mum said. 'Right now she's trying on her own and she needs to see how that works out for her. Maybe it'll all be great and then I'll be pleased for her, and we can figure out what she needs from us, but maybe she'll decide that she was a bit quick to strike out alone and that she'd rather have some support. All she has to do is ask.'

I thought about this for a while, peeling more potatoes. I can't imagine Alex asking for help – that'd be like admitting she was wrong or had failed.

'What if she doesn't ask?' I said to Mum. She stared out of the window and then told me that she had to let Alex make that choice on her own. That Mum would always be there when Alex decided that she wanted her.

This is why I'm not particularly looking forward to the holidays. Endless weeks wondering what Alex is doing, and hoping that she's OK, and trying not to think about other brilliant summers when we all went on holiday together and had so much fun.

I'm lying in the garden on a rug, trying to relax in the sunshine. Nobody has given us any homework for ages now, which means that I have absolutely nothing to do when I get home from school. I've decided that a person does not have to go all the way to Switzerland to enjoy good weather so I've dragged a rug on to the lawn and brought my book, and I'm trying to get into the holiday spirit.

Just as I start chapter six a shadow falls across my page. I groan – that is so utterly typical. It took me ages to get all sorted out here and now that I'm just starting to relax the sun has decided to disappear.

'That's a nice greeting!' says a voice and I look up to see Finn standing above me. 'Here's me bringing you a delicious ice cream and you just groan!'

I sit up quickly and take the dripping ice cream out of his hands.

'Yummy – thanks, Finn!' I say, licking the drips that are running down the cone and threatening to fall on to my hand. 'What's this for?'

'Can I not bring my favourite neighbour an ice cream on a hot day?' jokes Finn, sitting down next to me on the rug and stretching out his legs. He licks his own ice cream and we sit in silence for a moment, and the only sounds are the slurping noises we make as we try to beat the heat and eat the ice creams before they melt.

'And I felt a bit bad,' he says, finishing the last of his cone before I've even managed to get halfway. I don't know how boys manage to eat so quickly: it's like they don't want to enjoy their food, they just want it eaten.

'Why do you feel bad?' I ask him.

'Because I've not been over lately. Not since Alex – well, you know.'

'Don't worry about it,' I tell him. 'Everything's different since she left.'

I watch an ant scurrying across the grass towards a few drops of ice cream that have fallen on to the ground. Some friends quickly join it and I wonder what they're saying to each other. Maybe stuff like 'Come over here – there's an ice-cream mountain!' and 'It's a miracle, sent from heaven – quick, quick, eat it up before it goes for good!'

'But just because she's gone doesn't mean we can't still hang out, does it?' asks Finn and I look at him and smile. I know it won't happen really. Finn's got work and friends and band practice – he hasn't got time to hang around with me. But I've missed him a lot. I never realized how much time he spent in our house. I think about the fact that, when Alex left, we lost more than just her that day.

'We can hang out, Finn,' I tell him. 'But I need to warn you that I've got a crazy social life going on at the moment. I can't be there for you the way I used to be.'

Finn laughs and ruffles my hair and then stands up.

'See you around, Izzy,' he says.

'Yeah, yeah, whatever,' I reply, busying myself with smoothing my hair down so that he won't see me looking sad.

'You know where I am,' he tells me and then walks towards the garden gate.

'Thanks for the ice cream!' I yell after him and he puts his hand in the air, but keeps walking away. I hope this isn't going to be a theme for me: people leaving. I wonder when I'll be old enough to be the one who does the walking away.

Dear Mum,

It's been a fantastic day today. This morning we packed a picnic of cheese, bread, chocolate biscuits and oranges and went on a walk up a mountain. We followed a little path through the forest that ran alongside a really fast river. We never got to the top because around lunchtime we came out of the forest into a beautiful meadow full of flowers. It looked like something out of The Sound of Music! I was feeling a bit tired and the baby was kicking and it was really hot so we stayed there for hours, eating our picnic and sunbathing and splashing in the water — which is totally freezing by the way! It was an amazing way to spend my birthday. Can you believe it, I'm finally eighteen! Thanks so much for the money you sent — it'll come in really useful.

Can you believe that I can feel the baby move?! It's such a strange feeling, like having a stomach full of goldfish. I'm getting really fat now too and I had no idea that I'd feel so tired all the time.

Charlie's been talking to his Uncle Rob about what we'd have to do to stay out here for good. Uncle Rob is going to make enquiries for us and let us know. I know that you might not want to hear that, but everything's working out totally perfectly and we'd really like to live here and have the baby grow up in such a beautiful place.

I've been doing a bit of ironing for the hotel and have earned some of my own cash, which is great! And guess what I bought with my wages? A real, genuine cuckoo clock! Totally handmade in Switzerland! It works really well most of the time and it looks brilliant on the wall in our room. Charlie said I should have bought something more useful (it cost one whole week's wages) but I told him that it was a bargain because it's multi-purpose. It tells the time, makes our room look like a real home and makes me laugh every time the cuckoo pops out! Like three for the price of one, I told Charlie. He's an old grouch though and made me stop it at bedtime because he said he's tired enough without being woken up every hour by a stupid bird!

258

It's early evening now and Charlie's at work again. I'm sitting under a tree outside our chalet and it's still really hot. I'm going to visit the doctor any day now, as soon as Monique sorts out an appointment for me. Everyone is making me feel very looked after.

I hope you're both OK and getting used to me not being around. I'm still missing you, but it's all fine here.

Love you forever,
Alex xxx

PS Have you kept my bedroom the same? You said in your last email that you've done a major spring-clean — I hope you've not got rid of my stuff??!!

Roses Are Red, But Violets Are Not Actually Blue

Dear Alex,

I thought I'd write to you and tell you about what's going on at home. School has finished now so we're all on holiday, which is good. You're totally wrong about the weather here by the way — it's really hot and sunny and we've been spending most days outside in the garden.

Last week Mum completely surprised me. She said that we should get away and have a proper holiday after all the upset of the last few months. She said we should make the most of Granny and Grandpa having some extra help and that we could go camping for a few days. She dragged our old tent out of the attic and we went shopping in town and got a camping stove and a new sleeping bag for Mum (I used yours — Mum said you wouldn't mind).

It was SO MUCH FUN! I wasn't sure whether it'd be any good with just the two of us, but it was the best holiday ever! We drove for ages. Mum said it was a road trip and let me sit in the front with my feet up and the windows down and we put the radio on really loudly and sang along. You'd have loved it! Then we got to a campsite right on the beach — the only things between the sea and us were these amazing sand dunes. When we woke up every morning, we could hear the waves — it was the best sound to wake up to.

Every day was amazingly sunny. We swam in the sea and it wasn't freezing cold like it usually is. I bought a snorkel with my holiday money and spent ages floating around, looking at all the amazing creatures on the seabed. I'm thinking that I might go to university and study to be a marine biologist when I'm older.

One night we had a campfire and toasted marshmallows and told each other scary ghost stories. I got a bit freaked out when it got really dark, but it was OK because then I could just snuggle up next to Mum, all warm in your sleeping bag, and it felt like nothing could ever scare me again.

We went for a few long walks along the sand and Mum only wanted to talk about me. She asked me all about school and my friends and what I'd like to do with the rest of the holidays, and did I feel like she gave me enough attention. I feel like this holiday has been really good for us – we've never had so much time together before, just the two of us.

I'm glad it's all working out for you in Switzerland. Your chalet sounds great and I'd love to see the cuckoo clock – Mum told me about it. I hope Charlie's stopped being moody now, but boys can be like that, I know.

Write back soon,

Love Izzy xxx

Dear Izzy,

Thanks so much for your brilliant letter! Your camping holiday with Mum sounds fantastic. I wish I could have been there too. Of course I don't mind you borrowing my sleeping bag — you can take anything from my room (just make sure you put it back!).

I'm sitting outside our chalet in the sunshine because Charlie's inside having a rest. Thank goodness he's gone to sleep — I hope he wakes up in a nicer mood! I'm determined not to have an argument with him today. Still, I suppose I need someone to yell at and I haven't got you or Mum here so I'll just have to make do with Charlie! Like you say, boys can be moody.

He's tired all the time at the moment, but he says he has to work extra shifts because we need the money. It gets a bit boring for me sometimes because Uncle Rob won't let me do much work at all, which means I'm just sitting around doing nothing, on my own. Don't feel too sorry for me though — being bored in Paradise isn't the worst thing that could happen to a person!

Further adventures of a cuckoo clock:
yesterday, when Charlie was hammering up
a coat hook, it fell off the wall and all
its insides pinged out and it doesn't work at
all now. But I put it back up on the wall
because it still looks nice and homely, despite
the various bits and pieces hanging drunkenly
out of the bottom. I think 'passive' is about
the only word you could use to describe the
poor cuckoo now — he looks a bit floppy and
bewildered by it all!

Have you seen much of Finn? I've written to
him a few times, but I haven't heard anything
back. I guess he's still mad at me. If you see
him, tell him I said hello.

Do you know how Sara's getting on? I know
her exams will be over by now, but if you
happen to see her around tell her that if
she ever feels like writing a letter then I'm
desperate for news from home.

Tell Mum that I've sent her a birthday
card, but the post can be really slow, so not
to think I've forgotten if it hasn't arrived
by the fifteenth.

Take care, Izzy. I hope you guys are coping without me! Give my love to Granny and Grandpa.

Love you forever,
Alex xxxx

I never thought I'd be glad to be going back to school, but it feels like this summer holiday has lasted forever. I've spent so much time in the library in town that I could virtually run the place. I know all about how they organize the books and the other day, when I overheard a lady asking where she could find a book on gardening, I answered her before the librarian did. It was incredibly embarrassing.

Early on in the holidays Mum and I went camping. It was a complete disaster. It rained virtually every day and the only day that it was sunny I got stung by a wasp. Our tent is really old and has a rip in the roof so all our clothes got wet. I had to use Alex's sleeping bag and it was only a two season – but camping in England in the summer definitely requires more of a four-season attitude. Mum tried really hard to make it fun, but it was just too weird without Alex. Not that I'm going to tell Alex that. I don't want her thinking that we can't have a nice time unless she's there. So I wrote her a letter saying how amazing it all was. I didn't tell her anything about how I'm actually feeling because I can't trust her any more. Actually, I'm quite surprised by how easy it is to lie if you write the lies in a letter; it makes me wonder if everything Alex writes in her letters is the actual, honest truth. Maybe it isn't as fantastic in Switzerland as she says it is.

The weather's rubbish too. The second we broke up for the holidays it started to rain and it hasn't really let up. Even the ice-cream van has stopped coming down our road and he never normally lets a bit of bad weather put him off: one year I saw him out there in December, trying to sell ice lollies to kids wrapped up in gloves and hats and scarves.

I've seen Hannah a few times, but she went away to Spain for a fortnight with her family and then her cousin came to stay so she's not been around much. When we got back home from camping, Mum felt bad about leaving Granny and Grandpa, so we've spent most days popping over to their house. Mum and Granny mostly sit around talking non-stop about Alex and the baby. I've played my violin for Grandpa a few times, but I can't really be bothered to practise as much as I usually would; now there's no chance of me ever being a member of On the Rocks I can't really see the point of carrying on with the violin. The rest of the time I've just sat quietly, listening to them going on and on. I think it's fair to say that it has probably been the worst, most boring summer ever and I'm glad that school's starting tomorrow. Maybe life can get back to a bit of normality now.

Red Rag to a Bull

Dear Izzy,

It feels like it's been raining forever, but today it's finally stopped and the sun is shining. I'm outside on the grass, getting bitten to death by weird flies and probably sunburnt, but it's so nice to be able to sit out here after days stuck in our room.

Charlie had the day off yesterday so we took the bus to the nearest town. We'd decided that we wouldn't spend any money at all apart from the bus fare and we'd taken bread, cheese and tomatoes for our lunch. When we got there though, we saw a really lovely baby shop and we couldn't resist going inside to look at a child's carry seat — you know, the ones you wear on your back like a

rucksack? We really fell in love with it —
it's made out of dark green material with
orange bits on the sides. You can't put a
newborn baby in it, but it'll be perfect for
when he or she has grown a bit bigger. We
really do want to stay out here so we'll be
going on lots of long walks into the mountains
all the time, I suppose.

Charlie told the man in the shop that we
wouldn't be buying, we were just looking, but
then he asked the price and as soon as the
man told us we both said, 'See how much we've
got'! It was totally meant to be — we had
just enough to pay for it and our bus fare
home — so of course we ended up buying it.
It felt fantastic carrying it home and now
it's propped in the corner of our room and
it makes the baby seem very real, like it's
actually going to be here in a few months!!

Yesterday we went to visit Monique's nephew
Eric and his girlfriend Chrissie. They live in a
hut further up the mountain and Monique had
to drive us down the bumpiest track EVER
to get there. To reach their hut you have to

cross a stream (which is where they get all their water) on a rickety old plank bridge. They've got a vegetable garden and some hens and ducks and NO electricity!!!!! I spent ages talking to Chrissie (her English is great). She said that she's lived there for two years and doesn't even miss having electricity. When it started to get dark, she lit loads of candles and cooked us an amazing meal on a massive kitchen range that had a fire lit inside it.

It was such a romantic place and really cheap too. I think me and Charlie could live like that when the baby arrives. Monique tried to put me off and started talking about how difficult it'd be to look after a baby in conditions like that, but loads of people in the Third World do it, so I think we'd be fine.

The only downside was the toilet. It was outside and was just three wooden walls up against the house — the fourth side was completely open, not even a door! It looked out on to the stream and wasn't actually even a proper toilet, just a big box with a hole in the top. There I was, sitting quite happily admiring the view, with my knickers round my ankles, when along came a farmer, herding his fifty million cows home (well, probably not QUITE that many, but it seemed to take them all an extraordinarily long time to walk past me, all gazing at me with their freakily large cow eyes!).

I NEVER expected that anyone would come past, the place is so isolated, and I nearly fell into the box in horror. The farmer didn't seem even a little bit bothered though — he just gave me a cheery wave and kept herding his cows!

Even after that though, I'm dreaming of us having a home like Eric and Chrissie's.

Tell Mum that I've had a check-up with the doctor. He listened to the baby's heartbeat and said everything's fine.

Love you forever,
Alex xxxxx

I'm sitting on the bottom of the stairs and listening to Mum and Charlie's mum (apparently, her name is Marianne) talking about 'the situation' in our kitchen. After weeks of telephone conversations, Mum invited her over to our house so that they could talk properly and work out how they should deal with Alex and Charlie. I've been sent off to do my homework, but there is no WAY I'm missing this. Mum won't tell me what Marianne says and if Alex's baby is going to dominate my entire year then I definitely want to know what's going on.

Mum's made coffee and brought out the best biscuits; I think she's going all out to impress Marianne and make her think we're a 'nice' family. I don't think she knows that the red top and brown trousers that she put on just before Marianne arrived show that she's moody and anxious and likely to be easily annoyed. Marianne, on the other hand, is wearing a crimson-coloured shirt that shows she's a bit threatening and will demand to be listened to. There could be fireworks. So far, they've only talked about completely boring stuff like the weather and work and, bizarrely, the rising cost of fuel. Very strange. Now though they've sat down with their drinks and I can sense that they can't put it off any longer. Alex and

Charlie are making their uncomfortable presence felt, even though they're hundreds of miles away.

'Have you heard from Alex recently?' asks Marianne, diving in and getting straight to the point.

Mum sighs. 'She wrote a few weeks ago, and she's written a couple of times to Izzy. I spoke to her on Sunday night as usual, but the line was crackly and there's always people around at her end – I couldn't really get a lot out of her.'

'At least she writes to you,' says Marianne, and I can hear that she's trying to find something positive to say about Alex. 'Charlie hasn't written once – not if you don't count the miserable note he left us when they ran off, which I do not.'

There's a bit of quiet while they both slurp their coffee and then Mum takes charge of the conversation.

'The reason I thought it'd be better to get together to chat is because Alex is talking about them staying in Switzerland. For good.'

'I know,' says Marianne. 'Rob's been keeping me up to date. He's done his very best to show them how difficult it would be, but he says that they seem determined. It's a problem. The last thing any of us want to do is to make life harder for them, but I just don't think they've addressed the reality of their situation. They're still playing at being grown-ups and when the baby arrives they're going to be in for a nasty shock.'

'I agree,' says Mum. 'And I can't pretend I'm not hurt about how they've dealt with it all. Running away without talking to us. I lie awake at night wondering what I did to make Alex treat me like that.'

There's the sound of a cup being put on the table and I imagine Marianne reaching across and holding Mum's hand.

'You mustn't blame yourself,' she tells Mum. 'It's happened and we all just want them to take some responsibility and start working out how they can make this work in the real world.'

I hear Mum sniff and then clear her throat, as if she's trying not to cry.

'There are so many ways that this doesn't have to be a disaster for them. But they're going to need to ask for help – acknowledge that they're in too deep and can't do it alone.'

'Completely, which is why we have to be strong. Nobody ever said that being a mum was easy, and I don't know about you, but I'm kind of missing the stage when all I had to worry about was grazed knees and temper tantrums and arguments about watching too much TV.'

They both laugh and the tension flowing through the open kitchen door seems to ease a little bit.

'I've contacted school and they've said that they can help Charlie get a place at university for next year. He'll have to retake the exams he missed and there'll be a little bit of extra coursework, but they said that with his predicted grades, and his excellent conduct up until now, there shouldn't be a problem. A blip, that's what the head teacher said to me.'

There's a silence again and then Mum answers, her voice sounding slow and careful like she doesn't want to say the wrong thing.

'And the baby? Is that going to be just "a blip" for Charlie, do you think?'

'Oh, that's not what I meant! We'll do everything we can to support Charlie, to help him take responsibility for his actions. We're trying to see this whole awful experience as a life lesson for him – that everything he does has a consequence and that he needs to face up to that.'

'Hmmm.' Mum is making her thinking sound. 'Yes, that could be a good option!' She's starting to sound enthusiastic. 'I know that they both had offers from the same university – Alex could do the same and they could rent a little flat. There'd probably be some childcare available through the university and they could share the rest. It wouldn't be the same experience that their friends will be having, but it could work. That's a fantastic suggestion, Marianne!'

'That wasn't quite what we've been thinking about though,' says Marianne, her voice so quiet that I have to lean forward to catch everything she's saying. 'Oh, just imagine it. They'd have no sleep and no time for fun – it'd be all work and no play. Not the university experience we wanted for Charlie at all.'

'Well, no,' replies Mum, her voice now a tiny bit louder than before. 'But we've agreed that they need to take responsibility. It was you that mentioned "life lessons" a minute ago.'

'But the price you're suggesting is just too high!' says Marianne and I can hear a hardness in her voice. 'I'm not sure you fully understand our situation here. Charlie is a top student. He's set on being a doctor and there's no reason why he won't achieve that goal. A goal we've all been working towards for a very long time, incidentally. But the pressures of medical school are huge.

There's no way he could cope with a screaming baby at the same time. It's out of the question!'

'So who's going to be looking after this screaming baby while Charlie skips off to university?' I can tell that Marianne has just pushed Mum into very dangerous Mum-mode. Her voice sounds totally polite, but there's an undercurrent of menace that makes the hairs on my arms all stand up on end.

'Alex, of course,' says Marianne, sounding surprised. 'I'm sure you'll agree that one silly mistake with a daft girl is not a good enough reason to ruin the rest of Charlie's life.'

I hear a chair scrape back across the floor and tense my body, half hoping that Mum isn't about to thump Marianne and half hoping that she doesn't let her get away with making such terrible comments about my sister. There's a click of heels on the tiles and I scuttle further up the stairs just in time as Marianne walks out of the kitchen and to the front door, Mum just behind her. She turns to Mum as she opens the door, one hand on the handle.

'Don't worry, we'll make sure that Charlie keeps in contact and it goes without saying that his father and I will contribute to the upkeep of the child.'

'That won't be necessary,' murmurs Mum and I can tell she's using every bit of her self-control to stop herself from slapping Marianne.

Marianne steps on to the path and Mum watches her go. When she's about halfway down, Mum calls out and I wonder if this is when she's finally going to let rip.

'There *is* one thing you can do for me,' she shouts and Marianne stops and turns, looking towards the door. 'You can do whatever it takes to get my little girl home again.' Marianne holds up a hand in acknowledgement and trots off to her car.

'My silly, daft little girl,' mutters Mum, but Marianne is in her car and doesn't hear her.

Mum stays at the door to watch her leave, as if she's making sure that she's definitely gone. Then she backs inside and closes the door.

'Did you hear all of that?' she asks me without turning round.

'Yes,' I say, hoping that she doesn't yell at me for eavesdropping.

'Good,' she says, turning and looking up the stairs at me. 'We need to discuss something very important and I need to explain a few ideas I've had. I want to hear what you've got to say too – this is going to be a Family Stone decision.'

She gestures me down the stairs and into the kitchen. The plate of posh biscuits is still on the table. Mum sees me looking.

'She was on a diet,' she tells me. 'I should have known then that we were in for trouble. Never trust a woman who won't eat a luxury biscuit, Izzy – remember that.'

She clears away the coffee cups and grabs two glasses and a carton of orange juice. She puts them on the table, pushes the biscuits towards me and tells me her idea. And we talk and I make suggestions and, for the first time since this all started, I feel like we're back on track, back as a family.

Dear Mum,

I've put on so much weight – I wonder if you got this fat when you were pregnant with me.

I'm avoiding Charlie today because he's in a really bad mood. Are ALL boys totally unreasonable? He had a big chat with his Uncle Rob last night and he's been grouchy ever since. I'm trying to ignore him and hope he snaps out of it. I suppose I'm finding it a bit hard because I've never seen him being grumpy, not before we came out here anyway. I guess we didn't actually know each other as well as we thought we did.

I know that in an ideal world we'd have had time to get to know each other properly before we had to deal with things like money and jobs and heartburn and backache. We haven't GOT time though – every day is another day closer to being parents. I'm really excited about meeting our baby, but I'm starting to feel a bit worried too. How will we know what to do? I don't have a clue about how to look after a baby. What if I get it wrong? I've tried Googling it, but it's all really confusing and there's loads of choices. Some people say you must have a strict routine, other people say go with the flow; some sites go on and on about how, unless you're a planet-killer, you MUST use cloth nappies, but I've looked at them and it means you come into close contact with an awful lot of poo. I don't want choices any more – I just want someone to tell me what to do.

Charlie's mum isn't helping at all. Last week

she sent him a prospectus for the university that he'd got a place at. What was the point of doing that? We missed our A levels when we came here – he can't go to uni now, can he? She wrote him a letter too and he wouldn't let me read it, but I snuck a peek over his shoulder and saw that she'd written something about it 'not being too late'. I don't understand why she'd write that. Even if he did retake the exams, the baby is still going to be here. It's still going to need looking after. He's still going to be a dad, whether he likes it or not.

Sometimes I wish more than anything that I could sit down with you at our table in the kitchen and talk to you about everything. I've got a million questions to ask you – things about how I'm feeling and giving birth and the baby. Things that I don't know how to say in French. Even if I did I haven't got anyone here who I could ask, not even if my French was fluent.

I know that I really hurt you a lot when I left without telling you what was going on. I'm really grateful that you phone every week, but it's impossible to talk to you properly and I miss you. I expect you'd like to be around when your first grandchild is born, wouldn't you? Even if you are still mad at me. Even though you'd have wished for a different situation, I know you'll love our baby.

I feel it moving all the time now – it's really exciting and I wish I hadn't cut you out of all of this. Charlie is trying hard, but our room is tiny and I've got nobody else to talk to and we never have anything new to tell each other because nothing ever happens here. I spend most days cleaning and tidying our room (which doesn't take long) and when Charlie gets back I want to talk, but he's really tired and just wants to sleep.

Anyway, don't worry about me – I'm probably just in a grouchy mood. Charlie would say it's the hormones talking. (I don't think he's quite worked out that I want to push him in the river when he says stuff like that to me. He'll learn!) The weather is rubbish too and my suntan has completely washed off.

I just can't talk to you properly on the phone — I'm sorry if I sound distant. I feel a long way away from you right now and it's making me homesick.

Love you forever,
Alex xxxx

PS I saw the doctor again and he said the baby is definitely due at the end of November. So it'll be here for Christmas!!!

Red-letter Day

Dear Mum,

Thank you, thank you, thank you for your letter! I cried when I read it, which made Charlie really worried that something bad had happened! He was really pleased too when I told him what you'd written and says a big thank you! I keep rereading your letter to check it's really true!

I can't believe you're letting us come home! We can make my room into the perfect place for the baby and us. I know you said it'll be a bit squashed but, honestly, it's probably the same size as our whole teeny chalet here! I'm so excited that you're going to be there to help me. I've missed you and Izzy SO MUCH the last few months. Your letter came at the

perfect time. Monique has been having loads
of chats with me about how hard it'd be for
me to have the baby in Switzerland, and
Charlie's mum keeps phoning him and I don't
know what she says, Mum, but he's always a
bit fed up or sad or mad at me when he gets
off the phone. I've been really starting to
think that we made a mistake running away.

Thank you for forgiving me. (I'm guessing
that you HAVE forgiven me or you wouldn't be
letting me come home, would you?) I promise
things will be different when I'm back. I'm
different now — I've had to be. My baby
needs a proper mum, not someone who can't
even look after herself.

Charlie is going to get a job the minute we
get back. We'll pay our way for food and
things for the baby so you don't need to worry
about that. We're both so grateful to you.
It's going to make everything totally perfect
and I can really start to look forward to
this baby instead of feeling scared.

I'm going to be with you and Izzy in two
weeks — hurray!!!!! I'm going to forget the

cost and phone you up RIGHT NOW so we can make plans!!

Love you forever,
Alex and Charlie and Bump xxxxx

I am SO excited that Alex is coming home to live! It's going to be fantastic – just like it used to be. I'm pretty glad that we can start to get back to normal too because this year has been totally rubbish. I like it when you know what's going to happen, when the only surprises are nice surprises, but this year hasn't been like that at all.

I'm sitting in our den and relaxing. Mum and I have been working for hours today, painting Alex's room. Mum said it needed doing and if there's going to be a baby in there then it should be fresh and clean. We packed up all Alex's stuff and put it neatly in boxes in the bottom of the wardrobe. I don't know how she's going to manage sharing a room with Charlie and a baby, but I suppose babies are quite small so it probably won't take up much space, and Charlie's a boy so he probably doesn't have a lot of clothes and stuff.

Mum told me not to tell anyone what I'd heard Marianne saying that day in our kitchen, about Charlie going off to university while Alex looks after the baby. She said that Alex and Charlie needed to have a fresh start and a chance to make their own decisions, and that we needed to support them, but not choose for them. Then she muttered darkly about not everybody understanding that, but she didn't seem to want me to answer her so I pretended I hadn't heard.

I haven't told Hannah or anyone else that Alex is coming home. I don't want there to be a big fuss or anything so I'm just hoping that people will have forgotten what happened last term and not go on about it. We can just go back to normal.

If I peer through the branches of the fir tree, I can see Mum hanging out the washing on the line. She's been a lot happier since she told Alex that they could all live here with us. We've talked about it loads; Mum said that I had to be honest about how I felt about sharing our house with Charlie and a baby. I thought about it really hard, but I just don't think it's going to make much difference. Charlie will be out at work and he's so quiet that I don't think I'll notice when he IS here. And a baby isn't going to affect me very much. It won't be able to walk or talk or do anything at all really. Mum said that it will cry, but I'm sure tiny babies can't make *that* much noise and I can always close my bedroom door if it cries when I'm trying to sleep.

I think this is a new start for all of us. It's going to be totally fine.

Red Alert

I'm walking home in the pouring rain and the weather totally matches my mood. Although it's raining, I'm taking my time, even though I could bump into the nasty boys from school at any moment. It turns out that they hadn't forgotten about me after all – or maybe they had and all the drama with Alex reminded them about me again. Even though it's now October, the walk home from school is fraught with danger, knowing they could leap out and start making foul comments at any moment. They're getting braver too; last week one of them grabbed my arm when I walked past and hissed something awful into my ear.

But still I'm not desperate to get back to the house. Alex is back, although nobody would ever recognize her as the same Alex who left.

I can't believe that I thought things would go

back to normal when she came home. For starters she looks completely different. I couldn't stop staring at her stomach when she got out of the car. Mum and Charlie carried in all their bags and she just carried herself; she walked up our garden path with one hand on her back and this HUGE stomach jutting out in front of her. I was surprised that she didn't topple face first into the flower beds. She was wearing a long lavender-coloured tunic top and it's one of the first times that I've totally struggled to match a colour to the person. Lavender represents grace and elegance and those words definitely can't be used to describe Alex right now.

She shrieked my name when she saw me at the front door and staggered towards me and honestly, for a split second, I wanted to turn and run upstairs and hide under the bed – because even if she knew where I was there is NO WAY on this earth that she could squeeze under there with me. But then I saw her face and it was just Alex and I felt bad. So I ran down the path and gave her a hug and it felt weird hugging her when I couldn't reach past her massive stomach.

They call the baby 'Bump', but I think that's utterly ridiculous. It's like calling Mount Everest a hill. Alex keeps stroking her stomach and talking to it like it can actually understand her. She tried to make me say hello to it the other day, but I just couldn't. I wouldn't say hello to her arm or her leg, would I? I don't see how it's any different.

It was my thirteenth birthday a week after they got back and I thought having Alex home would be the best present ever. I was wrong. Just as I was about to blow out the candles on my cake, she started squealing that the baby was kicking and Mum and Charlie and Granny raced to be the first to put their hands on her stomach, while Grandpa started chanting 'baby, baby, baby' and hitting the kitchen table in time to his chant. I blew out the candles and made a wish. I wished that this stupid baby had decided to get born to some other family. When Mum asked though, I told her I'd wished for a proper music stand because I'd already seen it wrapped up in the living room. At least Mum felt happy on my birthday.

'Izzy!' I tense up when someone shouts my name, ready to start running. 'IZZY!'

The voice sounds familiar though so I risk squinting through the rain to see who it is and see Finn running up behind me. 'What planet were you on? I've been yelling at you for ages!'

I laugh as he bends over and rests his hands on his knees. 'I thought your new job on the building site was supposed to be keeping you fit?' I ask him.

'Cheeky!' he says. 'You might beat me in a race, but I reckon I could dig a trench quicker than you.'

I shrug at him. 'So what? Not a lot of call for trench-digging around here, in case you hadn't noticed!'

Finn mock-glares at me. 'Fine. Show me what you've got then.'

I look at him for a moment and then grin. He might be stronger than me, but I'm smaller than him – and small equals fast. Racing Finn suddenly seems like the perfect way to end today. I look across the road and point and the second that his attention is distracted I bolt, racing away from him down the pavement.

My school bag is banging against my side as I sprint down the road, Finn close behind me. Leaping a muddy puddle, I land safely on the other side and start sniggering as I hear Finn charge straight through it and curse as dirty water splashes up his legs. I decide to detour through the park and swing left between the gates. It's totally deserted in this weather and I find my pace, starting to enjoy the sensation of running in the rain. The water flowing down my face is refreshing. It feels like freedom.

Finn is next to me now and I glance at him and smile. He's forgotten that he was meant to be racing me and is enjoying the running as much as I am. Together we dodge puddles and the occasional hard-core dog-walker and run as fast as we can. By the time we come up our road, I'm puffing and panting, all thoughts of my weird, uneasy house pushed away.

I beckon Finn to follow me as I turn up our drive and together we bundle in through the front door, laughing and yelling and dripping water everywhere.

'Still reckon I'm horribly unfit?' puffs Finn, gasping for breath, but I'm too exhausted to reply. I drop my bag on the floor and start to unzip my coat.

'Hello there,' says Alex from the kitchen doorway. I look up, but she isn't talking to me. Finn shakes his head like a wet dog and drops of water fly off in every direction. Alex grins and disappears into the kitchen, returning a second later with a towel.

'Look at the state of you,' she says to Finn and hands him the towel. I stand there for a moment, drenching the hallway floor, until I realize that she has no intention of getting ME a towel. She'll be sorry if I get pneumonia and am too ill to babysit for her.

Finn takes the towel and dries his face. Then he looks at Alex, looks at all of her from her toes to her head.

'Look at the state of YOU,' he tells her and I freeze, waiting for Alex to bawl him out. But instead she just smiles and looks a bit shy.

'I know,' she says. 'I look awful. I'm probably the fattest person in this whole town.'

'You don't look awful. You look *different*. It's kind of amazing really – there's a real, live person living in there!'

It's not THAT amazing, I think to myself. And the baby isn't a proper person yet anyway. It doesn't know any words so it can't have any thoughts, not like we do. All it does all day is sleep and swim about and eat – and it doesn't even do that like a normal person. I don't know why people get so excited about babies; we've all been one so it's not like it's a special achievement or anything.

I'm starting to shiver and, as Alex is now completely absorbed in conversation with Finn about Switzerland and babies and his new job working for his dad as a builder and other totally boring things, I take off my wet shoes and go upstairs to get changed.

By the time I've dried off and come back down, Finn and Alex are sitting at the kitchen table, still talking. I grab a biscuit and have just started to make a drink when the back door opens and Mum rushes in.

'Disgusting weather out there today. Did you get home before the rain started, Izzy?' she says and then she spots Finn. 'Well, hello! Good to see you sitting at my table.'

Finn gets up and gives Mum a hug. She's surprised, but I can tell she's really pleased.

'I haven't done any baking, if that's what you're after!' she tells him.

'Oh, I might as well go home then,' he says, but Alex laughs and grabs his arm.

'Not a chance! We've got loads of catching up to do. You're not leaving here for hours yet, so just accept it and settle yourself down!'

Finn has got a funny look on his face – sort of worried and sort of massively delighted. He sits back down at the table and picks up his cup of dark, strong tea that Alex has made him.

'What time will Charlie be back?' he asks, trying to sound casual, but failing miserably. I realize that he doesn't want to see Charlie and I think Mum knows it too because she squeezes Finn's shoulder as she walks past on her way to the fridge.

'Oh, not for ages and ages yet,' says Alex, sounding breezy. Finn looks at her suspiciously, but he doesn't need to worry – Alex doesn't seem that bothered about Charlie these days. 'He'll go home to his parents for supper and he said he might stay the night there. He does sometimes; it's just a bit easier that way.'

I look at Mum in surprise, but she shakes her head at me very slightly and I remember that she said it all had to be their choice. That suits me perfectly. I've had enough of my sister's dramas to last me a decade.

'Anyway,' continues Alex, 'that means that there's no reason you can't stay for supper and tell me all about the band and what you've been up to and WHY you didn't write to me the whole time I was away!'

Finn goes a bit red at this, but Alex is still grinning so I guess she isn't that mad at him.

'Ooh – I nearly forgot,' says Mum. 'Look what I bought today!' She goes to her bag and takes out a neatly wrapped package. She hands it to Alex who puts it on the table and carefully unwraps it.

'Oh, Mum!' she gasps and I crane my neck to see what it is. I'm disappointed though because, instead of a chunky necklace or a funky vest top or a new scented candle, Alex has spread out a tiny piece of material on the table. It's hard to work out what it actually is for a moment other than it has red and white stripes. A weird colour combination of danger and energy and peace. Then Alex picks it up and I see that it's a hat.

'The baby will need to be wrapped up warm – it's going to be winter when it's born,' says Mum. 'We'll get lots of basic hats and blankets, but I really couldn't resist this and it's good for a girl or a boy.'

Finn reaches out and Alex puts the tiny hat into his large, upturned hand. He looks at it in awe and I leave the kitchen in quiet disgust. I was so happy to have Finn back in our lives, but not if I have to share him with the baby. As I stomp upstairs, I can hear them laughing and talking about whether they think it's a boy or a girl and how there's only six weeks to go, and a very bad feeling comes over me. I look at my mood ring and see that it has turned red. Danger is on its way. This baby is bad news.

In the Pink

The Bad-News-Baby is completely dominating every second of every day. Quite an achievement for someone who hasn't even been born yet. Mum has started racing home from work to check on Alex and Alex told me that she even phones during her lunch hour, just to make sure everything's OK. There are still four whole weeks to go until it arrives, but there's more preparation going on here than there would be if we were preparing for battle.

Even Charlie is starting to realize that something is about to happen. I heard him and Alex having a long talk in her room two weeks ago. Alex cried quite a lot and said that he wasn't being fair, that this baby deserved to have two parents who loved it, and that she didn't get pregnant all on her own so why should he expect her to bring it up all on her own? I don't know what Charlie said to that because I suddenly decided that it was time to stop eavesdropping and sneaking around. That actually, maybe, I don't need to know absolutely everything that's going on around here. From now on I'm going to trust Mum to tell me stuff on a need-to-know basis. And I really don't need to know what's going on between Alex and Charlie.

Anyway, Charlie moved out of our house and back to live with his parents. Alex cried for a day and Mum took the day off work and, by the time I got home from school, Alex was tired-looking and red-faced, but sort of calm. And actually it seems like it's working out OK. Charlie stayed away the first few days, but then he popped over one evening and since then he's been about quite a bit. This week he's behaving really weirdly though: he keeps turning up at random times of the day to see if the baby's decided to be born. Alex has told him about a hundred times that she'll ring him the second she feels the slightest twinge, but I don't think he believes her.

Mum goes on and on at Alex every night about making sure her phone is charged and has got lots of credit. I tried telling her that we live in

a civilized part of the world and it's highly unlikely
that Alex will end up giving birth curled up under
a hedge in a blizzard, but Mum told me off for
being sarcastic so I've kept my opinions to myself
since then.

I've got the day off today because my school
has a teacher-training day. I'm bored and I'm
feeling really sorry for myself, which is a good
job because nobody else is feeling sorry for me.
Mum's at work and Alex is lounging around in
the living room. She's told me to stop moping
about and find something to do, so I'm playing
my violin. I've got an exam in a few months and
I've decided that I might as well carry on with it;
it's one of the only things that I can do that Alex
can't, so it'd be a shame to waste all my hard
work and give up now.

'Izzy!' I can barely hear Alex calling me over
the sound of the scales that I'm playing. She's
probably going to moan at me AGAIN – she
hates the sound of my violin. I ignore her. I'm
totally within my rights to practise my violin in
the kitchen if I feel like it. I finish my scales and
move on to my music book.

'IZZY!' She's yelling at me now and her voice

sounds a bit strange. If this is some pathetic attempt at making me go in and change the TV channel because she can't be bothered to reach out for the remote, I'm actually going to go berserk at her.

I finish the piece that I'm playing and then I grudgingly trudge into the living room, but then stop dead in the doorway. Alex is leaning over the back of the sofa, her face totally white apart from two bright red spots on each cheek. She's panting loudly and looks like she's about to fall over.

'Alex?' I ask her, hoping that she's eaten one too many packets of stinky crisps and just has a stomach ache.

'Izzy!' she gasps again and I rush to her side, not sure what I should do. I put my hand on her arm, but she flicks it away and I back off a bit, starting to feel very scared.

'Are you ill?' I ask her. 'What's going on?'

'I think the baby's coming,' pants Alex and a giggle escapes my lips: the baby isn't due for another four weeks yet. Then I look at Alex again and I stop laughing. She isn't joking. The Bad-News-Baby is on its way and there's nobody here to help us.

My mind races desperately and I look at the hideous brown clock on the mantelpiece, hoping that it might give me some help. Mum has been grilling us every night about what we need to do if this happens when she's at work. I know I've got the answer somewhere in my brain, but I just can't join up all the dots. Alex starts whining, a high-pitched noise that makes my spine tingle. She's stopping me from thinking straight and I want to tell her to shush, but somehow I don't think she'd appreciate that.

'Hold on,' I tell her, backing out of the room. 'Just stay there.'

'Where else would I go?' I hear her muttering, but I ignore her and race to the phone in the hallway. The list of important numbers is still on the noticeboard next to the phone and I quickly dial Mum's mobile. I take a few deep breaths while the line connects and then I can hear Mum's phone ringing. In the kitchen.

In total disbelief I slam down the phone and run into the kitchen. Mum's phone is lying on top of the fridge – she must have left it there this morning. I want to snigger again: after all her military-style planning it's Mum who's messed up the system. But it isn't actually funny and I can hear Alex's groans getting louder so I run back to the phone and call Mum's school.

'Good afternoon. Darnfield Primary School. How can I help you?' says Definitely-Called-Margaret.

'It's Izzy Stone and I need you to pass an urgent message to my mum,' I gabble, desperate to get back to Alex in the living room.

'Of course, dear,' says Margaret. 'What's the message?'

'Tell her that Alex is having the baby NOW and she needs to come home because I don't know what to do,' I say and then I hang up the phone. Should I ring Granny and Grandpa? Granny can drive, but it takes ages to get Grandpa ready to leave the house and by the time they get here it could be too late. I run back into the living room.

'I've left a message for Mum,' I tell Alex. 'Just hang in there.'

'It's too early,' moans Alex. 'The baby's too early. We need to get to hospital, Izzy. I can't wait.'

'Hang on,' I tell her and, sprinting down the hallway, I fling open the front door in the hopes that Mum might be pulling into the driveway, even though I know she'll only just be getting the message. My eyes dart frantically up and down the street and when I see him I think for a moment that he's an illusion, that he's just a figment of my imagination, because seeing him right now would be just about perfect.

But then he waves at me as he steps into his van and starts to drive and I realize that he's not an illusion, he's actually here, but if I don't do something fast then he won't be here much longer. Flinging myself down the path, I charge out of the garden gate and stand in the middle of the road in my socks. Finn screeches to a halt just in front of me and leaps out of the van.

'What on –' he starts to shout at me, but I interrupt him.

'The baby!' I shout back at him. 'It's coming and Alex is scared and she's not OK and it's too early and I don't know what to do. Should I ring 999 because you get told off if you do that and it isn't an emergency, and I don't know if this is an emergency, but it feels like one?'

I stop to take a breath and Finn dashes past me and up the path, leaving his van in the middle of the road with the engine still running. I chase after him and together we run into the house. Alex has made it as far as the hallway and when she sees Finn her face collapses at the same time that she does. Finn grabs her just before she hits the floor and holds on to her as if she's a delicate little princess and not a great, hefty, eight-months-pregnant girl. All that trench-digging has come in handy, I think, and I remind myself to tell him later.

The sight of Finn makes Alex start crying, but he whispers into her ear and she nods and stops, wiping her eyes with the back of her sleeve. Suddenly I'm not sure if I'm looking at a grown woman who is about to have a baby or a scared little girl who doesn't know what's going on – it's all very confusing.

'Should I phone for an ambulance?' I ask Finn again, remembering the list of instructions that Mum had given me.

'I don't know,' he says, looking at Alex, and I see concern etched on his face. 'Maybe I should drive her. By the time they get here, we could be almost at the hospital. Or maybe that's stupid – what if she gives birth in the van? I don't know what to do!'

'What about your mum?' I ask him. 'We need a grown-up!'

'She's at work!' Finn's voice is getting squeaky and I can feel the panic starting to wash over me. Someone has to make their mind up and Alex can hardly speak and I'm only thirteen so it needs to be Finn.

I look at him desperately and he seems to have been having the same thoughts as me because he gives his shoulders a little shake and then stands up straighter.

'I'll drive her in,' he tells me, his voice lower now, but still sounding wobbly.

He half carries Alex down the path and I run ahead, opening the passenger door.

'She'll be OK,' he tells me, guiding Alex towards the door. 'I'll drive really carefully, don't worry.'

Finn eases Alex on to the seat and then leans in next to her. 'How often are the contractions coming?' he asks her. I can't hear her answer, but Finn looks worried. 'Wait here for your mum,' he says to me, 'and then follow us to the hospital. Make sure you pick up Alex's overnight bag and everything she's packed for the baby – nappies and sleepsuits and cotton wool and that kind of thing.'

He ruffles my hair quickly and then runs round the front, diving into the driving seat. I bend down next to Alex.

'It'll be OK,' I tell her, hoping that the terror I'm feeling isn't obvious in my voice. She looks at me and I think she might be trying to smile reassuringly to make me feel better, but it isn't working because her face is screwed up and all scrunchy. Looking at her doesn't make me feel any less scared.

'Phone Charlie,' she whispers, and then she doubles over, clutching her stomach and moaning. I slam the door closed and step back as Finn pulls away. I expect him to race off down our road at one hundred miles an hour, but he creeps away so slowly that a snail could overtake him, as if he's carrying the most precious cargo ever in his beaten-up, filthy old van.

I watch the van until it turns the corner and then go back to the house. I find Charlie's number on the list of important numbers on the wall and phone him. I barely manage to get past 'Alex is on her way to hospital' before he's hung up on me. I have no idea how long it takes to have a baby, but I hope Charlie gets to the hospital in time. Then I go and find Alex's bag, wondering how Finn knows so much about giving birth and babies all of a sudden. And it dawns on me that Mum isn't the only one who's been preparing for this day.

Little White Lie

The Bad-News-Baby is here. And it's a girl. I think it must take after Alex because, since the moment it arrived, it hasn't been quiet for one second. Not one single second.

Mum arrives home about fifteen minutes after Finn has left with Alex. I really hope the police aren't monitoring our road for speeding motorists because, the way she's going, she's not going to have a licence left before too long. I jump in the car and we race to the hospital, and it's all really exciting and a bit scary, and everything is happening so quickly and I don't really have time to think about what the outcome is actually going to be.

And then we get to the hospital and Finn dashes out and tells us where to find Alex, and Mum rushes in to see her, and Finn and I just stand and look at each other and don't really say anything. And then Charlie comes speeding into the corridor, looking like he's about to throw up, and Finn just points at the door where Alex is and Charlie goes in.

And then everything stops being fast. Mum joins us and we sit in a waiting room FOREVER, and eventually Charlie comes to find us and says that it's going to be ages yet and we should go home. Finn wants to stay, but Charlie scowls at him and then Mum insists that Finn comes back to our house for supper. She says it's the least she can do to say thank you for his heroic rescuing of Alex – even though it turned out that the baby was HOURS away from making an appearance. We eat fish and chips and all the time I'm wondering what Alex is doing and how she's feeling.

Today is Saturday and Mum and I are eating breakfast. I kept waking up in the night and thinking about Alex and once, when I got up to go to the bathroom, I saw the light on downstairs, so I don't think Mum could sleep either. It all seems to be taking a very long time and I want to ask Mum if this is normal – but before I can figure out how to say anything without making her worry, the phone rings.

Mum answers it and then promptly bursts into tears. She tells me the baby is here and it's a girl, and everyone is fine and that we can go in to visit later on this afternoon. I don't really know what I think about that – I'd kind of forgotten that there would be an actual baby at the end of all this – so I carry on buttering my toast while Mum phones Granny and goes on and on about how fantastic it all is and how she's SO happy. Then, when she finally puts the phone down, she starts moaning at me to hurry up because we've got to go shopping RIGHT NOW.

The shopping centre is heaving with people, but Mum is on a mission. I scurry to keep up with her as she weaves through shoppers, intent on getting to the toyshop by the shortest route possible. As we near the music shop, I remember that I need a new pot of rosin for my violin bow.

'Mum!' I call, trying to get her attention. 'Just stop a moment.' She slows slightly and turns her head to look at me, but I notice that she doesn't actually stop moving. 'Can we pop in here? I need more rosin.'

'Not today, Izzy,' she says, walking past the music shop door.

'But, Mum!' I say, hearing a slight whine in

my voice. 'I really need it and it'll only take a second.'

'No time,' says Mum, 'now hurry up. I don't want to rush choosing a teddy bear for the baby.'

She marches on and I sulkily follow her. It would have taken hardly ANY time to go into the music shop. It'll be all her fault if I fail my violin exam.

We arrive at the toyshop and Mum heads upstairs to the cuddly toy section. I'm still trying to show her how fed up I am, but then I get a bit distracted by the shelves and shelves of stuffed toys. There's every animal you could ever imagine here and some that you could never imagine too.

'What's this supposed to be?' I ask, picking up a green creature that has huge floppy ears and a long tail. 'It's definitely not a rabbit – it looks like some kind of genetic mutation!' We've been learning about genetics in science and I wonder what my science teacher would make of this freaky specimen. 'Oh, what about this one?'

I show Mum an amazing, cuddly, indigo-blue frog, moving my arm so it jumps through the air towards her. She scowls and shakes her head.

'No. It needs to be a teddy bear. Just like Grandpa gave to Alex when she was born.'

Hmmm. So it's going to be like that, is it? Nobody gave ME a teddy bear when I was born. Dolphins and kangaroos and rabbits were fine for me. History really is repeating itself. Alex got a teddy bear because she was first and special, and now her baby gets one because IT'S first and special. This does not seem fair to me at all.

I jump the frog back to its place on the shelf. 'Sorry,' I whisper to it. 'You're not special enough. Just like me.' It looks at me and its big beady eyes seem to be pleading with me. The tag on the shelf says 'poison arrow frog' and suddenly I really, really want to keep him for myself. I look away and focus on Mum, who is choosing teddy bear after teddy bear off the shelf and then discarding them for not being 'right'. Every time I look back though, the poison arrow frog is still watching me until I can't bear it any longer and I grab him, holding him tightly to my chest.

'Mum? Can I buy this?' I ask.

She glances in my direction as she throws another inadequate teddy bear back on the shelf. 'No, Izzy! We're here to buy a "welcome to the world" present for the baby. Not something for you!'

'Please, Mum,' I beg. 'I'll pay for it with my own pocket money.'

Mum gives up on the teddy bears and walks over to me. 'Why on earth do you want that?' she asks me. 'You're a bit old for cuddly toys, aren't you?'

I feel my cheeks start to flush red, but I stand my ground. I have no idea why this suddenly matters to me so much, but I do know that this frog is meant to be mine. She glances at the price tag. 'It's really expensive – more than your pocket money.'

'So take it out of next month's allowance!' I cry. 'Please, Mum. I really, really want to buy him!'

Mum hesitates for a second and I hold my breath. 'Oh, if it means that much to you,' she says and I smile for the first time all day. 'But you've got to help me find something for the baby! None of these teddy bears look right.'

I'm surprised by how relieved I am that she's letting me have the frog and I'm keen to help her now. Together we search the shelves, but she's right: all the teddy bears are wrong. It might be their eyes or the fluffiness of their bodies or the perkiness of their ears, but none of them are as nice as Mr Cuddles.

Eventually Mum looks at her watch and does a

little squeak. 'There's no more time if we're going to get to the hospital for the start of visiting time. We'll just have to get something for now and I'll keep searching for a teddy bear.'

We leave town with a box of chocolates and a bunch of flowers for Alex and a cardigan and a cuddly monkey for the baby. I'm happy that Mum didn't find a teddy bear. I don't want this baby to be any more special than me.

I don't really know what to think when we walk on to the hospital ward, except that I didn't think it would be so noisy. We walk past loads of cubicles and in each one is a tired-looking woman holding a screaming baby and a freaked-out-looking man who doesn't seem to know what to do. I start to find it quite funny and then suddenly we're looking at yet another exhausted-looking mum and a scared-looking dad and I realize it's Alex and Charlie. And the screaming bundle of blankets in Alex's arms is what all the fuss has been about.

Mum rushes forward and hugs Alex and hugs Charlie, and then she peeks inside the bundle of blankets and starts welling up and saying, 'Oh, Alex,' in a teary voice. And Alex passes her the blankets and gazes at Mum as Mum coos and ahs and kisses whatever's inside until it goes quiet. I don't really know what to do so I stand quietly at the end of the bed until Mum asks me if I want to meet my new niece.

I walk over and Mum bends down and peels back the blankets a bit further and there inside is the most scrunched-up, miserable-looking face I've ever seen.

'Isn't she the most beautiful baby you've ever seen?' coos Mum and, as I haven't actually ever really seen any other babies properly, I think it wouldn't be too much of a terrible lie to agree.

'Do you want to hold her?' asks Alex and before I know what's happening I'm sitting in a low chair and Mum has placed the bundle of blankets in my arms and the Bad-News-Baby is staring up at me. Her face is red and wrinkly and her eyes are scrunched up tight like she doesn't want to look at me. She feels heavy in my arms and I want to give her straight back to Mum and get out of here. A camera flashes and I look up in time to see Charlie taking a photograph, a goofy-looking smile on his tired face.

'You can have her back now if you like,' I offer to Mum. 'My arms are aching – she weighs a ton.'

For some reason this makes Alex and Charlie

and Mum laugh really loudly. Their noise startles Bad-News and she opens her eyes. They are the bluest eyes I have ever seen in my life, like staring into a deep pot of indigo paint. With her eyes open, she doesn't look quite so weird and I find myself gently stroking my finger against her cheek. It's so soft that I'm not sure I'm actually touching her at all.

'Stop laughing,' I tell them all. 'You're scaring her.' This makes Charlie laugh even louder, but Mum and Alex calm down a bit, and Mum comes and perches on the arm of the chair next to me.

'She's not scared, Izzy,' she says. 'She's interested. She wants to meet us all. Look how she's staring at you!'

'I think she likes you, Izzy,' says Alex and for a moment everything feels warm and good and hopeful. And then the baby starts crying – a loud, piercing, shocking sound that comes out of nowhere. I panic and thrust her at Mum before standing up and moving to the other side of the room.

'I didn't do anything!' I splutter, wondering what has caused so much screaming. Mum passes the baby back to Alex and she stops crying straight away, snuggling up tight inside the blankets.

'It's fine, don't panic,' says Mum, coming to stand next to me. 'She's just making herself heard, letting us know that she needs something, like a clean nappy or a feed or an extra blanket. Right now she just needs her mum – who is doing an excellent job!' She directs this last bit across the room to Alex, who looks up for a second and beams at Mum before going back to gazing at the baby.

'Don't worry, Izzy, you didn't do anything wrong. Babies cry and they do it a lot!'

Oh, they do, do they? Well, I'm not convinced that this is going to work then because that noise was nothing like the quiet little squeaking that you'd have thought something that small would make.

Alex has put the baby into a tiny cot next to her bed and now they're all standing round, admiring every bit of her. There's nothing about her that is too small to comment on.

'Look at her darling little nose!' says Mum.

All the better to SMELL you with, my dear, I think to myself.

'And have you seen how huge her eyes are?' adds Charlie, sounding as proud as if he'd made them himself.

All the better to SEE you with, my dear.

'It's her gorgeous little rosebud lips that I love!' says Alex in a voice I've not heard before – all drippy and soft and gooey and pastel-coloured.

All the better to GOBBLE YOU UP, my dear. And that's exactly what is going to happen. She might be tiny and brand-new, but she doesn't fool me. She's got them all exactly where she wants them. I'm over here by the door, all on my own, while everybody looks at her like she's some kind of miracle. They're under her spell: she'll be able to get absolutely anything she wants and they're powerless to resist her.

'Can't you all see?' I want to shout. 'Look at yourselves! There's more going on than just this baby, you know. I got an A for my history assignment on Victorian England – that took a lot of work – but none of you are interested in that, are you?'

But I don't say a word. I stand by the door and pretend to be fascinated by a poster on how to wash your hands properly. Not that anybody notices – they're too busy watching the baby fall asleep. Once she makes a snuffling noise and they all nearly fall over each other in delight. I leave the cubicle in disgust and stand outside the curtain, trying not to listen to the ridiculous conversations that are going on around me about fingernails (yes – I have ten, but is anybody impressed?) and the contents of nappies (utterly gross and not something that should ever be discussed in public) and the amazing smell of a baby's head (excuse me? I wash my hair twice a week with shampoo that smells of coconut, but nobody's trying to take deep sniffs of my head – good job too).

Eventually a bell rings and visitors throughout the ward begin to gather up their bags and get ready to leave. I step back into the cubicle just as Mum starts to stand up.

'Where's Izzy?' she's saying, but not in a particularly worried or concerned way. 'Oh, you're there! Come and say goodbye to your niece before we go.' She leans over the cot and kisses the baby before moving round to the other side of the bed and talking quietly to Alex, showing her the cuddly monkey and the cardigan that we bought in town this morning. Charlie is raiding the box of chocolates that Mum had put on the table for Alex, so when I walk up to the cot there's nobody paying the slightest bit of attention to me.

She's awake again and as I bend over she fixes

me with her big eyes. I put my face right down next to her – anybody looking would think I was giving her a kiss. I usually try hard to be a nice person, but the feelings I'm having won't stay inside and there's nobody that I can tell, except the baby.

'Let's get one thing straight,' I murmur, so quietly that my lips are barely moving. 'I know what you're up to. And you may well be prettier and cuter and more interesting than me, but I know the truth about you.'

I move back slightly and see that she's looking at me like I'm the most fascinating thing in the world. I waver for a second – she actually is pretty cute – but then I remember how obsessed everyone is with her and how there's no room for me. How she's changed everything and I didn't have a choice. One of us needs to stay level-headed and see her for what she is: an imposter who will stop at nothing until she has the love and attention and adoration of the whole family. She won't let Alex go back to the Alex she was before.

'You're bad news, baby,' I tell her. 'I'm keeping my eye on you.'

Then Alex calls me over to her for a hug and it's time for us to go.

Mum tells me on the way home that they'll

probably be allowed to come home in a few days, once the baby has put on a bit of weight and is feeding regularly.

'We'll be a proper family again,' she says, her smile wide as she turns into our road.

I say nothing, which doesn't matter because she's full of her own thoughts about the baby, and about the house being full of chatter and laughter and noise and people. And all I can think is that nobody ever told me that we had stopped being a proper family.

Seeing Red

So this is how it is. The Bad-News-Baby wakes up every two hours all through the night because she needs a feed. Unfortunately, because she's incapable of keeping her hunger to herself and suffering in silence, she makes her needs known by screaming. Very, very loudly. Then, when my alarm clock goes off and it's time for me to get up for school, the Bad-News-Baby suddenly decides that she needs to sleep and I have to creep around the house, making sure that I don't slam any doors or even have a shower in case she wakes up. And there's no way I can play my violin: the Bad-News-Baby seems to sense when I even just open the case and starts screeching hysterically.

The house has been really busy with visitors, all desperate to catch a glimpse of Bad-News. Granny and Grandpa arrived the day after Alex came home from hospital and Grandpa just sat in the armchair, holding the baby in his arms as gently as if she was made of glass, and murmuring 'Alex, lovely Alex' over and over again. He had absolutely no idea that the baby was his great-grandchild and not actually Alex. Granny and Mum watched him and cried a bit, and Alex had a snooze on the sofa, and I just sat there wondering if this was how life was going to be from now on.

Finn has virtually moved in: he comes over every day after work and only goes home to sleep. The rest of the time he's here, changing nappies and cuddling the baby. He's no fun at all any more. Charlie pops in every day and all he does is stare at Bad-News as if she's done something wonderful like achieved world peace or found a cure for the common cold. It's very, very boring in our house.

Right now there's a rare moment of quiet. The baby is asleep in her basket in the living room and Alex is asleep on the sofa next to her. All she ever does is sleep; I haven't managed to have a proper conversation with her once since the baby arrived. Mum's at the shops and there's nobody else around. I'm not really sure what to do with myself. Whatever it is it'd better be silent because

I don't want to be responsible for waking up Bad-News. I've done that once and Alex was so unbelievably furious with me that I'd rather spend the day tiptoeing around than risk her getting so angry again.

I'm trying to decide between writing a new poem about imposter babies who steal all the attention and writing my Christmas present list when there's a loud banging on the front door. I wince, hold my breath and cross my fingers at the same time, but it does no good: there's a high-pitched screeching noise from the living room followed by the sound of Alex groaning.

'Who on earth is making that racket?' Alex calls towards the stairs, where I'm standing, working out if I can escape to my room.

'I have no idea,' I call back, 'on account of the fact that I do not possess psychic powers.' I whisper the last bit because Alex is always seriously grumpy when she's just woken up.

Whoever it is, they're very determined to get our attention. I can see their outline through the glass door and a hand, bashing the doorknocker up and down.

'Well, answer it!' yells Alex. 'I've got to deal with the baby!'

I walk slowly down the stairs. I am so sick of being Alex's slave. I wonder if I'll ever have a younger person of my own to boss about. Maybe the baby could be MY slave – that'd be kind of fair, if you think about it. I open the front door, but before I can register who's standing there they have barged past me and into the hall.

'Hello, hello! Bet you can't believe I'm here!' she shouts. Oh. It's Sara. My heart sinks; she seems completely out of place in our house. Her hair has changed colour since I last saw her – she's got all these blonde streaks running through it – and her clothes look different too. She looks edgy and funky and confident – and she seems too big for our front hall, even though she's actually quite small.

'So where is she then?' she screeches at me. 'Lead me to her!' I nod in the direction of the living room and Sara strides towards the door, me trailing behind her with a bad feeling.

'Babe!' she cries, racing up to Alex and stopping a few steps in front of her. 'Look at you! You look super exhausted. You poor thing. At least you're not so fat any more – although you've got a bit more weight to lose, hey, hon?' She laughs. 'Remind me to give you the name of this brilliant workout class in town. I bumped into Nadia a few weeks ago – you remember, Nadia from school? Anyway, she's totally gorgeous now and she's lost loads of weight and she said she'd started working out. It'd be great for you, babe – just what you need to lose that last bit of chub!'

Sara plonks herself down on the sofa and exhales loudly. Alex looks like someone's just slapped her in the face, which I suppose they sort of have. She looks at Sara and I can tell that she's having a whole speedy conversation with herself in her head, but after a moment of hesitating she sits down next to Sara and smiles at her.

'Thanks for coming over,' Alex says.

'Oh, no worries, babe! I was home anyway for Lee's party tonight. It's going to be insane! I know I could have just caught up with you there, but I was at a bit of a loose end so I thought I'd pop in for a chat. So tell me everything! How's it going with you and Charlie?'

I quietly sit down on a beanbag near Bad-News's basket. I'm half expecting Alex to tell me to get lost, but neither of them seems to even notice I'm here. I don't actually know why I haven't gone up to my room; I've just got a feeling that Alex might need me. And I'm a bit nosy.

Alex looks down at her hands, as if she's wondering how much to tell Sara.

'Come on!' says Sara. 'Tell me all the gossip!'

'There's no gossip really,' says Alex. 'We're not together any more, but –'

'I KNEW it!' screams Sara. 'I heard a rumour, but I couldn't be sure until I'd spoken to you! Is it someone else? Who did he go off with? I knew you wouldn't keep him long – no offence!'

'It's nothing like that,' says Alex quickly. 'We just decided it'd be better if we didn't commit to something that didn't feel right. We're still friends. He still comes over to see her.'

Sara reaches across the sofa and pulls Alex into a hug that doesn't look particularly comfortable.

'Oh, you poor, poor thing. You must feel so sad and unwanted.'

Alex sits up. 'Not really –' she starts, but Sara interrupts her.

'But look on the bright side, hon!' she says cheerfully 'You're free and single! And Lee's party tonight is the perfect opportunity to let your hair down and have some fun!'

'I'm not –'

'What are you going to wear?' squawks Sara. 'You're going to need some new clothes because you CANNOT go out looking like that! We're going to have to be clever – figure out a look that hides your tum, but doesn't make you look like someone's mum!'

'I AM someone's mum,' says Alex, standing up and looking down at Sara. 'And I'm not going to Lee's party tonight.'

I'm not sure what course Sara is doing at university, but it must be quite an easy one because she's not very bright. Not bright enough to hear the steely tone in Alex's voice that means she's not happy. Definitely not bright enough to shut up.

'Oh, babe!' she wails, looking up at Alex and opening her eyes very wide. 'What's happened to you? The old Alex would never turn down a party!'

'Did you just ask what's happened to me?' says Alex, sounding gobsmacked. 'I've had a baby, Sara. I can't just leave her to go to a party.'

'But how are you ever going to meet any boys if you don't go out?' asks Sara, sounding genuinely worried.

'I don't need to meet any boys, Sara – that's what I'm trying to tell you!' Alex has started walking round the living room and I can tell that she's really upset. I sink further into my beanbag and hope that Sara goes home soon.

'You're just scared because you're out of practice,' states Sara in a bossy voice. 'I bet you haven't spoken to a single boy except Charlie in months! You've turned into a hermit, hiding away in here. Well, never fear, I'm here to help you get back out into the world!'

'I don't need your help,' says Alex, but Sara just raises her eyebrows at her. 'I don't! And I have spoken to other boys actually. I speak to Finn all the time.'

Sara puts her head in her hands and moans dramatically, and I remember why she and Alex used to be friends. 'Finn! He doesn't count as a boy! Seriously, Alex, you need help!'

Sara stands up and grabs Alex's hand. 'Come on! Let's go into town now and I'll do you a make-over – you won't recognize yourself when I'm done with you!' She tries to drag Alex across the room, but Alex stops her.

'I can't, Sara! I can't just *leave* her.'

Sara turns and looks at me for the first time. I stare back at her, willing her to disappear. I don't like how she's talking to Alex.

'Oh, she'll be fine on her own,' she says, waving

her hand dismissively in my direction. 'She must be in Year Eight now surely? Come on! If we go now, we'll have plenty of time to get ready.'

'I wasn't talking about Izzy,' says Alex and I can hear the frustration in her voice. She looks at me and I grimace back at her in support. This visit is not going very well. Alex takes a deep breath and tries to smile.

'Do you want to meet her?' she asks Sara, moving towards the basket where Bad-News has been lying quietly.

'Meet who?' says Sara, sounding sulky and grabbing her bag off the sofa.

'My baby!' says Alex. 'Sara, meet the newest member of the Stone family.'

She gestures towards Bad-News and Sara walks slowly across the room and peers suspiciously into the basket.

'Oh!' she says. 'Look at it!'

'I know,' says Alex. 'Isn't she the most beautiful baby you've ever seen in your whole life?'

'I guess,' says Sara, but she doesn't sound very convinced. I stand up and join them next to the basket. Bad-News is babbling to herself and gazing up at the ceiling, totally transfixed. Sara glances up and then looks at Alex, a strange look on her face.

'Is it OK?' she asks.

'What do you mean?'

'I MEAN, is it all there?' Sara hisses this last bit as if she's talking about something not very nice. Alex looks at her, confused. 'I don't mean to be unkind, Alex, but it's looking at the ceiling and there's nothing even there. It's a bit odd, don't you think?'

Sara looks up again and then stares at the baby. Alex starts laughing. 'She's looking at the light reflections on the ceiling!' she tells Sara. 'There's nothing wrong with her.'

Sara scowls. 'Well, it shouldn't stare like that. It makes it look strange, like there's something wrong with it. Its eyes are a bit squinty too – you should probably get them checked. Although you can get glasses for little kids and, I have to say, they do look pretty cute in them.'

Alex moves in between Sara and the basket, blocking Bad-News from Sara's doubtful gaze. She looks Sara right in the eye and when she speaks her voice is clear and firm. 'She doesn't look strange. She looks like a newborn baby, which is exactly what she is. And it's why I'm not going shopping or partying or anything else right now. I'm staying here with her and keeping her safe.'

Sara shrugs. 'Well, it's your choice.' She leans forward and kisses Alex – a peck on each cheek like French people do. Then she turns and walks towards the door. 'Text me if you change your mind – you know my number.'

'Thanks for coming, Sara,' says Alex, opening the living-room door and guiding her out into the hall.

'Well, I won't see you for ages now,' I hear Sara say. 'I'm at uni the day after tomorrow and I won't be coming back to this dive of a town until it's absolutely necessary. You should think about going to uni, Alex – it's fantastic! I could tell you stories that you wouldn't believe!'

Alex mutters something that I can't hear and then the front door opens.

'Ciao!' calls Sara.

'Bye,' says Alex and then she slams the door closed and comes back into the living room, flopping down on the sofa. 'I can't remember why we were ever friends,' she says. 'She's changed so much since we left school.'

I look down at Bad-News. 'You've changed too,' I tell Alex. 'You're always busy with the baby now. I hardly ever get to talk to you!'

'That's not true,' says Alex and her voice sounds hurt. 'We talk loads.'

'Yeah, about the baby and how you're feeling and gory details about giving birth that I don't want to hear,' I tell her. 'We don't talk about anything actually important. I can't tell you about things like I used to.'

I don't know why I'm saying this to Alex right now. I can see that she's upset by Sara's visit and that I should probably be making her a cup of tea and offering to look after the baby or something. But I just want the old Alex back – MY Alex who was annoying and noisy and frustrating, but who was always there for me if I needed her.

Alex runs her hand over her face and looks at me. 'I'm sorry you don't think my baby is important,' she says in a very quiet voice.

'That's not what I meant,' I say, but I'm too late: the damage has been done.

'It's EXACTLY what you meant!' cries Alex, and then she swears at me under her breath, but I still hear her. 'I've got enough to worry about without you telling me that I'm not being a good enough sister. News flash, Izzy – I'm worried stupid that I'm not going to be a good enough mum, so being there for you right now is fairly low down on my list of priorities! I love this baby

MORE THAN ANYTHING and I've got to get this right!'

I stare at her in shock. I didn't really mean it. I know Alex loves her baby, but I didn't think that actually meant that she didn't love me any more. I was just feeling a bit narky that we never get time to chat, that every single thing is about Bad-News. And she's just told me that I'm not important at all. The baby has completely replaced me. Alex hasn't got room for me.

Izzy

My sister looks just the same as always,
but really she's changed.
The space inside her heart that she kept for
me
has been invaded, taken over,
and I have been evicted.
She's got no time to
talk
listen
laugh with me
any more.
Now it's all
nappies
milk
blankets and
sleep.

The baby is triumphant, victorious.
Ruler of all things,
like a tiny queen of the world.
Like the tiny queen of Alex's world.

Now, when the aggro boys make
rude comments
that make my legs tingle
and my ears buzz,
there are no footsteps
behind me.

No supporter, protector, defender,
just me and them.
If I try to ignore them like Mum told me,
it just makes them
worse,
baiting,
waiting
for a reaction.
If I shout back at them like Alex told me,
it just makes them
cry with laughter,
doubled-over, knee-grabbing howls.
If I cry, if I let the tears bubble out,
it just annoys them,

embarrasses them,
scares them,
and they mutter dark threats about
what they will do to me if I
make a complaint.

I don't bother telling Alex.
She wouldn't be able to
hear me anyway.
She is deafened
by the sounds of
cooing
crying
gurgling.
She is blinded
by the sight of
tiny fingers and toes and a
sticky-out tummy button.
Her ears and eyes belong only to
the baby.

Love Is Golden

I had planned to keep well out of the way of the baby after our argument, but then Alex had a bit of a meltdown and spent two whole days sobbing. Mum told me that she's just exhausted and overwhelmed and Sara coming over didn't help. She said that it would pass, but that we needed to help Alex rest so that she could look after the baby properly. I felt really guilty. Mum doesn't know anything about the argument and, even though Alex tried to call me back that day, I ignored her and ran out of the room crying. Part of me wanted her to see what it feels like when you're left all on your own.

But I didn't want to make her that upset. I still love her even if she doesn't love me any more. So we've developed a bit of a routine. When I get home from school, Alex has just finished feeding the baby so she puts her in a bouncy chair and I watch her in the kitchen while I do my homework. Alex has a little sleep and then, when Mum gets home, I wake Alex up and we all juggle making the supper and looking after the baby and doing our schoolwork.

The first time I was on my own with Bad-News I was quite terrified. She slept most of the time though and I started to relax a bit. Even so, it's quite hard to get any homework done because she's started sucking her fingers when she's asleep and she looks so gorgeous – it's quite distracting. I'm still determined not to fall for her charms; she's pretty good at being a cute baby, but I'm not fooled: she's probably planning world domination behind those long, flickering eyelashes.

I've looked forward to today all week. Charlie is leaving work early and taking Alex and Bad-News over to visit his parents. No crying or screaming or pooing for a whole two hours. As I walk up the front path and put my key in the door, I think about how much work I'm going to get done. In complete and utter peace and quiet.

I open the front door and step inside, calling 'hello' just in case their plans have changed and

Bad-News is waiting somewhere to leap out at me. But the house is silent and I feel a shiver of something unusual flood through me. I put my shoes neatly in the corner and walk into the kitchen, trying to shake off the odd feeling that is everywhere. Bad-News's bouncy chair is by the back door and it looks strange without her in it. I go to put the kettle on and see her bottle next to the sink. I am completely unprepared for the panic that follows: what if Alex forgot to take any milk? I look at the clock. Bad-News will be starving by now. I pace the kitchen, unsure what to do until I realize that I can't do anything.

I make a drink and get out my homework, but it isn't the same without my foot bouncing the chair up and down. I consider putting her chair next to me anyway, but decide that would be just too weird. I try for a few more minutes, but my attention isn't there. All I can think about is whether Bad-News is hungry and if Charlie's parents are being nice to her or treating her like a 'blip' – that's what Charlie's mum said that day in our kitchen.

By the time I hear Charlie's car pull up on the road, I've virtually worn out the carpet in front of the living room window. I make myself wait while

Alex gets out of the car and Charlie unstraps the car seat, and then I watch as Alex waves goodbye to Charlie and walks up the front path. Then I run to the front door and yank it open, grabbing the car seat out of her hands and putting it down on the hallway floor.

'Steady!' laughs Alex. 'You're keen today.'

I undo the straps and gently lift Bad-News out of her seat, looking at her carefully.

'Have you fed her?' I demand.

'Er – yes, Izzy,' says Alex, shrugging herself out of her coat.

'And were they nice to her?' I ask, snuggling her next to me and sniffing her head. It turns out that they knew what they were talking about. Bad-News's head smells way better than any shampoo ever could.

'They loved her,' says Alex, crouching down next to me. 'What's wrong, Izzy? I thought she was just a bit of a nuisance to you?'

I rest Bad-News on my knees and put my hands over her ears, glaring at Alex.

'Don't say things like that in front of her!' I say. 'You'll make her feel sad. She IS a little bit of a nuisance, but she's our nuisance.' I look at Bad-News and feel a surge of love running through my body. I will never, ever let anything happen to this baby, even if she is a complete pain and noisy and actually quite smelly.

'I missed you,' I whisper and I'm not sure if I'm talking to Alex or Bad-News or maybe both.

Alex puts her arm round me and we sit on the floor together, looking at the scrunched-up face in front of us.

'We missed you too, Izzy,' Alex whispers back. 'I can't do this without you. I could start saying sorry for all the things I've got wrong, but if I do I'll still be saying sorry when I'm an old lady.'

'I'm sorry too,' I tell her. She laughs.

'You've got nothing to be sorry for! I just need you to promise me one thing.'

'Anything,' I say, looking up at her and holding Bad-News tight.

'Even when I'm being a cow, don't forget that I love you. Forever.'

I should feel happy, but I don't. I look down at Bad-News again and think about how to ask Alex the question that's been bothering me for a while.

'What about the baby? You told me that you love her more than anything. It's OK – I understand if you love her more than me. She is pretty special.'

343

Alex pulls me closer to her. 'I DO love her more than anything. But she hasn't taken any of the love I have for you away, Izzy. It's totally different. You're YOU, Izzy – the most amazing, unique, precious and special little sister in the universe. I love you for being YOU just like I love her for being HER! And I love you both more than anything, just in different ways.'

I think about that for a moment. And, actually, that makes some kind of sense. Life is different now, but if different means having Alex AND Bad-News to love then different is OK. I think I like different.

A Golden Opportunity

We're sitting having supper and Mum is putting her foot down. This conversation has been going on for weeks and she's had enough.

'She's four weeks old!' she says to Alex. 'She needs a name.'

'Your mum's right,' says Finn, shovelling a forkful of peas into his mouth and earning himself a smile from Mum. 'We can't just keep on calling her "Baby" all the time.'

I say nothing. Bad-News and I have come to an understanding over the last few weeks. I'll look out for her and keep her safe, and be there to rescue her when Mum and Alex are being grown-up and boring and won't let her do anything cool – and she'll make a real effort to stop being such a drama queen and screaming the place down just because she's a bit bored or has a wet nappy. I think it's going to work out for the two of us. And I've kind of got used to calling her 'Bad-News' too – I think it suits her. My mood ring has been brown for days now and I know that our home is the right place for Alex and Bad-News to be, safe here with us. There's a lot to be said for brown: it's safe and comforting.

'You and Charlie have got to register her birth by the time she's six weeks old anyway,' Mum continues. 'You need to choose a name, Alex. It's not fair on the poor child.'

Alex groans and looks at Finn for support, but he just shrugs at her and keeps eating. He still spends most of his spare time at our house; it almost feels like Bad-News brought Finn back to us.

'Fine,' says Alex theatrically. 'It's just such a big responsibility. I want to get it right.'

'Of course you do,' says Mum, trying (and failing) to sound sympathetic. 'But you've had a while to think about it. Didn't you and Charlie talk about baby names when you were in Switzerland?'

Alex grimaces. 'Seriously, Mum, you do NOT want to hear his suggestions! Poor kid will be a laughing stock if he gets to name her.'

'All the same,' says Mum, standing up, 'he's her dad and you need to make this decision together.'

Mum starts to stack up the supper plates and Finn gets up to help her. Bad-News is squawking in her chair so I go over and pick her up and bring her back to the table.

'What do *you* want to be called?' I ask her.

'Why don't we all make a list of suggestions?' says Mum, turning to look at Alex. 'Tell Charlie and invite him here for supper tomorrow night. Let's have a naming party and get this sorted once and for all.'

Alex looks worried.

'I suppose we could,' she says. 'But I've got very firm ideas about what I want her name to represent.'

'I'm sure you have, darling,' mutters Mum and I see Finn trying not to grin. 'Well, tell us what you want and we'll all get together tomorrow and choose her name.'

'OK,' says Alex, sitting up straight and ticking off each point she makes on her fingers. 'Well, she's definitely going to be creative so I want a name that represents imagination and creativity. And life isn't always easy so I want her to be brave – she needs to have courage.'

'That's lovely,' says Mum, looking a bit pale, but Alex hasn't finished.

'She's unique, one of a kind, so we need to choose something that demonstrates those qualities. And she'll definitely be independent: she knows her own mind already so her name must help her to always remember how strong she is and to trust in herself.'

'This is reminding me of that bit in *Sleeping Beauty* when the fairies all give Princess Aurora different gifts like being beautiful and good at singing,' I say. Alex scowls at me, but Finn bursts out laughing and Mum looks like it's taking all her effort not to join in. I grin and hug Bad-News closer to me.

'And lastly,' says Alex loudly, making sure she has everyone's attention, 'her name must mean that she's always loved and reaches her full potential in life. And she must always, always be happy!'

Alex sinks back into her chair. Mum wipes her hands on a tea towel and clears her throat.

'You don't think that's quite a lot to ask from a name?' she asks Alex gently. 'Your name means "defender or protector" and I've always loved that, but you're so much more than just the meaning of your name. Don't you think you should choose a name that you and Charlie both like and that suits the baby?'

We all turn to look at Bad-News who chooses this moment to sneeze, screwing her face up hard and making herself look utterly ridiculous.

'Oh, I don't know!' groans Alex. 'Maybe you're right. Just find some names and we'll choose tomorrow. You'll come, right?' She says this last bit to Finn who looks startled but pleased.

'If you want me to,' he says.

'Well, you're virtually part of the family which means you're part of her family – so you can come as long as you bring a list of names,' Alex tells him.

'No problem!' says Finn, his eyes lighting up and, as soon as the washing up is done, he says goodbye and heads home, and I know he's going to spend hours trying to think of the perfect name for Bad-News.

Alex goes to phone Charlie and tell him the plan and I cuddle the baby for a little while longer, wondering what name I would give her if I had the choice. I think about Alex's crazy list of qualities and suddenly I know. I look at Bad-News and can see immediately that it would suit her completely brilliantly.

When Alex comes back into the kitchen, she takes the baby and I go upstairs to find a piece of paper and my old set of paints.

Every Cloud Has a Silver Lining

'We are gathered here today –' says Finn in a serious voice, and Alex elbows him in the ribs.

'This is no laughing matter, Finn,' she scolds him. 'We're about to decide the name for my daughter – sorry, OUR daughter.' She looks at Charlie here, but he just smiles at her. Things seem to be OK with them. He comes to visit when he can and when he starts university next year he says that he'll keep in touch in the holidays. Alex doesn't seem to mind. I think she's glad that they aren't always fighting any more.

'Sorry,' says Finn, and gets his piece of paper out of his back pocket.

We've eaten supper and cleared the table and Bad-News is snoozing in Grandpa's arms. When he's around, the rest of us have no chance of cuddling her; it seems to make him feel calm and he hasn't wandered off once since she was born.

Granny leans forward and picks up her cup of tea.

'Oh, look at the little dear,' she says. 'She's totally unaware that her future is about to be decided by you lot. Poor little lamb!'

'Yes, thank you, Granny,' says Alex. Granny grins; she never lets Alex get away with being too uppity.

'Right then, who wants to go first?' Alex demands. She has appointed herself chairperson of this meeting and hasn't made a list of her own. We're all suddenly a bit scared: Alex has high expectations and her list of requirements was quite demanding. Nobody wants to be the first to make their suggestions.

'How about you go first, Charlie?' says Mum. She tries to make it sound as if she's being kind, but I know better and look down at the table so that nobody sees me grin. Charlie looks at his list a bit uncomfortably and then rattles off four names so fast that I can barely understand them.

'SavannahParisMelodyChelsea,' he says, and then slaps his piece of paper on the table, relieved to have done his bit. There's silence for a moment while we all work out what he has suggested. I look at Alex; her face is steely and she's glaring at Charlie.

'We've had this conversation before,' she says, sounding as if her teeth are gritted. 'I don't want her to have a trendy name. There'll be millions of girls with those names in her class when she starts school.'

Charlie just looks at her, as if he doesn't really understand what her problem is. Mum is looking concerned and I can tell she's crossing her fingers under the table that Bad-News doesn't end up with one of those names. So am I actually. She'd be better off keeping the name I've given her – at least she'll be the only Bad-News in her class.

'I must say, those are quite "cheap" names, dear,' says Granny.

'Why don't I tell you my suggestions?' says Mum in a breezy voice, trying to drown out Granny's words, and Alex stops frowning at Charlie and turns to Mum.

'Please do,' she says. Mum looks down at her list, and it might just be my imagination, but her face seems a bit white and her hands seem to be shaking just a little.

'I think you can't go wrong with classic names,' she tells Alex, who scowls suspiciously. 'Some names never go out of fashion, so I thought Rose, Charlotte or Sophie.'

'Oh, lovely!' cries Granny. 'Your great-great-grandmother was called Rose. How perfect to choose a family name!'

Mum shoots a warning look at Granny and then looks anxiously at Alex, who is pulling her 'thinking' face and looking at Bad-News who has started making little snoring sounds.

'They're good names, Mum. I just don't think they're right for her. Do you know what I mean?'

Mum nods, but as soon as Alex turn away I see Mum's face fall and I can almost hear her brain screaming, 'No! I do NOT know what you mean! JUST PICK A NAME FOR YOUR BABY!' Granny grins again. I'm getting the distinct impression that this is the most fun she's had in ages.

Finn's up next, which is a good job because he can barely sit still in his chair, he's so excited about his choice of names – although he keeps shooting nervous looks across the table at Charlie, who just looks straight back at him. Alex nods at Finn and he clears his throat.

'So I thought about what you want her name to mean,' he tells Alex and she smiles, starting to look interested. 'You want her to be brave and unique and independent, right?' Alex is nodding and trying to crane her neck round so that she can read Finn's list, but he's holding it close to his body, ready for the big reveal. 'I thought about the women I know who represent all of these things and the answer was obvious.'

'It was?' breathes Alex and we all lean in closer in anticipation.

'Female rock singers!' says Finn and slams his piece of paper on to the table.

I get up and stand behind Alex so that I can read the list over her shoulder. It's impressive – he's managed seven names.

Pearl	Daisy
Emmylou	Avril
Courtney	Siouxsie
Stevie	

Mum has read the list and is muttering to herself just under her breath. Granny is finally quiet. Finn's suggestions have stunned her into silence. Alex looks at Finn in disbelief.

'How do you say that one?' asks Charlie, pointing to the last name.

'Suzie,' Finn tells him.

'So why is it spelt like that?' Charlie looks puzzled and I feel a bit sorry for him. I think he just wants this to be over and the baby to finally have a proper name.

'It's like "Sioux" – the Native American tribe. They pronounce it "Sue". Siouxsie Sioux is a rock singer.'

Charlie still looks confused and Finn turns to Alex.

'You don't like my names, do you?' he asks her.

'It's not that I don't LIKE them,' says Alex. 'Although seriously – are you genuinely suggesting that my daughter looks like an Emmylou? It's just that –'

'I know, I know,' says Finn, sounding exasperated. 'None of them look like her. I get it.'

'What now?' asks Mum. 'We're still no closer to choosing and she really needs to have a name!' Her voice goes higher towards the end of her sentence and I wonder if it's time to share my idea.

Alex is looking totally miserable, Charlie looks like he's about to do a runner, while Finn and Mum look completely and utterly fed up. Even

Granny is starting to look a bit concerned. Only Grandpa seems happy, singing under his breath to Bad-News.

'I've got a name for her,' I tell them and they all look at me in surprise. I try to ignore the slight feeling of hurt this causes; honestly, they all seem to think I'm more like Bad-News than like them. It's about time they realized there's only one baby around here – and she needs a name she can be proud of.

'Let's hear it,' says Alex, and Mum nods at me encouragingly. I feel suddenly nervous. I spent hours on this last night and if Alex is rude about it then I don't want to embarrass myself by crying. I hesitate for a second – maybe I won't show them – but then I look at Bad-News lying in Grandpa's arms. She's awake again and is looking at me with her beautiful eyes that are turning more and more purple every day, although I think I'm the only one who has noticed.

As I look at her, she smiles. Her very first smile and it's at me. I heard Mum and Alex talking about when she'd do this and Mum said it wouldn't be for a while yet, but I just saw her smile, absolutely definitely for certain, and it was a smile meant just for me. And I know in this instant that I have to be the one to name her, that she'll love my choice of name far more than any of those other suggestions. Because she is not a Charlotte or a Savannah. She is most definitely not an Emmylou. I know her and I know who she is.

Walking across to the fridge, I take down the large piece of paper that I hid there earlier and put it on the kitchen table. Then I stand back and watch.

Five people crane over the table and for a moment all I can see are the tops of their heads. Then Finn looks up at me and gives me a nod, followed by Charlie who smiles. Mum and Granny are next, looking teary-eyed, and then Alex has leapt out of her seat and is hugging me and laughing.

'It's perfect, Izzy – totally perfect!' she says, spinning me round the kitchen and bringing me to a stop in front of my artwork. I painted the name in the right colour and then drew pictures round the outside. Delicate, small flowers in one corner. Alex's fountain pen in another.

And there, in the middle, the name that I think will suit Bad-News more than any other name on the earth. Violet.

'It's beautiful, Izzy,' says Mum, wiping a tear off her cheek.

'Just perfect,' agrees Granny.

'It means all of the things that you wanted her name to mean,' I tell Alex. 'But you knew that already because it's your colour. You just listed all the colour meanings of violet.'

Alex's eyes are shining and she looks at Charlie.

'What do you think?' she asks and for the first time in ages it sounds like she's desperate for him to agree with her. 'Can we call her Violet?'

'I think it's a brilliant name,' says Charlie, getting up and taking Bad-News from Grandpa. 'It really suits her.'

Alex whoops and spins me round again. Then she stops and plonks herself down next to Finn, who is still looking at my piece of paper.

'Finn?' she says. 'What do you reckon?'

Finn looks at Alex and then across at Bad-News. 'I reckon you've got a very clever little sister,' he says and I feel myself flushing with pride. 'Violet is definitely a name that will take her a long way. Maybe even rock-star status!'

'My gorgeous baby girl is not going to be a rock star, Finn!' shrieks Alex, punching him in the shoulder. 'Don't you ever dare suggest such a thing – not where she can hear you. She's going to stay at home with her mummy forever and ever and never leave me and never cause me any trouble. Got it?'

I look across at Mum who is smiling at Alex.

'I seem to remember saying a similar thing when you were a cute little baby,' she tells her, but her voice is teasing, and when Alex goes across the room and scoops Mum into a big hug I see Mum close her eyes and rest her head on Alex's shoulder, a happy, contented smile on her face.

'And I said exactly the same thing about you,' Granny says to Mum. Mum looks up and makes eye contact with Granny over Alex's shoulder. 'And I wouldn't want to change a single thing that's happened,' Granny continues, smiling gently at Mum. 'Life has a funny way of doing just what it wants – and if things had been done differently we might not all be here together right now.'

We're all quiet for a moment, each thinking about what Granny has said. I look at the four generations in our kitchen and wonder if Violet will ever love the rest of us the way that we all love her.

'Is it time for her to go to bed?' says Charlie, and I freeze, thinking for a minute that he's talking about me, and that once again I'm going to be packed off like a baby. But then I realize that he's actually talking about the real baby and I laugh at myself for being so quick to leap to conclusions.

'Can I put her to bed?' I ask, and Charlie looks at me, uncertain. Mum comes forward and touches my arm.

'That's a lovely thought, sweetheart, but you've not done it before. Why not let Alex do it tonight and she can show you how it's done tomorrow?' I nod and start to step back, but Alex stops me.

'No, I'd love it if Izzy put her to bed. I think it's a great idea and she was the one to choose the perfect name after all.'

'Are you sure?' I ask her. 'I know how to change her nappy and I'll put a clean sleepsuit on her. I'll be really careful.'

Alex laughs. 'I know you will. You're the best Aunty Izzy in the universe. She's a very lucky baby to have someone like you. Her very own darkness-destroyer!'

Charlie kisses the baby's head and puts her in my arms and slowly, very carefully, I walk round the kitchen, stopping so that Mum, Granny, Grandpa and then Alex can give her a kiss. When I walk past Finn, he ruffles the fluffy hair on her

head and I see him look over at Charlie. A look
fizzes between them and I can't work out what it
means, but then Charlie nods at Finn and Finn
smiles and looks relieved. Then, with all of them
watching me, I walk upstairs and into Alex's
room.

The lamp is on and the whole room has a cosy
glow. It feels safe – like a good place for a baby to
sleep. I put her on the bed and ease her plump
little arms and legs out of her clothes. She lies on
the changing mat, her legs kicking in the air and
gazing at the room around her, as if it's the best,
most wonderful place she's ever seen.

I laugh, watching her tire herself out with her
kicking, and then I change her nappy and slide a
fresh sleepsuit under her body, pulling the sleeves
over her arms. It takes a while to get her feet into
the legs of the suit because she keeps kicking them
out, but I get there eventually and do up the
poppers at the front. Then I pick her up and hold
her close to me while I look round the room. It's
really hard to remember what this room was like
before and I truly can't imagine a home without
her in it.

She's almost asleep so I tiptoe across to her cot
and lie her down. There's a worrying moment

when I think she's going to start crying, but then she finds her fingers and starts sucking, and within seconds she's completely gone. Fast asleep.

I watch her for a few more minutes, just to be sure, and then I creep out of the room and into my own bedroom. From downstairs I can hear the sound of Alex and Finn singing a song that they used to play in their band and I wonder if Alex might go back and rejoin On the Rocks. I could help Mum with the babysitting. I can hear Mum and Charlie walking Granny and Grandpa to the front door and Mum telling Granny to ring if she needs her, and Charlie laughing with Grandpa as he helps them down the front path, and it feels good to be part of such a funny, messy family.

In my room I kneel down and pull out the wooden box where Alex kept the letters she wrote to me. She left it inside the laundry basket when she ran away and I rescued it, but I wasn't sure why. I put it on my bed and find the new notebook and the pen with the indigo ink that I bought yesterday with my pocket money. But there's still one thing left to do, so before I can start writing I take Mr Cuddles off my pillow, where he's sitting next to my poison arrow frog that I got the day that Bad-News was born. Then I go back into Alex's room.

Bad-News is dreaming – I can see her eyelids flickering and I hope it's a dream about something good. I put Mr Cuddles at the bottom of her cot. I don't want to scare her if she wakes up and sees one freaky eye staring at her. Then I lean over the cot and whisper to her.

'I was wrong. You're not bad news at all. In fact, you're the best thing that's ever happened to me – probably to our whole family. Mr Cuddles belongs to you now. Take care of him, and welcome to the world, Violet.'

I look down at my mood ring. It's yellow and I remember nearly a whole year ago when I decided that this year would be the Year of Yellow. Yellow for happiness and joy, hope and friendship. Yellow for being me – for mattering and being important to somebody else.

'We got there, Violet,' I tell her. 'We made it yellow.'

Then I walk back to my room and sit on my bed and start writing down the story of you. So that one day, Violet, even if you think that life's unfair and nobody likes you and you always get everything wrong, you will know how totally and completely and utterly loved you are. You will know that I trust only you with my words and my thoughts. And you will know that I will always be here to keep you safe and scare away the dark and love you. Forever.

Love Izzy xxxx

Acknowledgements

When I was in my late teens, my granny gave me a packet of letters that she had been keeping for me to read when I was old enough. Those letters are some of my most treasured possessions. Thank you, Mum, Granny and Granpa, for sharing your stories and memories and love with me.

Many thanks to Lizzy and Polly for once again reading an early draft and giving me lots of brilliant advice. And to Julie B, Flor, Julie N, Kate and Niki who gave their time to read this book and share their thoughts with me.

I also need to thank Holly, Erin and Eliza, three fantastic readers whose opinions were well considered, thoughtful, honest and incredibly valuable.

Thank you to Julia and Alex, for your support.

Acknowledgements

And thanks to my amazing family – Adam, Zachary, Georgia and Reuben – for your constant excitement and enthusiasm.

READ ON FOR
INSIDE INFORMATION AND ACTIVITIES FROM

REBECCA WESTCOTT

Writing Activity

Alex is a letter writer. She says nobody writes letters any more but that they should because letters are special. She says you can hold a letter and keep it close to you and read it any time you want. Emails can be wiped and texts are gone if you lose your phone – but letters stay forever.

I totally agree with Alex. When I was a child, I used to love the sound of the postman pushing the post through our front door. I lived in eternal hope that there might be a letter for me, and sometimes there actually was. My nana and my granny used to write to me and later, when I was at university, my mum and my little sister wrote to me all the time. I've kept all those letters and they are really special to me.

We don't send as many letters today – I suppose

it's just easier (and cheaper) to email or send a text. I still think letter writing is fun, though, and it's a good way to practise your writing skills and make someone's day a bit nicer!

Try these letter-writing ideas – and if you haven't got a stamp just leave them on the pillow of someone who lives in your house. It'll give them a brilliant surprise and, if you're lucky, they might write back . . .

1. Write a letter to someone who is important to you. Tell them why they mean so much to you and why you're glad that you know them.

2. Write a funny letter describing the most embarrassing day of your life. You'll make someone laugh and, you never know, it might be therapeutic for you to put down your excruciating experiences on paper. (I know what I'm talking about here. Let's just say that the basketball scene and Izzy's subsequent total humiliation was based on a VERY personal experience. Except I wasn't twelve – I was sixteen . . .)

3. Write a letter to yourself in the future. Include details of everything that matters

to you now: the TV programmes you watch, the music you listen to, the books you're reading, the people you like (and don't like). Then describe what you'd like to be doing in ten years' time – your hopes and predictions for yourself. After that, seal it up in an envelope, put your name and the year in which it can be opened on the front and put it somewhere safe. You'll be really glad you did this when you stumble upon it in the 2020s!

Reading-group Questions

1. Do you think the title *Violet Ink* works for this story? Would you have given the book a different title? If so, what would it be?

2. *Violet Ink* is told from Izzy's point of view, but do you think it is *her* story? Which character do you feel that you get to know best – Izzy or Alex?

3. Izzy says she thinks that words are really important and some of her free verses are included in the book. Do you think that the verses add anything to the story? Choose your favourite line from Izzy's writing and explain what you like about it.

4. Izzy writes in one of her verses that: 'Guilty has a twin sister. Her name is Memories.' What do you think she means? How does

this personification of emotion give us more detail about what life is like after Alex has gone?

5. Have you ever experienced a situation where something unexpected has happened and it changes your life forever? Sometimes it can be a really small thing that causes the biggest changes. How did you react? Did you feel like Izzy, as if you had no control, or did you behave differently?

6. Did you feel that Mum's reaction was believable when she discovered the truth about what was going on with Alex?

7. In her citizenship lesson, Izzy has to answer a question – who would she choose to save if there were four people tied to a train track and a train was coming? What would your answer be?

8. In the same lesson, Izzy learns that dilemmas are usually dealt with in one of four ways: trusting your gut instinct; getting some advice; asking for the opinion of everyone involved or tossing a coin. Which strategy do you tend to use when you've got a difficult problem to solve? Discuss the pros and cons of each strategy.

9. How do you think Finn feels about Izzy? What do you think he feels for Alex? What do you think will happen next?

10. Were there any times that you disagreed with the actions of one of the characters? What would you have liked them to have done differently?

11. Did you guess the name that Izzy chooses for the Bad-News Baby? Do you think that 'Violet' is an appropriate choice or would you have chosen another name? Explain your reasons.

12. How is the theme of *colour* used throughout *Violet Ink*? Do you think that this adds anything to the narrative?

13. What are the differences between Charlie and Finn? Create a pen portrait of them both, describing their characteristics and personalities. Who do you prefer?

14. Did you like the ending? How would you have liked it to end? Are you keen to find out what happens next to Izzy, Alex, Finn, Charlie and Violet? Describe what you think they'll each be doing in ten years' time.

Questions for Rebecca

How long did it take you to write *Dandelion Clocks* and *Violet Ink*?

I tend to write a first draft quite quickly – it takes me about six to eight weeks, writing after work in the evenings and at weekends. Being a teacher is great because I get lots of writing time during the holidays, which helps! Once the first draft is written I'll take my time on the edit, really developing the voice of the main character and making sure that there are no inconsistencies in the plot.

Does anyone read your books while you are in the process of writing them?

I'm really lucky to have an incredibly supportive family, who read everything that I write (and have an opinion on everything I write too!). My eleven-year-old daughter was the first person to read both books. In fact, it was a conversation that I had with her in our garden one day last spring that gave me the idea for *Dandelion Clocks*. She also helped me to write some of Izzy's poems in *Violet Ink*. Once I'm happy with what I've written, I'll ask people to have a read and give me their thoughts. My husband, mum, sister and lovely friends are great at doing this!

Which authors have inspired you?
One of my favourite authors is Robert Cormier. He writes about topics that are quite grown up in a way that younger readers can access, without being patronizing. I often find his books chilling – they always leave me with a list of questions and wanting more.

When I was a child, I loved Judy Blume. I would read her books and feel as if I completely knew the characters, even though their lives were so different to mine.

Now, I enjoy reading books by authors like Patrick Ness, Meg Rosoff and John Green. They aren't afraid of tackling 'big' issues. After all, life happens to everyone – not just to adults.

What is your favourite way to spend a day off from teaching and writing?

I love spending time with my family. We are all big fans of camping and what I enjoy most is sitting in the sunshine watching my husband cook us an amazing campfire meal while our three children race around on their bikes (I'm not completely lazy though – I do the washing-up!).

In the winter, if I'm not writing then I'm probably reading, while my husband cooks us a meal and the children create chaos with Nerf guns. (You can probably tell that I really, really hate cooking.) Actually, I'm not that fond of housework either, so at the weekends we play a card game after supper – the loser has to wash up.

I want to be a writer. What are your top tips for getting published?

Write for fun! When I wrote *Dandelion Clocks* I was so excited by the idea that I wanted to write it down just to find out if I could create a story from beginning to end. I didn't write to get published – I wrote because it made me feel happy.

Sometimes, write as quickly as you possibly can. Don't worry about whether it's perfect – just enjoy the excitement of writing your words down.

And then leave it. One of my favourite things about writing is returning to read something I wrote a while ago. It's a great way of figuring out what works in your writing.

Write for lots of different reasons. Being a writer doesn't mean that you are writing a book. It means that you communicate and record information using written words. So write a diary, write letters, write emails, send texts. Make lists, write a poem that you'll only ever show one person, leave notes for your family on the fridge in magnetic letters. Write using as many exciting, interesting words as you can and then write using only twenty words. Play about – they're your words and there aren't any rules.

Don't give up. If someone gives you feedback on your writing (it could be your friends, family or a teacher), then listen to what they have to say. Try out their ideas and decide if it improves your writing. If it does, then great – you've developed your skills. If it doesn't, then you haven't lost anything.

Rebecca's Top 5 Best Books

Goodnight Mister Tom by Michelle Magorian
After the First Death by Robert Cormier
Wonder by R. J. Palacio
A Monster Calls by Patrick Ness
Skallagrigg by William Horwood

(But really, it's impossible to choose just five! I have always loved The Dark Is Rising trilogy by Susan Cooper and I've recently started reading books by John Green. When I was growing up my reading included Enid Blyton, Judy Blume, Willard Price, Lynne Reid Banks and Lucy M. Boston to name just a few. I've just read *Grace* by Morris Gleitzman and thought it was amazing.)

Three Months After

I sometimes think about the box buried deep at the back of my wardrobe and wonder if I'll ever open it up again. I wonder if her soul is in there, desperate to get out and be free. I wonder what she'd say to me if she could see how I've become – but I don't think about this for too long because I think I know what she'd say and I don't agree with her. To laugh, to enjoy, to live is to forget – and I will never forgive myself if I allow that to happen. And actually, she left me so she doesn't get a chance to have an opinion. If she wanted to have a say in how I live my life then she should have stayed, shouldn't she? She shouldn't have left me alone with a box of old, rubbish diaries that are no use to me at all.

She shouldn't have gone.

Thirteen Weeks
Before

If it were possible to actually die of embarrass-ment, then right now, I would be officially *dead*. There should be some sort of Charter, or human rights Act, that stops every mum from behaving as if she is the first person in the world to become a mother. It's like my mum has no idea that women the world over have been parenting forever and have not felt the need to interfere in every teeny little detail of a child's life. People grow up every day, even without their interfering mothers and their totally unwanted help and 'advice'.

I so nearly got away with it as well. I've been planning for ages and saving my allowance so that I didn't have to ask Mum or Dad for extra – I knew they'd go mental if they thought that I'd gone against their wishes *and* got them to pay for it into the bargain.

I'd done all my research – which wasn't that hard as the only place in this miserable town that you can get your ears pierced is Hair & Things, a totally lame girly shop that sells jewellery and hairbands and lots and lots of pots of nail varnish in neon colours – and Alice called for me this morning as we'd agreed.

When we got to the shop there was a queue. I started to feel a bit nervous and wished I'd brought my camera. Taking photos always clears my mind of everything else and the girl waiting in front of me had this amazing purple and pink hair that would have made a brilliant photograph. Alice told me that it wouldn't hurt any more than the time I was stung by a bee at Sports Day – which wasn't actually reassuring cos that was agony. Anyway, it came to my turn and I sat on the stool in the window.

I've never been sure why they put the stool in the window – but I know now. It's so that when your nosy, bossy mother happens to walk past on her way to the supermarket and sees you sitting there about to 'violate your beautiful body', she can push her way into the shop, yelling at the top of her voice and demanding that the, frankly terrified, shop assistant explain herself 'this very instant, young lady'.

She then went on to ask, in a piercing voice that carried all the way to the back of the shop (where I definitely saw some girls from school lurking and sniggering), how a reputable shop could allow a young girl to disfigure herself. The shop manager had bustled over by this time and started telling Mum that I'd said I was over sixteen, but Mum burst out laughing in a not-very-amused way and asked the manager to take a good look at me and did I *look* like I could possibly be over sixteen? The manager said that no, now that she thought about it, I looked nowhere near sixteen and could she offer Mum a £5 gift voucher to make up for the mistake?

I have no idea what Mum said in response as I was too busy dealing with shrinking into the floor.

By now the girls from school were openly listening to every comment and nudging each other and laughing. Alice, star that she is, stayed by my side but had turned a particularly unflattering shade of pink.

Mum, having made mincemeat of the manager and vowing never to darken the door of Hair & Things again as long as she lived, turned and stormed back out on to the street.

It was obvious that she expected me and Alice

to follow her, which we did. Mum was waiting for us outside and without saying a single word, walked us to the car. The whole way back to Alice's nobody said a thing. Alice and I kept looking at each other – I half wanted to laugh but every time I thought about what had just happened, and how it would have spread round Facebook like wildfire by the time I went to school on Monday morning, I lost my sense of humour. Alice just looked petrified – my mum can be pretty scary when she wants to be.

We dropped Alice off at her house, Mum still not speaking. Alice gave my hand a squeeze and mouthed 'Good luck' at me. We both knew that I was really going to need it.

Mum drove off but then she stopped the car round the corner. I braced myself. The thing about my mum is that she talks. And talks. I reckon the armed forces have missed a trick when it comes to fighting terrorism and defending the free world – they should send Mum in and let her lecture the enemy into surrendering. A couple of hours with her and they'd be begging to be released with eternal promises of good behaviour and a firm understanding of the consequences if they stepped out of line . . .